DAN BROWN

ISBN 979-8-88644-746-0 (Paperback)
ISBN 979-8-88644-747-7 (Digital)

Covenant Books
11661 Hwy 707
Murrells Inlet, SC 29576
www.covenantbooks.com

Everyone during some point in their lives has been humiliated and embarrassed by someone. It may happen during their school years, during their marriage, or during their years in the workplace. *Sweet Revenge* is a collection of twenty-one short stories that involves cases where a person has been humiliated and the means by which the offended person gets revenge! An amazing analysis of the issues of humiliation and getting justice.

CONTENTS

THE MIDNITE CALLER

She had no idea when she answered the phone that late Friday night what she was getting into by merely picking up the phone and saying hello.

A nice voice on the other end of the line asked, "Is this Katie?" His voice was soft and smooth and quite masculine. She liked the sound of his voice so much she didn't get angry at being aroused from a deep sleep. She sat up on the side of the bed, trying to figure out who could be calling at this late hour. She instantly thought, *Bad news!* Maybe it was a wrong number? Regardless that she was barely awake, she was doing her best to sound sensible to the charming voice.

She caught the name "Katie" and responded as quickly as she could.

"No, this is not Katie. I'm afraid you have the wrong number," she said, trying to make her voice sound equally as pleasant as his.

"Oh, I am so sorry to make such a blunder at this late hour. I hope you don't have an early appointment? If you do, I will never be able to forgive myself."

What a perfect gentleman, she thought as she scrambled for words to make him feel better about dialing the wrong number.

"Really, it is okay! I don't have an early appointment, and if I sound agitated, it's because I was in a deep sleep. It takes me a few minutes to clear my mind. I am a real sleepyhead at this time of night." Now it sounded like she was apologizing to him. He did not answer her right back, and for a moment she thought he had hung up the phone. The silence continued as she hung on the phone with a tight clench as if it was a very important call. Then she said, "My name is Kathy." She had never given her name out like this to any stranger over the phone before, but there was something in his voice that made her want to stay on the line and learn more about him. She could not understand her own emotions at the time.

She heard him clear his throat. "You sound like a very considerate lady. When you said you weren't Katie, I just knew I was in for an earful! In fact, I have never gotten a wrong number that is so polite."

"Why get angry?" she said, knowing well that she was being deceiving to this great-sounding voice. "Anyone can make a mistake.

Besides, I am sure it is very important that you reach Katie, or you would not be calling at this hour."

"Yes," he assured her. "It is very important that I reach her tonight. Could you give me your number so I can check it out with the number that I have for Katie?"

She promptly gave him her number. He repeated it back to her, telling her that he indeed had misdialed. "I must be more tired than I thought," adding, "I am looking at my watch, and it's after 2:00 a.m. I am usually in bed by this time."

The thought of this handsome man lying in bed perked her imagination ever more. She would give a week's salary for a quick glimpse of him right now. Could this be her lucky night? Maybe he was Mr. Right, and how amusing that they were meeting over the phone like this. What an incredible story to tell her friends and family about how she met the love of her life with a misdialed call. She had been looking for Mr. Right for a long time, and so far nothing had happened! She and her best friend, Cara, had been making every party they were invited to and sometimes crashing the scene where they were not on the guest list. It had been fun to troll the bars late at night on the weekends looking for Mr. Right. The men they had met so far were only looking for a one-night stand, or they were complete nerds. They both had tired of the bar scene and decided the right place to meet a man would be doing some type of volunteer work. After a little bit of research, they both signed up to do charity work for charity. This would be a noble cause. She turned her attention back to the man on the phone. What would this man think if he knew she was trying to reel him in like a fish? She was beginning to feel like the predator. No doubt he would think she was a scheming witch or a desperate woman and hang up immediately. Suddenly, she was at a loss for words thinking about how devious she was being.

"You have gotten quiet, Kathy! Have I put you to sleep with my endless chatter? I really don't want to hang up the phone. You sound so sweet. To hang up and disconnect would be a shame! I would really like to meet you." His voice was so sincere.

All the time he was talking, she was making a mental picture of what this intriguing man must look like. Tall, dark, and handsome. If he looked half as good as he sounded, she would be truly satisfied.

"Well, Kathy, I have taken up enough of your time. I need to let you get back to bed. Please accept my apology for waking you up in the middle of the night."

"I will be all right," she said. "I do have to work tomorrow, but it should be an easy day. Nothing I can't handle."

"What is your line of work?" he asked quickly. "No, let me guess. By the sound of your voice, I think you are a highly intelligent and successful person. I think you are probably a professional?"

"You can tell all that about me by just my voice?" she asked. She giggled softly. The more he talked, the more fascinated she became with him. He was definitely trying to compliment her.

"Yes, I'm one of those people who can read into a personality by their voice and catch a glimpse of the true person. I've been told I am physic!" His voice sounded so confident, like he knew exactly who he was and what he wanted.

"I'm quite good at this," he said. "Now let me think for a minute." He began humming a snappy little tune that she couldn't identify, then a pause.

"Don't tell me just yet. I mean, don't give me any clues." He was humming again. She was holding her breath to hear what kind of image he had conjured up in his mind. "I have got it! Let me describe what I think you look like. Now you have to be honest with me. No little lies or put-downs about yourself. And if I am correct in describing you, you have to admit it."

"Okay," she said. "Let's hear what you think I look like."

"Well, I think you are about five feet eight and weigh around 125 pounds. You have dark hair and beautiful brown eyes. I think you are a very beautiful woman!"

She wished now that he hadn't aimed so high with his description. Maybe he wouldn't think she was beautiful? Maybe not even pretty. And she certainly weighed more than 125 pounds. She had pushed the scales past one hundred fifty in the last six months. She felt let down at his expectations.

"What if I am a plain Jane and weigh three hundred pounds?" she responded. "Would you still want to meet me?" She was now laughing almost to the point of sounding intoxicated. He had shot her right out of the saddle, and it hurt her. He was expecting someone beautiful. She considered herself to be a plain Jane!

She hoped he was not laughing at her. She could picture him grinning from ear to ear as their conversation progressed. He quickly answered, "I don't think for one minute that you would be a plain Jane. Remember, beauty is in the eye of the beholder." Then he said softly, "Beauty on the outside fades, but beauty on the inside lasts forever!"

She adored his answers. On a scale of one to ten, he was a perfect ten! He definitely was a smooth operator, almost as smooth as his voice. "I am glad that you dialed the wrong number," she said sweetly back to him. She meant every word of it.

"Maybe I haven't," he answered back. "Maybe you are the right number. Perhaps it is destiny! Would you like to find out, Kathy? Would you take a chance on meeting me?"

Not wanting to sound over anxious, she replied, "Yes, this highly intelligent and confident woman is going to take a chance." Her head was spinning. What a wonderful misdialed call. Was she on her way to meeting someone fantastic! She truly believed she might be. She could tell that he was pleased that he had talked his way into her heart.

"Where would you like to meet?" he asked. "Make it some place that you feel comfortable. Some place where there are other people." He was melting her heart with his concerns. "I don't want you to have any doubts at all," he said. "You know I could be Jack the Ripper!"

The thought of him being something sinister jolted her. She quickly remembered the murdered woman that had been found a few blocks from where she worked.

"Yes, you could be Jack the Ripper! I could be Aileen Wuornos," she replied.

"Who is Aileen Wuornos?" he asked.

"She is that lady serial killer in Florida! She killed eight men and didn't bat an eye. When men got rough with her, she gave them a good dose of their own medicine. She didn't let them put anything over on her. She would pull a gun out of her purse and shoot them in the head! They would never know what was coming down! You know what? In my opinion, she was justified in what she was doing! Don't you?" she asked.

There was silence on the end of the phone. She repeated her comment. "I said, I think she was justified, don't you?"

There was dead silence on the other end of the line. After about thirty seconds of silence, she heard a loud click on the other end of the phone, and the line went dead. She felt dumbfounded for a moment.

What had just happened? Evidently, she had said the wrong thing at the wrong time. She felt a bit clumsy for getting so caught up in the moment over a wrong number. Maybe Aileen Wuornos had run into a few clowns like this late-night caller, smooth and charming under a hidden mask of evil! She sat on the edge of the bed thinking about the recently murdered woman that had been found in a vacant building downtown. A wrecking crew tearing down the old building had discovered her decomposed body. It had been the talk of the six o'clock news for weeks. The whole town was terrified. Women walked in groups to their cars or had family pick them up after work. She too had been scared half to death walking home to her apartment after work. It had been over a month now, and no one had been arrested in the case. Whoever had committed the murder had probably left town by now.

The dead woman was identified as Norma Weedle. Norma worked in a large hotel downtown as a night auditor. She went missing early one morning after her night shift. Her car was found down by the river. Her driver's license and credit cards were found on Highway 90 about a week after she disappeared. The police had a description of the suspect. A tall thin man that looked to be was seen hanging around the hotel lobby where Norma worked, braid down his back. His clothes were wrinkled and dirty. He didn't look like clientele that would be staying or dining at the hotel. People thought he stuck out like a sore thumb. He had been seen talking to Weedle, who was described as a soft touch. She had given him money for food because he looked so down. Kathy did not want to do something foolish and end up like poor Norma Weedle. She sat there on the end of her bed trying to make sense of the call.

Probably she had just saved her own life by calling his bluff. After all, he was the one that started talking about Jack the Ripper. Why would he even be thinking such things? It was obvious that he was trying to get her to trust him by suggesting a public place to meet. Also, voices could be so deceiving! He probably was grossly overweight and had the face of a walrus! Even worse, he could be the killer that the police were looking for in murder case! A shiver suddenly ran down her spine!

This is probably how the killer meets women before the crime. Kathy lay back down in bed and pulled the cover up around her neck, still shivering from the idea that she had just talked to a killer!

The chance that the midnight caller was a cold-blooded killer was so remote to the point of being ridiculous.

"Oh well," she muttered to herself, "I wonder if Aileen Wuornos started her life of crime with a late-night call like this one? Who knows what crazy things some women will do when they are looking for a man!" Right now, she didn't want to think about it anymore. It made her so uncomfortable. She felt rattled and stupid for taking the call so seriously.

When she woke the next morning, Kathy remembered the call first thing. The sound of his voice played over and over in her troubled mind. He had added excitement to her dull night, and she had enjoyed feeling so special. She wished he would call again. Now that she had her head on straight, she could make better judgment about his intentions. Why couldn't she have another crack at meeting him and finding out what he was like in person. She stared at the phone, wishing it would ring again. Total silence! She double-checked to make sure she had not left it off the hook.

Weeks passed, and Kathy felt like an idiot. Why was she still thinking about him? Was her life that boring! She had to admit, her life was boring. She hated herself for being so blunt with him and causing him to hang up the phone. What harm would there have been by meeting him in person at some nice restaurant. He was being totally sensible. She was being a nut. He was making it easy for them to meet. No wonder she was all of thirty-one years of age and still single. Kathy was far too suspicious of everyone and every little thing. She still looked in the closets and under the bed when she came home from work or after late-night outings. She had been doing this as long as she could remember. "You can't be too careful," she'd warned her friend Cara when she found out that Cara had met a man online. She truly expected Cara to turn up missing since she was convinced the online man was up to no good. It turned out he was a nice guy with money. They were getting married, and she had never seen Cara happier. That could be happening to her if she wasn't so paranoid.

The next three weeks passed, and Kathy had given up completely on the midnight caller. He was not going to call again. She felt stupid about how she had handled the whole situation. She had messed up the chance to find a man that might be just as good as Cara's husband. The midnight caller had all but come riding through her kitchen on a white horse, and she had stopped him in his tracks.

To satisfy her own curiosity, she decided that she would retrieve old newspaper clipping about the murdered woman. She owed it to Norma Weedle to find out everything she could since it appeared the police were not making any progress in the case. No arrests. Nothing. Kathy liked the idea of a private detective like Joe Mannix or Barnaby Jones!

To her dismay, Kathy found pitifully little about the case in the newspapers. Did the police know more than they were letting the news media in on? She talked her friend Cara into having lunch at the hotel where the murdered woman had worked. Maybe this murderer would show up again, and they could be the heroes. She doubted the police were putting that much effort into finding him. She and Cara had lunch at the hotel three times that month. They saw no one that was remotely close to the description given to the police about the suspect. After Cara told her it was a lost cause, she continued to go alone. Without any luck, she decided to change the time she scoped out the hotel. She would go in the evening, have dinner, and keep a watchful eye on the hotel lobby. She certainly wasn't going to solve anything by staying home and chewing on her fingernails. Kathy was spending too many evenings home by herself. She was bored to death!

That night as she had dinner at the hotel, she noticed a very nice-looking man staring at her from across the dining room. There was something familiar about his face that made him seem like an old friend or someone she had known in the past. Where had she seen this man before? She began to think about her college days or previous jobs. She rolled her food around on her plate as she racked her brain. Then she remembered. She had seen him on the office elevator at work. She had also seen him in the coffee shop downstairs in her office building. He was extremely handsome, with dark hair and Johnny Depp eyes. She realized he was the image of what she though the midnight caller would look like. She had a feeling with the way he was looking at her that he was interested in her also. The waiter brought more coffee, and she ate in silence knowing his eyes were on her. He smiled, and she smiled back. This went on for over thirty minutes. If he should approach her table, she was going to go for it. She had been too cautious way too long. She ate slowly, hoping she could make a connection with him before she finished her dinner. Soon, she saw him writing something on a note. He smiled as he handed the note to the waiter and pointed to her table. The waiter brought it over immediately along with a dessert menu. Kathy would order some dessert so she could linger.

Kathy unfolded the note and read it as she waited on her dessert. The note said, "Will you meet me in the lobby after dinner for a drink?" She nodded yes to him with her best smile. Kathy finished her dessert, trying not to act overjoyed at his attention. This was the most excitement that she had seen in a long while! At least she could see who she was dealing with now. He looked ever so good. She left money on the table plus a generous tip for the waiter and made her way to the restroom. Kathy wanted to make sure there was no roast beef stuck in her teeth. The restroom was at the far end of the lobby, which was a good little walk from the restaurant. The walk there helped her to tame her excitement. She didn't want to make a fool of herself. She wished she had taken more time in getting dressed. Snagging a date had been the last thing on her mind that night.

Her trips to the hotel had paid off. She hadn't located the killer, but that was fine. She had found a man to spend some time with! Once inside the restroom, she ran her fingers through her hair, trying to pouf it up for a little height on top. She reapplied her lipstick. She felt so proud of herself for finding the courage to take a chance. This was what life was all about, taking chances at the right time. She made her way back to the lobby and seated herself in plain view of the dining room. She pulled out her cell phone and checked for messages to put herself more at ease. She was just killing time until he was through with his dinner. Her mind raced as she looked up ever few seconds. Maybe he would change his mind and not come. Maybe he was a slow eater like herself. Then she saw him walking toward her. His shoulders were broad, his walk full of confidence. At a point about twenty feet away from her in the lobby, three men rushed out of nowhere and grabbed him. One man flashed a badge in his face. The other two men grabbed his arms and began reading him his Miranda rights. They were arresting the man right in front of her in the lobby of the hotel. Kathy was in a state of shock. The man's hands were pulled behind his back, and he was handcuffed. Everyone in the lobby was staring in that direction and gawking at the man that had been subdued. As the detectives put the handcuffs on him, she heard the man say, "What is going on here? You have the wrong man!" Kathy froze at the sound of his voice.

She thought, *Oh my god! It is him! The midnight caller!*

The unforgettable voice that she played over and over in her mind! That was the voice of her midnight caller! There was no way she could be wrong! She would recognize that voice anywhere. Suddenly, she knew that he had been stalking her at work!

Somehow, he had gotten her phone number. She had almost taken the bait! Just like Norma Weedle. As Kathy walked past the man being arrested, she muttered loudly, "Thank God for Aileen Wuornos!"

The detectives looked up at her as if she was crazy and off her rocker! She knew they didn't understand her muttering!

The next morning, she got up and drove downtown. Her first stop, a pawn shop. What did she buy at the pawn shop? A .38-caliber handgun. She would be prepared if the midnight caller decided to pay her a visit after dark.

She then drove down to the police station and filled out a Citizens Complaint form to have that idiot arrested so he would stop bothering women like her. She was smart to be so cautious. It had saved her life. He had counted on her being a fool! She had called his bluff! She smiled. She was definitely a smart, confident woman, maybe a little too cautious at times. Maybe he had laughed at her on the phone that night! Now she was getting the last laugh!

POETIC JUSTICE

The August sun was sizzling hot but not hot enough to keep the kids from lining the street of a small town named Carrington. Eagerly, they waited for the ice cream man to arrive with a refrigerated box full of frozen treats. Mark Spaulding drove slowly down each street, handing out fudge bars by the dozens. He enjoyed seeing the joy on their faces, flushed red by the sweltering heat when he handed them either a multicolored popsicle or his best-seller, the fudge bar. They showed gratitude as they waited patiently for their turn to grasp the frozen treat on a stick in exchange for a nickel. His best customers were the dirty-faced kids that lived on the poor side of town. It was the best time of the day from them. Usually, they held the exact change in their small hands.

Sometimes he would need to dip into the sack that he carried his change in to break a bill. Tommy Andrews, who lived on Pine Street, sometimes gave him a dollar bill. The kid would get so excited about the ice cream that he failed to pay attention to the change he got back. One day, Mark shortchanged him a nickel. Tommy's mother met him the next day demanding the correct amount back. Mark, who already knew that he was ahead a nickel, promptly gave her the shortfall and apologized as she left in a huff. A nickel made a difference to these families. The error in change, of course, was not intentional. Mark was a very honest young man, and it was important for him to do a good job. He knew what it was like to be poor, and many times he felt saddened to see the conditions in which they lived.

During the summer months, when school was out, Mark drove a large portion of the day with his father at his side. Sometimes, his father was too drunk to drive. He desperately hoped the kids didn't notice his intoxication. If they did, they didn't say anything. There were days that Mark didn't finish his ice cream route until after eight o'clock. He would go home, take a shower, and watch a little television. Then he would go to bed by ten o'clock and get back up to start the same schedule over again. First, Mark would go to the distributor to pick up the ice cream he would need for his daily run. Then he would go to the bank and get a roll of nickels in case he had to make change. Someday he got only pennies. He kept a large bucket on the truck to collect them in. At the end of the week, he would take them to the bank and exchange them for crisp dollar bills. Then he would hand all the money over to his mother to pay their living expenses. He handed it over most willingly. She showed him nothing but love and respect. She did her best to make life good for them in spite of their limited income. The poor side of town was a far cry from what the upper-class side of town looked like. A rich kid named Kenny Harris lived in one of the upscale homes. Mark and Kenny were the same age and in the same grade at school. Mark was tall and handsome while Kenny was an ugly kid that had become the bully at school. Kenny taunted him daily at school every opportunity he got.

One of his favorite terms was the word *nerd*! When Mark didn't react to being called a nerd, Kenny came up with the one that really cut deep. The term was Polly Wally Doddle! Mark felt embarrassed to drive the big white ice cream vendor truck up and down the streets, but it was the only income the family had at times, especially in the summertime. He wished with all his heart that he could go to work at some local business and leave the ice cream truck to his dad. But that wasn't going to happen since his dad had a problem with alcohol. Mark's best friend, Lonnie Parks, told him about a job where he worked part-time after school and the weekends for Brodie's Grocery Store. He would put in a good word for Mark if he wanted it. Mark would have taken the job in a heartbeat, but he had little choice. The money from the ice cream truck was good during the summertime, and his dad had a problem with keeping a regular job because of the drinking. Mark welcomed the thought of the season coming to a close. It was the final dog days of summer, and school would soon be starting up again. For the seventeen-year-old boy, it couldn't end soon enough. Mark had one more year in high school and then off to college. Mark wanted to be a medical doctor, and his teachers were encouraging him.

Mark arose early that August morning, counting the number of days left to drive the ice cream truck that embarrassed him so much. His father would be getting his driver's license back by the end of August if he could stay sober. Hopefully, his dad could finish the end of the season by himself. This would free Mark up to mow more yards and save some extra money. Mark had worked at mowing lawns in the early spring and during the summer months after his ice cream route was finished. Mark had put the money in the bank for his college expenses, but lately, it was going to pay for his dad's lawyer fees. Mark didn't let the setback bother him too much. He would do whatever it took to get into college. With his excellent grades, he knew that he could get a scholarship. Mark wanted more than anything to get a good education and move up in the world. He wanted a better life for himself and especially his mother. Being a medical doctor would be a far cry from driving an ice cream truck.

Mark's determination showed, and it bothered Kenny Harris to no end. He couldn't stand the thought of Mark being successful. For whatever reason, Kenny Harris was out to do all the damage he could. Kenny was a cruel person! He had done so much to create havoc in Carrington, and he always seemed to get away with it! Kenny's behavior would go unpunished because of his wealthy family and his social status. Mark wondered why there was so much injustice in the world and how money could buy power and allow evil people opportunities to take advantage of those that were less fortunate! There was always a different set of rules for people with money! Mark thought that his only saving grace was to get a good education and make something out of himself!

The hot day had gone by pretty fast. Most of the kids had the exact change, and nearly every one of them wanted a multicolored popsicle. Today, Tommy Andrews ordered two—one for himself, one for his brother! Usually his little brother, Teddy, was standing right behind him. Tommy told Mark that little Teddy had a sore throat, and he thought the frozen treat would make his throat feel better. All the children liked Mark. Sometimes they wanted to hang around and talk to him for a little while. But time was of the essence, and Mark had to move on. There were other kids waiting on the hot street with strained ears waiting to hear the tune of the familiar song. If only those kids knew how this song embarrassed Mark, they would have probably cried along with him.

It was right after the delivery on Oak Street that Mark looked up and saw Kenny Harris with a group of his friends walking to his ice cream truck.

"Hey, here comes Polly Wally Doodle," Kenny yelled. Then they began to laugh and poke fun at him and how ridiculous he looked behind the wheel. Marks's face burned with embarrassment. Mark felt that he looked just like a nerd. "Hey, Polly Wally, have you got any popsicles left?" A group of boys were now standing in the middle of the street so that Mark had no choice but to stop.

"Hey, you, stop!" Barney Matthews snorted. Mark was surprised to see Barney as one of the gang. Barney was a good kid, and he didn't belong with the likes of Kenny. But like every kid, Barney sought acceptance from the cool group. Barney was a pudgy, pimpled-faced kid that was super religious. In all the time Mark had known Barney, he had always been a decent type of person. Barney never studied for tests because he was convinced the world was coming to an end before he graduated high school and it would be a big waste of time to study. If anyone fit the description of nerd, it was Barney Matthews.

Mark pulled over to the side of the street and stopped. He opened the freezer and took out a popsicle. He handed it to Barney, and Barney pulled a nickel from his pocket. Kenny Harris, who was standing a few feet behind Barney, came up behind him and grabbed the popsicle. "This is not what he ordered," Kenny shouted. He then grabbed the popsicle out of Barney's hand and threw it down in the street.

"You don't have to pay for something you didn't order," Kenny mimicked. "Don't you all agree?"

They all shook their heads in agreement with their leader. Everyone except Barney Matthews.

"Hey, guy! I did order a popsicle." Barney spoke up. "Why are you giving him such a hard time?" Now Barney was beginning to look scared as a rabbit standing there with the gang huddled all around him.

Mark could see the anger on Kenny's twisted face. He was not used to anyone crossing him. "If we say you didn't, then you didn't,"

Kenny yelled. He was standing in the middle of the street, trying to figure out what punishment he should execute on poor Barney. "You must be one of those nerds like Polly Wally Doddle here," he said, pointing at Mark. "I tell you what, nerd!" Kenny said, walking over to where the popsicle was and crushing it with his foot. "Now pick that up and eat it!" he ordered. Kenny was now strutting with all eyes on him. Mark could see the anxiety in poor Barney's face. The gang of boys gathered around Barney. Now it was an order, and they would help Kenny back it up. Not knowing what else to do, Barney picked up the smashed popsicle and began eating it. He was about to finished what was left of the smashed treat when Kenny yelled for Mark to throw down another one. "I don't think he has learned his lesson. Throw down another one, Polly Wally!"

Mark started up the motor to his truck. He didn't want to see another minute of Barney's humiliation.

"I have learned my lesson," Barney said sadly. He looked like a whipped puppy. Mark had never felt so sorry or anyone in his life.

"Say it louder," Kenny Harris demanded. Barney repeated what he was told to say. But the worst wasn't over for Barney. Mark knew he was in for a beating, but there was nothing he could do. He pressed his foot on the accelerator, and the ice cream truck moved forward slowly. He quickly glanced back. In his rearview mirror, he could see them pounding on Barney's head. Mark felt like a total coward, leaving Barney to the street gang of Kenny and his hoodlum friends. He should have jumped from his truck and helped him. He would have taken a beating also. Surely, the blows could not hurt more than his conscience. The vision stayed in his head long after the ice cream route was over. He hoped that Barney was okay. He wanted to phone Barney later and tell him how sorry he was for not coming to his defense. Mark felt more exhausted that day than he had ever felt. In fact, he was sick to his stomach. Being bullied by Kenny had taken a toll on him. He thought, how much more of this crap should he endure?

It was around nine o'clock when he made his way back home. He drove the vehicle across the grass in the front yard and parked at the side of the house. His mother fussed at him for parking there, but if he left the truck on the street, it was more likely to be vandalized. Mark's mother usually sat at the kitchen table working a crossword puzzle. She could see Mark pull up into the yard from the kitchen window. This was her cue to put his dinner on the table. He ate a quick meal of fried chicken and mashed potatoes. His mom had cooked green beans fresh from the garden just the way he liked, steamed with lots of butter. His mother came to the table and sat down by him. She could tell that something was bothering him. She figured it had something to do with Kenny Harris and his friends. She knew how they tormented her son about driving the ice cream truck.

It broke her heart to know that her son was being bullied. There was nothing she could do. It was comforting to know that Mark had only his senior year left in school. Then he could move on. "What happened today?" she asked in a soft voice.

Mark loved the sound of her voice because it always made him feel better. She had a way with making everything seem all right.

"Nothing much," Mark told her. "Just a long hot, grueling day at work. I will be glad when this summer is over," he replied. Mark had a feeling that she knew something had happened, but at that time he didn't want to talk about it. He gave her a kiss on the cheek. "The chicken was delicious, and the green beans fantastic." He knew she love compliments on her cooking. He ate everything on his plate even though he was not particularly hungry. He didn't have much of an appetite after what he had witnessed that day. He smiled up at his mother as he took the plate to the sink. She knew him well. She would not pester him to talk until he was ready. She watched him as he raked the chicken bones into the trash. He was always cleaning up after himself. She had done well in bringing him up. She could not have been prouder of him and his good grades at school. She had a feeling that he would go far in life. After cleaning the table, he told her that nothing sounded more soothing than a quick dip in the lake to cool off. The day had been so hot and stressful. He would call his best friend, Lonnie Parks, to see if he was available to go with him.

Mark changed his clothes and grabbed a large beach towel. He told his mother that he would drop by Lonnie's house and pick him up. At that time, Mark did not know for sure if Lonnie was home. But he would tell his mother that Lonnie was going to keep her from worrying. She did not like for her son to go out alone at night, especially the lake area. The summer had been bad. There was been lots of criminal activity. The police were getting a large number of calls about fighting and drinking at the lake with the teenage crowd. Mark didn't relish going to the lake alone. He had the feeling that Kenny Harris would like nothing better than to find him alone. Mark wouldn't put anything past him. Kenny's anger had festered for a long time. He was mad at the world and out to prove himself tough at any cost. Mark was disappointed when Lonnie's mother answered the phone. She told him Lonnie was working late that night, restocking the shelves at the grocery store. Hanging up the phone, he quickly decided he would go just for a quick dip by himself. Swimming relaxed him more than anything. He would be careful. He planned on going to a secluded place that he and Lonnie had found earlier that summer. He would swim for a few minutes, then be back home before his mother could worry that much. The lake was nearby. No more than a thirty-minute drive at the most. As he drove, he noticed how full the August moon was that night. He felt a little eerie at being alone. Traffic was light on Cedar Lake Road.

It was rather late, but not too late for the rough crowd that like to hang out and drink. He desperately wished that Lonnie had come along with him. Maybe he should turn around and go back home. Then the vision of Barney popped into his head. He kept on driving until he came to the turn off road. He parked the old red Ford pickup behind a large mound of trees. He found his way to the secluded spot and spread out the towel. The stars were bright, and he could see the water glistening. He heard a splash and saw a turtle swim out into the water. This gave him a little shiver because cottonmouth snakes were known to come out after dark and crawl along the shoreline. He thought about the snakes, then about Kenny Harris. If he had a choice, he would rather encounter a snake then Kenny. He was removing his pants when he looked down and saw something lying to the side of a small mound of dirt. He walked closer. It looked like a young girl lying there. The first thing that came to mind was that she was drunk and had passed out. He bent over him and called out, "Hello." There was no response. Then he called out "Are you okay?"

No response. He stood there for a minute, thinking it must be a mannequin! Maybe someone was playing a trick on him. Maybe Lonnie Parks. No one else to his knowledge knew the secret location. He called out hello again. Suddenly, he realized the object lying there was not going to answer. He pulled his jeans back up and hopped to the truck. He needed a minute to think what to do. If it was a dead girl, then he would be in a lot of trouble. He took some deep breaths and tried to calm himself. He needed a flashlight to check things out before he really panicked. His dad always kept a flashlight under the seat. He reached under and grabbed it. He then switched it on. Thank heavens, it was working. The light was strong and gave good visibility. He shivered, hoping no one would see the light. He ran back to where the girl lay. He shined the light directly on her face. His findings were sickening! The girl had long brown hair that hung in curls down her slender neck. Her blouse had been ripped off and discarded to the side. Her breasts were showing. Sweeping the light down to her feet, he could see that her jeans had been pulled down around her ankles. She wore pink socks. One tennis shoe lay next to her. He shined the light back up to her face. He did not recognize her as anyone from high school. It was hard to recognize who she was since her face had been beaten and swollen so badly! The brutality of the murder was horrible. Her appearance was shocking, to say the least! Her eyes were big swollen mounds of black and blue bulges. There was bruising on her neck and chest area. He did not see any blood on the body. She had probably died from strangulation. He began to sweat profusely as he continued to look down at the body. What was he going to do? How could he possibly explain being at the lake at this time of night by himself with a dead girl? No one would believe him! Even his mother would have her doubts. He ran back to the truck to search for a pair of gloves. His mind was screaming! Don't touch the body! Don't leave any fingerprints!

After running his hand under the seat back and forth, he found the gloves. He put them on and ran back to the body. Whatever he did, he had to do it quick. He grabbed up the beach towel and rolled her stiff body onto it. Rigor mortis had not already set in! This meant that the body had not been dead all that long. His mouth went dry as he crouched over the body. Then another thought struck him. What if the killer was still there? Could he be the next victim! He wished he had a gun with him. The night seemed so unreal. He listened carefully for anything that moved. All he heard was sounds of the lake, a few noises in the water, perhaps a turtle or a cottonmouth. A million crickets were singing. He rose to his feet, thinking he should look around to see if he could find anything that might provide a clue as to what happened. He walked the short trail back to the road. After walking a few feet, he spotted a green Chevy pulled to the side of the road, like someone was trying to hide it. He crept up slowly and looked inside the car. He did not recognize the vehicle. Usually, he knew what kid drove what car. Shining the light inside, he saw a key ring lying on the front seat next to a tote bag. He opened the door and pick up the bag. All he found was a tube of lipstick and some eye shadow. No billfold, no driver's license or anything to identify who the dead girl was. When he made his way back to the body, he could see more clearly. His eyes had adjusted to the darkness, making things more visible. He kneeled down again by the body. She looked like she was a young girl, maybe eighteen or twenty years of age. He surely didn't recognize the face as being anyone from town. The fact that the car had been left at the lake probably meant that she had driven there herself to meet someone. The next thing that came to mind was Kenny Harris! Kenny was always bragging about meeting all these hot chicks at a bar called the Doll House! Kenny was so full of hot air that no one knew what was true and what was not true. Kenny was not good-looking. He was such a bigmouth! Kenny's mouth turned most of the girls off. Kenny didn't like rejection. If this girl had gone with him tonight, she probably hadn't realized what she was getting into until it was too late! Rejection brought Kenny to the boiling point. Mark had a feeling all along that it was just a matter of time before Kenny snapped. Mark swatted at the bugs that were beginning to swarm around him. He didn't have another minute to waste. Maybe his mother might come looking for him if he stayed too long. Mark covered the body with the towel. He could not bear to look at her face another minute. He went back to the green Chevy and got the key ring. He prayed the key was the right one. He pushed it into the ignition. It fired right up. Mark drove the car up to the water as close as possible. There were two other keys left on the ring. He hoped one was to the trunk. It was! He went back to the corpse and gently laid her in the trunk, beside the spare tire. He had to get rid of the body or spend the rest of his life in prison or worse. He got back into the car and drove it into the water. He panicked, thinking that the car might go into the lake with him in it!

He got out and stood at the side. He left the car in drive and pushed with all his might. The car moved forward slowly, plunging and into the water.

He watched the car sink out slowly out of sight. He could still hear bubbling sounds as the car sank with the dead girl in it. He looked out over the lake at the darkness. The water had swallowed the girl and the car up as if they never existed! The lake returned to calm waters. He stood there silently and said a prayer for the dead girl. He knew in his heart that Kenny Harris had done this terrible thing.

Mark ran back to the truck and drove without headlight until he reached the main road. He didn't want the risk of being seen so late that night. When he got back home, his mother was still up. She looked up at her handsome son and wanted to tear into him for worrying her half to death. Like all mothers, she was so glad to have his back safe and sound that she said nothing! She just went to bed.

Mark went to bed that night wondering what the next day would bring. Before he went to bed, he retrieved the license plate that he had taken from the car. He pulled a box from under the bed and hid the license plate in it. He would dispose of it tomorrow. As he lay there, he began to construct a plan. If Kenny Harris was charged with anything, his family was rich and they would buy his way out like they always did. On the other hand, if he was charged with murder, he would not stand a chance. His public defender law-yer would not be wearing a three-piece suit and carrying a leather briefcase. The taxpayers would be burdened with his legal fees. He would be reduced in the courtroom to the same social creature that life had so unjustly molded him—poor and without a prayer. With this in mind, he began to form what would be real justice, a plan that would point a finger at Kenny Harris, thc bully, the monster that he really was! He had never paid for any of his misbehavior, and now it was time for justice!

It was almost dawn before he fell asleep. His racing mind had been razor-sharp all night. Mark's planning was precise. He would plant evidence that would lead them to Kenny Harris. There would be no way that Kenny could explain what he was doing with the dead girl's license plate! Of course, he would not be convicted with his family's money and power. But it could put a dent in his behavior for a while. He would dig a big legal hole for Kenny Harris and make sure that Kenny would spend a good part of his life behind bars.

Mark ate a late breakfast of bacon and eggs as his mother trotted back and forth across the kitchen floor. As she paced, she preached a short sermon to him about how he was going to get himself into trouble if he continued going to the lake so late at night. He wanted to tell her that he was already in trouble and way over his head, but he could not let his mind go in that direction.

He had to stay positive. He simply had to function today as he normally did to not draw attention to his anxieties. After eating breakfast, he made his usual trip to the distributor and then to the bank. He felt a bit nauseous as he tried to act normal. After what he witnessed at the lake, he knew he would never be the same again. After a few smiles from the teller at the bank, he began to feel a little better. It didn't seem that anyone noticed how nervous he was. No one was screaming at him, "I know what you did last night" or "I know what you did with that dead girl." Everybody was acting the same as usual. He tried to act as normal as he could.

After he left the bank, he felt like he was in a trance. He was an impostor, putting up a good front. The children were okay for small talk. They were only interested in receiving a frozen treat. The day went by slowly. Around two o'clock, he parked the ice cream truck under a shade tree on Oak Street. He took a cheese sandwich from the cooler along with a Coke and sat in the shade while he ate his late lunch. He did not have much of an appetite. He began to feel sick again. Sooner or later, the missing girl's information and picture would be in the news, and everyone would be talking about it. Things like this just didn't happen in this small community. He would keep his eyes and ears open for any breaking news. As he ate his cheese sandwich, he wished he had never heard of Cedar Lake.

It was exactly one week after finding the dead girl that he heard a bit of news. Mark had stopped by Lonnie's place of employment to visit with him. Lonnie was in the stockroom, opening boxes of canned food to restock the shelves.

"Hey, bro, did you hear the news about the girl that is missing?" Lonnie was talking as fast as he was working. "This missing girl's father is a bigwig in Carrington, and he is looking all over town for her. Get this, bro, the last place this girl was seen was at the Doll House. Isn't that the bar the Kenny Harris is always bragging about picking up girls there!" Lonnie had a glint in his blue eyes. He hated Kenny as much a Mark did. Kenny has not gone easy on Lonnie either. Lonnie stood with two can of green beans in his hands. "I have a feeling that Kenny Harris had something to do with that girl's disappearance."

That was pure music to Mark's ears. Already people were looking at Kenny as a suspect. The pressure began to fall from Mark's chest. It felt so good to know that someone knew about the missing girl except him. He hoped Lonnie would keep talking. His words were resurrecting the dead girl. Now all he had to do was find a way to plant the license plate in Kenny's possession. He thought about hiding it under Kenny's front porch, but someone might see him messing around the property. He could not take that chance. Then the magic thought came to him! Kenny hung out at the Doll House every Saturday night. The tag could be planted easily!

If Harris left his car unlocked, he could slide the license plate under the car seat. Since she had been seen talking to Kenny the night she disappeared, the police would surely search Kenny's car at some point. The more he thought about it, the more logical it became. Mark would drive around town and watch for a good opportunity to plant the smoking gun!

It was around midnight some two weeks after the girl went missing that Mark spotted Kenny's Pontiac at the Doll House. He drove around the block, trying to wait until the right moment. He waited as late as possible, feeling that this would be the best time to make his move. The bar should stay open for another hour or so. And by now, everyone should be good and drunk. He heard through the grapevine that the bar stayed open all night if the crowd was spending their money freely. He pulled over to the side of the street. He was at least a good block from the bar, and he felt safe in parking his old red pickup there. Everyone in town knew his old jalopy when they saw it. He had to be careful! At this hour, the drunks were not that observant.

The night air was hot and humid. His heart was racing as he placed the license plate under his shirt. He began to feel sick, just like he had the night he found her. The night seemed unreal as he walked toward Kenny's car. He saw no one outside, but the closer he came to the bar, the more he could hear laughing and loud talking. He knew he was taking a big chance in what he was about to do. If one person walked out of the bar and recognized him, it could be doomsday for him. He clutched his chest as he approached the car. The parking lot was crowded as usual. It was a watering hole for the rough crowd, and Kenny Harris fit right in better than anyone. He walked up to the Pontiac and pulled on the left back door. It was unlocked, the way that he had prayed it would be. He pulled the license plate from under his shirt and carefully shoved it way back under the car seat. No one would see if unless they were searching for it, like the police. He wiped his forehead as he walked back to his truck. With the license plate out of his possession, he felt like the weight of the world had been lifted off his shoulders. Although he had nothing to do with the girl's death. No would believe him if they found out he was at the lake that night!

The next morning was Sunday. He usually went with his mother to church. But this Sunday morning, he wanted to sleep and sleep. He had already told his mother the night before that he would not be accompanying her to church. He just wanted to sleep late for once. Somehow, the thought of hearing a sermon and gospel singing didn't appeal to him. He heard his mother leave for church. He rolled over in bed and wondered how long it would take for the police to find the license plate and start questioning Kenny. It would be pure heaven for him and a lot of people to finish their senior year without Kenny bullying them.

He would no longer have to endure the digs that Kenny made about the ice cream truck and calling him Polly Wally Doodle. Mark tried to sleep, but he simply could not fall asleep. Mark's mind was racing. He got out of bed and poured himself a cup of coffee.

The coffee was hot and strong, the way he liked it. He was on his second cup with the phone started ringing. It was Lonnie Parks. "Hey, bro, did you hear what happened last night? You are not going to believe this! You know that missing girl?"

Mark could hardly breathe.

"The law put the heat on old Kenny Harris because everyone saw him leave the bar with her that night!" Lonnie went on more excited than ever. "Old Kenny got pulled over for drunk driving last night after he left the Doll House bar. They arrested him for drunk driving and impounded his car. During the impoundment process, they inventoried the contents of his car and found a lot of stuff!"

Mark was so excited.

"What did they find inside the girl's car?" Mark asked.

Lonnie was now talking louder than ever. "They found the dead girl's driver's license and her wallet. And get this, bro, they found the license plate that he had taken off her car! Can you believe that?" Lonnie exclaimed.

Mark felt like he was going to faint. He tried to talk, but his voice sounded like it was coming from a deep well.

Lonnie kept right on talking. "They really put the heat on him, and all he could do was to confess to the murder! He killed her out at the lake! Can you believe this? Old Kenny Harris is in jail! The charge is first-degree murder!"

Mark found himself speechless!

"Hey, bro, are you still there? I know this is a lot of news to digest! Hey, man, justice has finally arrived in Carrington, America!" Lonnie proclaimed.

Mark's head was spinning. He had pulled it off. He knew the whole town would be happy to hear that Kenny was behind bars. He hung up the phone. Lonnie would probably want to go to the lake and help search for the girl if Kenny told them where he left her. He sat back down at the breakfast his mother has left for him. It was now cold. He pushed the eggs around on the plate with his fork. Would the girl's body ever be found? Maybe it would happen this week! He took a bite of his eggs. Suddenly, food never tasted so good! Suddenly, he was no longer Polly Wally Doodle. He was Mark Spaulding, a brilliant young man who intended on becoming a doctor and helping those in need. He took another big bite. What a day! Now the future looked great! Justice had been finally delivered to Kenny Harris!

THE DEAD BODY
IN THE CELLAR

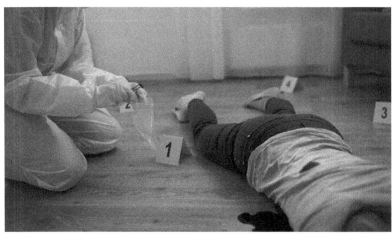

I was surprised that our flight took off during a terrible storm after sitting more than thirty minutes on the runway. I felt unsafe with the pilot's decision and wondered if he'd had a few too many drinks before boarding the plane. I almost got off the plane but decided that if it was okay with the rest of the passengers, then I should try to calm down. I found a seat over the wing, which is supposed to be the safest spot on the plane. I said a prayer and tried to think about all the trips the flight attendants had taken and how they were still alive and smiling. I buckled my seat belt and grabbed a magazine that I knew I wouldn't read. I was too nervous to concentrate on *SkyMall*. I should have downed a few stiff drinks before boarding the aircraft, but Mom was with me, and she didn't approve of drinking. I closed my eyes as the plane rushed down the runway. I simple hated liftoff. As the plane climbed higher into the sky, my stomach was in knots. I sat there digging my nails into the arm of my chair. Like this was going to save me if the plane crashed.

After what seemed like endless climbing, the sign to unfasten the seat belt came on. The flight attendants began moving about the cabin, taking drink orders. I took my first good breath since takeoff. I ordered a glass of wine and let my mind wander to the nice visit Mom and I had. I was so happy that she had moved from the small town of Naples, Arkansas, back to St. Louis, Missouri. This was where she grew up and felt at home. She had two sister and a brother still living in St. Louis, and it was an easy decision for her to make.

During our visit, I didn't tell Mom the real reason that I had come to visit. I didn't tell her that I thought Max was planning on killing me and that I needed a safe place to flee for the moment, that I needed some time to think and figure out what to do next. No, I certainly did not tell her that. If I had, she would have never let me board the plane or she would have accompanied me back home to face Max with a gun. I did tell Mom about Max having affairs with other woman and about his strange relationship with his number 1 assistant at the office, a girl named Kelly Babb.

Kelly was a short, dumpy girl with mousy brown hair that never looked clean. She wore threeinch heels that made her fat short legs look even more stumpy. Her saving grace, she was much smarter than pretty. But I still didn't understand. There were many other female employees that were both smart and pretty, but for some reason, he preferred Kelly. I could only speculate why he made such allowances for her. Maybe that's what everyone said when he married me. I may not have been a trophy wife, but I was certainly better looking than Kelly Babb. I attributed the allowances to Kelly's super intelligence. Max loved smart women with more than one degree to hang on the wall. I learned, through accident, that Kelly was only a high school graduate like myself. For the time being, I placated myself with the fact that I was fifteen years his junior, not that you could tell it by looking. I was beginning to get dark circles under my eyes, and I had put on weight.

Max was an extremely good-looking man. He would pass for someone in their thirties. He worked hard at maintaining his good looks. He watched what he ate, ran every day, and spent time on his hobbies, which were golfing and fishing.

I was not allowed to spend any time at the office where Max worked. But that was okay with me. I knew I didn't fit in. Deep down I felt he was embarrassed of me. I don't think anyone knew much about me except Kelly. Our wedding was a quick trip to Vegas. My family was more than livid when they found out there would be no church wedding. I must admit, I felt relieved because I knew his family was rich and they would not approve of him marrying beneath him. He came from a large metropolitan area, and I lived most of my life in a little rural town. He made me promise I would never tell anyone where I grew up. I can only imagine all the lies that Max and Kelly told the corporation about his young wife and why I didn't associate like the other wives did. I think he had conjured up a big story about me being mentally unstable and how he was trying to protect me until things got better for me.

It was not far into our marriage, less than a year, when I realized that our marriage was crowded with other women. With the exception of Kelly, I found these women to be incredibly beautiful, the James Bond type that turned men heads and made stay-at-homes wives very anxious about their husband's whereabouts. It was not just the women that worried me. It was also his cruelty. One night after getting home from dinner with two of his business associates, he became very angry with me. He said my bad table manners were deplorable and that I embarrassed him. I think I used the wrong fork to eat my salad. He made a big issue out of it. He also told me how "hicky" that I sounded during the conversation. He said I sounded countrified. As punishment, he made me sleep all night in the garage. I would have left that night, gone to a hotel, but I knew it would be more hell when I came back the next day. This was not the first time that Max had shown a lot of anger at something I did. To let me know when he was dissatisfied with me and that he thought I was being a bit of a hick, he would call me Poke Salad Annie. This hurt my feelings something awful. Another hurtful thing he did to humiliate me was to accuse me of not flushing the toilet. One evening he grabbed me by the shoulders for no reason at all and marched me to the bathroom. He took my hand and showed me how to flush as if I were a child. There was no reason for it. The toilet had not been left unflushed. It was just another way of making me feel bad about myself. I began to have second thoughts about him. How could anyone love such a man? Was I desperate for love?

If that were the truth, then I would feel less sorry for myself. That wasn't the meaning of true love in my book, and maybe he had figured this out. Was it evident what I was after? Was I being a parasite looking for a big bank account? The real truth was that I didn't know for sure. In the meantime, I was trying to figure out my true motives and if I was a good person.

Nevertheless I was one of those stay-at-home wives who worried constantly about what he wanted and how to make him happy. I cooked the meals he wanted, dressed the way he wanted, tried to act the way he wanted. What he wanted was demanded, not requested. Max made sure I quit my job immediately after we got married. The only reason he gave me was that I didn't need to work, which was true. It was also true that he wanted to control me in every way. I was okay with that for a while. I had access to money for things I needed or just wanted for that matter. I love this part of being married to him. I lived the life of luxury, and this was my priority for the time being. I had no interest in going back to middle class. We lived in a beautiful house in North Little Rock, which he bought while I was out of town visiting my family. His excuse for not involving me in purchasing the house was that it was being sold out from under him and there was no time to waste. It was a must-have house to him. I didn't give him any flak. In fact, I never gave him any flak. I wanted more than anything to please him. Staying home was easier now. I busied myself with decorating the house, buying new furniture, and planting a flower garden. He liked nothing I did and ended up sending all the new furniture back and hiring a decorator. I swallowed my pride and hid my hurt feelings.

Whenever he had to be out of town, he would set me up with some useless project involving charity work at the elementary schools or some church just to keep me occupied. He made me feel it was an obligation because of his standing in the community. He knew a lot of influential people in Little Rock, and it wasn't difficult to get something lined up for me to that would keep me busy during his business trips. I must admit that I enjoyed time out in the public because I was lonely and I'd never felt more isolated in my life. I wanted desperately to tell some of the women who worked with me about my husband's strange ways. I wanted to tell another living person what my marriage was like. I almost did one morning when we were making gifts baskets to take to elderly church members who were shut-ins. I brought up Max's name, and the next things out of Mrs. Bowman's mouth was what a great man he was, always donating money and helping the needy and the poor. I saw my story would be a lost cause. If I said anything, it would probably get back to him. I didn't need any more of his wrath down on me.

Early one morning after having coffee out on the terrace, I began to feel something sinister was going on. He was acting stranger than usual. Like he was stressed about something. I saw his briefcase lying there, and I felt compelled to look inside!

Getting a look in his briefcase was not an easy task. He was careful to keep it out of my reach, guarding it like a Doberman. I got a chance to look inside when he was in the shower one Saturday morning before he left on a trip. The policy was for an enormous amount. My life had been insured, and he was the sole beneficiary.

Oh my god! Were Kelly and my husband cooking up a scheme to kill me and get all the money that would be paid out under the policy?

After finding the insurance policy, I knew I had to get away for my safety. Red flags were going up everywhere. It would do no good to confront him; he was a habitual liar—a very good one at that. In fact, he was so good I still had trouble sorting out the truth from the lies. Lies rolled off his lips like water off a duck's back. I knew I was no match for him intellectually. I would have to beat him at his game with common sense.

I had to think of something quick, and it had to be something that wouldn't make him suspicious, something that would not tip him off that I was on to him. So I cooked up a story about my mother being sick and needing me. I figured if he was real stressed out with something, he would go along with me to put me off for a while. My hunch paid off. He looked at me with his dark smoldering eyes. I knew he hated the sight of me.

"When did she get sick?" he asked. Like he was concerned.

"She called last night and told me she was sick as a horse." I looked away as I lied. I was afraid he might sense my anxiety! didn't say that she asked me to come. If I had, he would probably have said no to be spiteful. Instead, he looked at me for a few seconds, then he said, "I think I can spare you for a few days." By now he was fully dressed and ready to walk out the door. The minute I heard the door close behind him, I began to pack my bags.

While the cat is away, the mouse will play, I thought to myself. *And this mouse better come up with a plan.*

After packing lightly, I decided to call a cab. I felt anxious and wasn't in any mood to deal with the hassle of parking and wait for a shuttle to the terminal. I hated flying just about more than anything I can think of. I hated it much as I hated Max, if that were possible. I asked myself over and over, *How did I get into such a mess?*

I wondered how he would try to kill me. Probably hire a hit man from some unknown part of the world. He had the money to do so. Then he would come back from a trip and find his wife dead. The trip would help him establish a good alibi. I would probably be strangled. I could see visions of my broken body lying on the floor, the hit man standing over me in a black trench coat and a black hat, his face pure evil. My mind was racing, playing back parts of our dark relationship and all the cruel, inhumane things he did to me. The plane shook, and I grabbed the arms of my seat. Maybe I should go to the police, but that would do no good. Buying a large insurance policy on your wife was not a crime.

I didn't tell her about the lie I told Max. I didn't want her to worry. She was surprised to see me. We spent most of our time out shopping and eating, and Mom asked me what was wrong. She said I wasn't acting myself. I told her about Max's womanizing and nothing else. She told me again to leave him. After two sleepless nights, I came to the conclusion that I would fly back home, pack the clothes that I wanted to keep, and leave the rest to him. He could have the house. All I wanted was my car, a divorce, and my freedom. I would leave as quickly as I came. Now all I had to do was get the flight back home over with. I had my mother drive me to the airport despite the bad weather forecast. Probably the flight would be delayed. I was hoping it would be, but the pilot had different ideas. We took off in dreadful weather. The man who sat next to me looked a bit nervous for a while, then he settled back with a book.

We were now more than halfway through our flight. Lightning still lit up the sky. I watched the flight attendants to see if they looked nervous. They did not. They were busy serving drinks.

I ordered a glass of wine as soon as possible to calm my nerves. I drank it down fast and ordered another. When the plane landed, and not a minute too soon, I was the first one to deplane. Before landing, the pilot let us know the weather was bad on the ground. A tornado warning had been issued. After deplaning, I got my bags hurriedly and went outside to grab a cab. The rain was pouring. I was lucky to get one. The cabdriver told me that I was going to be his last pickup of the evening. It was now around ten o'clock due to our delayed flight. He informed me that he was going home because of the weather alerts.

On the way home, I felt he was driving much too fast. I started to say something but held my tongue. I was exhausted from all the delays. The drive seemed to take forever. The streets were flooding, and we had to make some detours. The driver wasted no time in getting my bags out of the trunk. He carried them to the front door, and I quickly pushed a $50 bill in his hand and told him to kept the change. When I finally got to my front door, the sirens were screaming. I practically threw my bags down and turned on the TV. The weatherman was telling everyone to take cover underground if possible. The thought of going to the cellar by myself made me scared. I grabbed my purse, a bottle of water from the refrigerator, and ran to the storm cellar, which was about seventy-five feet behind our house. It was now raining so hard I could barely see. I felt for the cellar door and pulled with all my strength, and it flew open. I made my way down the steps. Darkness had fallen on the city, and it was pitch black in the cellar with the exception of the flashes of lightning.

Stumbling in the dark, I tried to find the light string. I could not find it. We had lived in this house for over a year, and this was the first time I had even been to the cellar. I saw a chair between flashes of lightning and sat down. My mouth felt dry, so I opened the bottle of water and drank about half. I was sitting there when I felt something in my hair. I let out a slight scream and swatted at whatever it was. I ended up holding the light string. When I realized what it was, I pulled the light on. The cellar looked clean but had a musty odor. The only other items in the cellar were another chair and a large blue tarp that was lying in the corner. I didn't like the looks of it. I could see a large bump, and I couldn't imagine what it could be. I sat silently in the musty cellar until the storm started to subside before I dared to move. The flashes became farther away, and the thunder was sounding distant. Finally, the rain stopped. I opened the door and looked out. The storm had passed. I went back down the steps to the large heap that lay under the tarp. I tried to remove it, but it was rolled round and round whatever was inside. I felt the lump. Whatever it was, was quite large and firm. I grabbed an end of the tarp and pulled on it. It began to unroll. I pulled and pulled on the thick blue tarp until it began to unroll. It looked like a large stuffed bear at first, then I saw a mountain of long blonde hair spilling out and then came hands with dark painted nails and slender legs. I heard a scream. I would later come to realize it was mine. At my feet lay a dead woman in a deep red suit. The color of blood. The next thing I saw was deep purple bruising around her neck.

My head began to spin, and my knees felt wobbly. I sat back down in the chair. My heart felt like it was going to beat out of my chest. When I gained a little composure, I looked again at the body. Her head was turned, so I could only see the left side of her face. Her long blonde hair was scattered across her face. I reached out and grabbed her slender shoulders and turned her around so I could see her face more clearly. It was not Kelly. Suddenly a new kind of energy kicked in. What was a dead woman doing in our cellar! My first inclination was to call the police. I made it halfway to the house and turned back again to the cellar. The only reasonable thought: Max had something to do with it. I shivered as I stood there above the dead woman. She looked so peaceful in death. Even with all the madness going through my mind, I knew that Max was due home anytime. If he found me here, he would have no other choice but to kill me to keep me quiet. I wondered who the dead lady could be.

I took another long look at her face again, then wrapped the dead lady back up. I wondered if she was one of his lovers that had crossed him in some way that he felt too threatened. I drank a few more sips out of my water bottle, then I began to devise a plan. I had to act fast!

Max would be home any minute. I didn't have a minute to waste. I had to do something with the body. Hide it from Max, make him wonder what had happened to it. Now the game was changing, and I was in the driver's seat. I was more the surprised that I was able to drag the dead lady up the steps and get her body into the back of my van. I ran back to the house in a panic. I grab my unpacked bags and put them into my car. The rain had begun to fall again. I backed out of my driveway and started driving down Beacon Street. I prayed that I could get out of the neighborhood without passing Max coming home. The only car I saw on the street was a police car. He waved, and I waved back. If only he knew what I had in my trunk. I looked at the gas gauge. The car was almost empty. I pulled in the nearest service station, one that I had used many times before. I hope

I wouldn't see anyone I knew. There was only one other person at the pump.

"What a storm," a friendly man said. He began to point out where the flooded streets were. I told him I wasn't going that way. I filled my tank to capacity, not knowing my exact destination. As I drove away, I wondered if I was the only woman in Little Rock looking for a place to hide a dead body. I turned on the radio and found an old rock-and-roll station. I sang along with the music as I drove and drove.

I soon was on Interstate 40 going west. I had no idea where I was going. I thought maybe a little rural town between Little Rock and Fort Smith. I knew I was crazy but not any crazier than the way I had been existing. Now I had something on Max. He would be glad to give me a divorce and pay me off. I had bargaining power now. I would not ask for too much. It would make him all the more determined to kill me. I wondered if he was home yet and what he was thinking. Had he gone to the cellar to check on the body? I would love to see his face when he found her missing. The first thing he would do would be to call me to see if I was still in St. Louis. I had driven a few more miles when my cell phone rang. It was Max. I did not answer it. I kept driving. I passed a sign that said, "Newton-10 miles." I drove on a little farther and saw lights in the distance. I took the first exit I came to. I then saw a sign that said, "Landfill—5 miles." It pointed to the left.

I took that road and drove probably another two or three miles. I then saw a gate—it was open. I pulled through the wrought iron gate, and I could see debris scattered across a very large area. The smell was awful. I knew I had reached the landfill. There were several posts with lights that allowed me to see the area. I turned the car around and backed up to where I saw a large pile of debris. I opened the truck and pulled the body out with the tarp. I grabbed the rake and began covering the body. It took me forever to cover the corpse with filthy clutter. The smell alone made me gag. I threw the rake down and rolled up the tarp. I thought a tarp might be suspicious lying out in plain sight. I put the tarp back in my car and headed for the first motel I could find. I was more than exhausted.

I drove back to Newton and got a room at Town and Country Motel. It was a seedy little room that made me nervous. I set the alarm clock for five hours of sleep. I did not undress or get my bags out of the car. At the sound of the alarm, I got up and ran a comb through my hair. I left the motel before daylight. I drove about a mile up the street and came to a truck stop. It was around five thirty, and there were a few truckers having breakfast. I felt famished. I couldn't remember when I last ate. I had coffee and scrambled eggs. By then daylight was breaking. I was amazed to see how much rain had fallen. The streets were still flooded somewhat, so I was very careful. I drove down Main Street and then got off on a side street which took me to a back to Interstate 40. I drove on a few more miles until I crossed a bridge called White Water River. I took the exit to the flooded river. I parked my car and stood on the banks and watched the swift current washing objects down the river. I saw lawn chairs, a table, trash cans with the lids still on bobbing in the water. I saw fallen trees and all kinds of debris. I pulled the blue tarp from my truck and rolled it up more tightly and walked as close as I dared to the edge of the river. I tossed it in and watched the strong current swirl it alongside mountain of trash floating down the river. I felt relieved. With such a flood, no one would think anything of seeing a tarp float.

My cell phone rang for the first time that morning. It was Max. I answered.

"Where are you?" he said, demanding I give him account of my whereabouts.

"Is something wrong?" I asked him in a sarcastic way.

He did not answer.

"Well, I'm not going to tell you where I am, but I will tell you where I am going to be in a seven o'clock tomorrow evening."

"Where?" he said.

"I am going to be at the Marriott hotel, in the lobby. Meet me there and bring a lot of money," I stated.

"How much money?" he asked.

"Two hundred fifty thousand dollars," I replied. "Then I will go away. You will never see me again. I'm giving you the time to raise the money. Trust me, you don't have any other option. No tricks. I'm not kidding."

Neither of us said anything about a body. He looked terrified when I met him at the Marriott. Not his confident self. He carried a large briefcase. Not his usual one. He laid it on the table.

"I'm not even going to look inside," I told him. "I trust you, considering your options."

He rubbed at his red eyes. I picked up the briefcase.

"It's been nice knowing you, Max," I said "I have learned so much from you. Like how to flush the toilet, the right fork to use, and how to not talk like a hick."

If looks could kill, I would be dead. But I loved holding the aces. We still did not discuss the body.

"I would have dinner with you, but I don't think they have poke salad on the menu here, and you know how us hillbillies love our poke salad." I picked up the briefcase and walked away. I still didn't understand if I had ever loved him or if it had been pure greed. It did not matter now! I was out of there, heading to a life at a warm beach resort to enjoy the good life!

SWEET REVENGE

E very morning with the exception of Saturday and Sunday, Laken Lane made her morning trip to the Walmart neighborhood market. The visit served two purposes. First, it gave her a chance to get some exercise by walking the three blocks from her house to the store. Second, she liked to get fresh fruit and veggies to eat every day. According to her doctor, walking was the best exercise possible for a woman that was going on sixty-five years of age. Laken walked out of her house and locked the door, making a mental note of every item that she needed to buy at the market. Some apples, pineapple, bananas, and celery, of course! Celery was at the top of her list. Celery was an absolute necessity for her afternoon drink—a Bloody Mary! She absolutely needed that stalk of celery to swish the drink around. Her drink had to properly mixed in order for it to taste just right.

The morning promised a nice day with blue skies and a cool breeze that made the leaves on the trees move around. After the three-block walk, she arrived at the store. The parking lot was nearly empty. There were relatively few shoppers in the store this weekday morning. Laken pulled a shopping cart out of the rack and started moving down the fresh produce aisle. She checked out the blueberries the first thing. The berries looked fresh, and the price was right. Laken got a plastic bag and filled it full with the fresh blueberries. Checking them on the weight scale, she determined that she had two pounds. That was quite enough, more than she could eat before the berries became stale. Moving on down the produce aisle, Laken checked out the cantaloupes. She picked up two different cantaloupes, giving each one of them a loud thump to determine whether either one was ripe. Lucy selected the smaller cantaloupe and placed it into her shopping cart, certain that it was ripe and ready to eat.

Laken proceeded to push her shopping cart down the produce aisle when she heard a voice from across the aisle say, "Hello, young lady. Do I know you?"

She looked up, and there he was: Remington Wheeler, the boy that broke her heart while she was in high school. Remy, short for Remington, was the most popular boy in high school. Every girl wanted to go out with him! She never got the chance! Remy was always attached to one of the school cheerleaders and never showed any interest in a plain girl like herself! Remington was tall, had dark hair and smoldering eyes. Remy was the captain of the football team, class president, and voted by fellow seniors to be the most likely to succeed! To snag a date with Remy would put any girl high on the social ladder at Parkland High School. Laken was totally in love with Remy, even to the point of it adversely impacting her grades. She went from an A student to a C student! Sometimes, when Laken saw Remy in the hallway, she would become so distracted that she would walk into the wrong classroom for the next class. Other classmates would laugh at her, knowing her head was in the clouds.

Laken never was able to summon up the nerves to talk to Remy about her feelings for him. She started to write a note to him express-ing her feelings about how great he was and that she would like to hook up with him sometime, but she got cold feet and threw the note in the trash. Then one morning, it happened! Remy stopped by her locker between classes and asked, "Would you be interested in meet-ing somewhere after school?"

Laken nearly passed out from the shock that his question posed to her. She smiled and replied, "Where at?"

Remy paused a moment and then said, "How about the Starlight Hotel, downtown?"

Like a fool, she accepted the offer without giving it a second thought! "Sure," she replied. "See you there." Laken could not con-centrate for the rest of the school day. How could she possibly be so lucky? Her dream had come true, Remy had finally noticed her. Remy was her knight in shining armor. Laken knew that she might be considered easy because she accepted the date quickly without giving it much thought. After thinking about it for an hour or so, she decided that she would go ahead and meet him at the motel and explain to him that she was not that kind of a girl. Surely, he would respect her for that! She thought that he was probably tired of girls throwing themselves at him. He would like a girlfriend that had high morals and a girl that went to church instead of drinking parties. Laken rushed home after the last class and applied fresh makeup and touched up her hair. Putting on a pencil skirt and a tight sweater, she rushed out the door, telling her mom that she was going to study at the library with a friend. She was so excited. It would take her only a few minutes to get from where she lived to the Starlight Hotel. The Starlight was an old building right at the end of town on the west side. It was one of the oldest hotels in Parkland. The new owner had done a facelift on the building by painting it a dark green. With the new paint and all the neon lights flashing brightly overhead, it gave the place a charming look. Laken picked up her pace as she neared the hotel. Laken parked her car in the visitors parking lot on the side of the hotel. Shutting off the engine, Laken glanced in the mirror one more time to make sure how she looked. She loved the way she looked. Laken exited her car and headed into the entrance to the hotel. Remy was waiting for her on a seat near the front door. Seeing her enter, Remy jumped to his feet and met her in the lobby. "I already got the key to our room. We are all set."

Remy led her to the elevator and escorted her on it. Remy pushed the button for the second floor. Remy led Laken down the hall to the room. Opening the door, Remy showed her into the suite.

"Why don't you go ahead and make yourself comfortable in the bed," he said. "Let me know when you are ready and I will come in," he concluded.

Laken complied with his request. Closing the door, Laken took her clothes off and jumped naked into the large bed. "I am ready. Come on in," Laken exclaimed.

A few seconds later, the door opened, and Laken was shocked to see several boys enter the room, making fun of Laken. Laken was humiliated as she grabbed her clothes and ran out of the room as fast as she could. She cried as she left through the side entry to the hotel, totally humiliated at what happened!

Running out the door, Laken cried all the way home. She cried herself to sleep that night, promising herself that one day she would get revenge on Remy if it took the rest of her life! The next few months were a total nightmare for Laken! She thought that she would die before graduation. The humiliation, gossip, and talk about her was terrible! She thought that she was going to have a nervous breakdown. She kept her head down and maintained a low profile.

Her friends deserted her. Nobody would talk to her at school anymore. Everybody was afraid to be seen with her. There was always laughter in the hallway when she walked by.

The years came and went. The pain subsided, but the anger remained for many years. Twenty years later, she still seethed when she thought about the laughter and ridicule that she got from her classmates. Laken later met and married Sam, who gave her fifteen years of happiness before suddenly dying from a heart attack two years ago.

After all these years, she still carried a grudge against Remington. The laughter and ridicule that she experienced after the incident remained vivid in her memory even twenty years later. Almost every day, she would sit on her patio and sip a Bloody Mary and think about how the incident had impacted her life for over twenty years. Seeing him today at the grocery store just renewed her anger, frustration, and resentment of the devil. She had brushed him off at the store, telling him, "I am sorry, sir. You must have me mistaken for someone else. I have never seen you before in my life!"

Remington responded, "I am sorry, lady. I must be wrong. I thought that you were one of my old high school classmates from thirty years age. From Cherokee High School."

Laken responded with a curt answer. "You are wrong, mister. I went to high school in Fresno, California. My name is Ruby, Ruby Taylor! I am sorry that you are mistaken. Have a good day," Laken said as she pushed her cart quickly down the aisle to the checkout stand. Laken glanced back at him and noticed that he had a look of total confusion on his face. She smiled to herself, leaving him with the thought that he was suffering from dementia.

Arriving back home, Laken unpacked her groceries and sat down to rest. Turning on the television, she flipped through the program guide without finding anything worth watching on the television. Laken decided to fix herself a drink. A Bloody Mary with a stick of celery, an excellent way to relax! Laken stepped out on to the patio and sat down in her favorite chair. Reflecting on the encounter in the grocery store, Laken felt so bad. She had plotted revenge against Remington all these years, and today she had blown her big chance in the grocery store. Laken had thought that Remington would have aged badly, with a potbelly and with gray hair. It hurt her to see how well he had aged. Today, hc looked like the same Greek God as he did in high school. When she gave him the Ruby Taylor line, he'd had the most bewildered look on his face. A smile covered her face with that thought.

Maybe today was just the first step toward total redemption. She concluded that if Remy was back in town, she would see him again, probably at the grocery store. She would get another chance to get her revenge! A few days later, Laken returned to Walmart to stock up on her fresh fruit and vegetables again. Maybe she would see Remington again. Sure enough, Laken found Remington in the frozen food aisle, looking at the frozen dinners.

"Are you passing through town, or do you live here?" she inquired.

Glancing up, Remington spotted her and smile. "Oh, it is you again, the lady from Fresno," he said. "I am sorry about the other day. I thought you were an old classmate!"

She smiled and asked, "An old classmate or an old girlfriend whose name that you forgot? Maybe both!"

Remington responded with a smile, "I don't know, maybe both. It has been more than twenty years."

"That's okay, my memory is not as it was twenty-five years ago," she said.

Remington and Laken headed to the checkout counter together. Laken went first, followed by Remington. "To make up for my mistake, let me take you out for dinner at that seafood place down at the wharf on the river?" Remington asked. "I understand that they are having some sort of music festival down there tonight. Would you like to go?" he asked.

After thinking about it for a moment, Laken answered, "Yes, I would like to go. I love crab legs!"

Remington said, "Good. We can have a nice dinner, enjoy the ocean breeze, and listen to the bands play."

"Sounds good," Laken said.

"What time?"

"Is 7:00 p.m. okay?"

Remington answered, "That's fine. Let me have your address and I will pick you at seven."

At his request, Laken got a piece of paper out of her purse and wrote down her address. She handed it to him. "See you at seven sharp. Don't be late," she said as she walked out the door.

"I will be there at seven sharp," he responded, smiling as she walked slowly out the door, admiring her great figure and long, slender legs.

Quickly loading her groceries into her car, Laken exited the parking lot, driving away with a big smile on her face. For the first time in a long time, Laken felt like that she floating on a cloud! Laken sped her car up, racing down the streets leading to her house. She had not been this excited in a long time. Maybe a day of justice had finally arrived for her. Arriving home, Laken quickly put her fruit and vegetables in the refrigerator. She was too excited to eat. She sat down for a moment to catch her breath. Her mind went back to Mrs. Denton, the biology teacher that had helped her stay in school and graduate with her class. Mrs. Denton had told her, "You are not the first young girl to something stupid. Forgive yourself and move on with your life. You have your whole life ahead of you!"

Laken remembered those words of wisdom from Mrs. Denton. Those words were so true, even twenty years later. Laken would never forget that good advice.

Laken kept herself busy the rest of the day, dusting everything in the house. After everything was clean, Laken went through her closets, cleaning out and throwing away many items that she no longer needed. Laken was down to the last closet when she opened a drawer in the closet. Suddenly, she remembered the gun! A .38 Smith & Wesson pistol lay in the closet drawer. Her husband, Sam, had bought the gun more than ten years ago for her protection when he was away from home on business. Laken had never fired a gun and did not know the slightest thing about gun safety. She pulled the gun out of the drawer and laid it on the kitchen table. Laken sat down at the table and picked up the gun, trying to get a feel for the gun and how to handle it. She opened the chamber of the gun to see it was loaded. It was! Five shells inside! It was ready for her to use it. Glancing at the clock, she realized that she needed to clean up, take a bath, and get ready for the evening. Laken looked around, trying to decide where to place the gun for the time being. Finding the large drawer where the silverware was stored, she slipped it inside and closed the drawer.

Laken went into the bathroom and turned the water on, drawing a large tub of warm water. She had time to take her bath and relax with a Bloody Mary. Twenty minutes later, Laken stepped out of the tub, fully relaxed. The bath and the Bloody Mary had done wonders for her nerves. Laken dried herself off and slipped on a soft robe. Glancing up at the clock, she observed that it was 7:00 p.m.

A few seconds later, there was a knock at the door. Getting up from her chair, Laken walked up near the door. "Is that you, Remington?" she asked.

"Yes," he said, "it's me."

"Remington," she asked in a soft sweet voice, "the front door is stuck. It has been raining, and the wood has swelled. Can you go to the back and come in the patio door?"

"Sure," he said.

Laken moved slowly through the house to the back area where the patio door was located. She waited until she saw him coming around the corner of the house. When he got to the back corner of the house, Laken stepped outside with a wooden stick and broke a pane of glass. The glass fell inside the house. Remington heard the sound of the breaking glass and yelled out, "What's going on? Are you okay?"

Laken replied, "I was sweeping off the back step, and I hit the glass with the broom handle. Guess that I am a klutz!" She stepped back and tried to open the patio door. "Oh my goodness," she said. "I accidentally locked us out of the house. Can you reach inside and open the door for us?"

"Sure," Remington replied as he stepped forward to unlock the door from the inside. He gave it a twist and pushed the door open. Like a gentleman, he stepped back and allowed Laken to enter the house ahead of him. Remington followed her into the house, stepping like a proud peacock that had saved the damsel in distress. He stopped in the den to brush himself off. Laken walked into the kitchen. "I will check the back door and then see if I can fix the front door for you," Remington said. Laken was not listening to a word that he said. She had another item in mind.

Laken walked back into the den and raised the .38-caliber pistol, pointing it directly at Remington. Stepping back in shock, Remington asked, "What the hell is going on here?"

Laken looked at him with cold staring eyes. "My name is not Ruby Taylor! My name is Laken Lane! Remember me? I am the naive girl that you lured to the Starlight Motel and embarrassed me in front of a dozen members of our high school class! Remember me now?"

He began to back up as she took aim with the gun. "No, please don't shoot me, please," Remington pleaded with her.

Laken pulled the trigger and shot him twice. Remington fell to the floor. Blood spilled out everywhere. Laken could not stand the sight of blood. She looked away as she walked to the phone and dialed 911.

A woman answered, "This is 911. What is your emergency?"

Laken, sounding hysterical, shouted, "I just shot an intruder that was trying to break into my house. Help me!" Laken hung up the phone and waited for the police to arrive. Laken moved to the refrigerator and fixed herself a Bloody Mary. She waited for almost thirty minutes before the police and an ambulance arrived at the crime scene. A young uniformed police officer knocked on the door, and she opened it and pointed over to the dead man that was lying in the floor in the den.

After examining the body, the officer said, "He is dead!" Getting up, he said, "Miss, why don't we step out on the front porch and let me ask you a few questions."

"Okay," Laken replied, following the officer out onto the porch as the emergency personnel entered the home to take control and secure the scene.

"Sit down there," the officer said, directing her to a lawn chair on the front porch. Laken moved over and sat down in the chair, carefully carrying her Bloody Mary so as to not spill a drop of it. "What happened here?" the officer asked.

Laken, after taking a sip of her drink, answered slowly and carefully, "I had just finished taking my evening bath when I heard a noise near the back porch. I glanced out the window and saw a shadowy-looking figure on my back patio. Thinking that it might be a burglar, I went to the kitchen and retrieved my husband's gun. Walking into the den, I confronted him as he broke into the house after breaking the glass of the patio door. I told him, 'Stop, don't move!' The man came toward me, trying to reach the gun. Raising the gun, I fired two shots. He fell to the floor, and I called 911!"

Laken took another sip of her Bloody Mary. The police officer stood up and said, "I will have to call the detectives and crime scene analysts out to examine the evidence and make a determination of what happened. I am sure that the district attorney will make the final determination on what should be done on the filing of any charges." The officer rose to make his call for the detectives.

Laken mumbled, "I can't believe that I did it!"

The officer turned around, stunned at what she was saying. He turned back and asked her, "What do you mean, lady?" The officer was expecting the obvious answer! That she had murdered the man in cold blood.

Laken mumbled the same thing again, "I just can't believe that I did it! I can't believe that I forgot the celery!"

A DEADLY LESSON

Elsie Dunlap was a retired math teacher who was tremendously enjoying her retirement with her black cat, Benjamin; her two parakeets, Jack and Jill; and her best friend, Shirley Bolen, who lived next door. The two women had been friends since childhood. They both had one thing in common, and that was their love for animals. Elsie had considered becoming a veterinarian after graduating high school but changed her mind during her college years. She discovered her love for teaching was stronger. A job was waiting for her at a local high school when she got her college degree. She jumped into teaching math to students who never believed they could master it so easily. She loved working with children of all ages but found high school to be the biggest challenge. Unfortunately, Elsie and her husband, Ed, also a teacher, did not have any children. But that was okay. She considered the kids at school her kids, and in a sense they were. Her friend Shirley had two children, both boys. The youngest son, Clay, was a park ranger who liked animals, just like his mother. It was not unusual for him to bring a stray dog or cat home until he could find a permanent home. His mother sometimes balked at the intrusion, especially if it was some kind of animal out of the ordinary for house pets like an owl or raccoon. She would take the poor wounded animal for a week or so, then put the pressure on the tender-hearted park ranger to find other accommodation for the injured animal. Elsie, on the other hand, was a bit more adventurous. Clay brought home a skunk one day with its front paws wrapped in bandages. He swore up and down the skunk had been de-odorized. His mother, not wanting to take a chance, said, "No way"! Skunks were not her style. Clay immediately took the skunk over to Elsie's place. One looked at the heavily bandaged paws sent Elsie into "take care of the poor thing" mode. Elsie told Clay that if the animal was still full of skunk perfume, she would deal with him later. Clay smiled his little-boy smile at her and told her to relax! Disregarding that it was a skunk, Elsie rolled up her sleeves and took excellent care of the bushy-tailed animal until he could be returned to the wilds. She was quite anxious to say goodbye to the skunk and felt a sense of pride for having tackled such a task.

Elsie was a petite little woman, barely standing five feet tall. She had volumes of thick brown hair that had turned completely gray. Her once soft voice had become gravelly over the years. Unlike her friend Shirley Bolen, who was stout and still going at full steam ahead, Elsie was suffering from severe arthritis. Her days of lengthy travel had been cut to a minimum, and she could no longer keep up with her robust friend. But Elsie was determined not to let her disability get in the way of enjoying life. She followed her doctor's advice, exercising on daily basis. Every morning, she walked at least thirty minutes, sometimes with Shirley, sometimes by herself. She still was able to go on shopping trips and out to movies and dinner. Occasionally she took a short cruise with her friends, but she would stay on the ship watching movies in her room and let her friends do the excursions without her.

She was always glad to get back home, where she could sit on her front porch with her cat, Ben, and enjoy the fresh air. Ben was one of those strays that Clay, the park ranger, had brought home. Clay found Ben wandering in the park late one evening. The cat looked lost and afraid. The cat wasted no time in wrapping his furry body around Clay's leg and not letting go. Clay couldn't leave the cat alone in the park. It would be too cruel. He picked up the lonely-looking cat and took it to her mother. Clay did not have to ask twice if she would keep the cat. It was love at first sight. The cat was beautiful, with its enormous golden eyes looking right into her soul. Ben, yet to be named at the time, was a large black tomcat with white marking on his face. His eyes were a deep gold color that contrasted with his jet-black fur. His eyes were so large it gave him a most unique look. He was almost too beautiful to be real! Both Elsie and Shirley had fought over Ben. Elsie won the battle. Elsie had lost her dog, Elmer, to old age less than six month ago. Losing Elmer had been so painful! She had put off getting another animal—that is, until she saw the stray cat. She knew immediately she wanted him. Shirley was happy to see that Elsie so adored the cat that she let her have it. Elsie took the cat home and immediately named him Midnight. After a few days, she decided the name didn't fit the cat. The big cat made her think of her grandfather Ben, who was a giant of a man. She cherished the memories of all the good times she'd had with Grandpa Ben. The next morning, Shirley came over for a visit and asked how Midnight was doing. Elsie corrected her, telling Shirley that his name had been changed to Ben. Shirley could see a change in Elsie now that she had Ben. She seemed much more content. Ben was her constant companion as they sat on the porch in the mornings and evenings. He slept on the foot of her bed at night. Having the cat had definitely filled an empty space in Elsie's life since she had retired from work.

Elsie loved her free time during weekdays, but she still missed her kids at school. She had been an excellent math teacher. The kids loved her as well. She had a reputation among the students that she was a great teacher but she expected the best from each student. If she spotted a student that was having a hard time, she would tutor them after school or at her home on the weekend. Their success was her success; their failure was her failure! She did not accept pay for individual tutoring. Her reward was a student mastering the skill. She loved to see her students excel. One of her former students had gone on to become a state senator. She carried his picture in her pocket. Whenever she felt a little unappreciated, she would look at the picture. One day the senator came to visit her at school during class. He spoke to the kids and told them how important it was to study hard and get a good education. Elsie had a lump in her throat for weeks after the senator's visit.

Elsie did have a few problems with discipline back in her early day of teaching. But every teacher does! There is always a problem kid around to make the day tough. She learned the hard way to never make a promise or a threat if she couldn't carry through with it. This was especially true with the real troublemakers. Standing her ground was mandatory to the petite little woman. She was not only strict with her student but her pets as well. She constantly shooed Ben away from the parakeet's cage. "Don't even think about it," she would yell at the big black cat as he gracefully approached the caged birds. "That's not your dinner!" The sound of her voice sent Ben scampering away from the cage. Knowing that cats will be cats and their nature with birds, she was careful to keep the two yellow parakeets out of Ben's reach.

Elsie was beginning to settle more into retirement. No more early morning alarm clock sounding. Now she could sleep as late as she liked, have breakfast on the patio and watch one of her favorite daytime shows, *The Price Is Right*. Around eleven o'clock, she would work in her flower garden in the front yard if the sun was not too hot. She favored marigolds. She planted mounds and mounds of them. She was working in her garden one morning pulling weeds when a teenage kid walked past her yard. Being polite, she acknowledged his presence with a warm "good morning" as she pulled herself up right. He responded to her with a sour look on his face and walked on by. A few days later, she would learn the kid's name. His family had bought the house four houses down the street from Elsie. This was truly the start of a dreadful time for Elsie. The kid had looked so hostilely at her that it had startled her. She had dealt with her fair share of rebellious kids, and she felt the vibes. This was not going to be good for the neighborhood. She later learned his name was Paddington Mack. When she described him to her friend Shirley, she told her that he was a big fat ugly kid and there was no other way to describe him. He had an enormous round face with big puffy cheeks that were far too red for his pasty white face. His eyes were small and beady looking, with hints of yellow specks. His nose resembled a pig's snout. His large body matched his equally huge face. As she would tell Shirley, he does not look like he has missed any meals! On top of his repulsive looks, he had a large economy of obscene language. As he passed her house, she could hear him muttering foul words.

One morning, Elsie was sitting on her front porch with Shirley and Ben. They saw a group of teenage kids coming up the street. They recognized some of the kids and waved to them. Everyone waived back except Paddy Mack. He left the sidewalk and walked up toward the two elderly women.

"Hello, old women!" he yelled. "That sure is a strange-looking cat you have. He is about the ugliest cat I have even seen! He looks spooky like something from the *Black Lagoon*." He then muttered something under his breath, and the other boys began laughing as they walked on down the street. The ladies knew that it something vulgar.

As the boys walked away, Shirley told Elsie that she was going to talk the kids' parents about his vulgar language. "That's the kid I was telling you about," Elsie said to Shirley. Both women watched the kids disappear down the street. Paddy knew they were watching him. He turned around and yelled something back at them, but they could not understand what he was saying. They just knew it wasn't good.

That night around midnight, the doorbell rang. Elsie was in bed asleep when she heard the chimes. She put on a robe and went to the door. Who could be at her door that time of night? She turned on the porch light and peeked out the window. There was no one at her door. She went back to bed. In about fifteen minutes, the doorbell rang again. This time she opened the door (with the screen door locked) and looked out. She could not see anyone, but she could hear kids laughing. The doorbell kept ringing until after 1:00 a.m. She called the police and asked for a patrol to check the area. She stood by the window until she saw a police car drive by. After that, the night was quiet again, and she finally went back to sleep.

The next morning, Elsie met with her friend Shirley, and they went to the fourth house down the street to talk to his parents. Ms. Mack answered the door. She was not accepting when they told her about her son's rude behavior. She stood there in the doorway looking at them with a frown on her face.

"My son would never do such a thing," she said with her hands on both hips. "He's a straight A student. You are accusing him because we are new in the neighborhood. There are a lot of teenage boys around, and I don't see you at their door." Her voice sounded agitated. "If it will make you feel any better, I will talk to him. I don't know why you two are making such a fuss at something so trivial. Boys will be boys, you know." She slammed the door shut in their faces. The two women felt like they had hit a dry wall.

"Well, we tried," Shirley said to Elsie as they walked back home. Later that week, Elsie came home to find her flower garden totally destroyed. All the beautiful marigolds that she had put so much loving work into were scattered all about. Most of them were scattered on her front porch and all over the white wicker chairs. A large bunch had been stuffed into her mailbox. It was heartbreaking to see such mischief. She felt dizzy. She brushed the flowers from her chair and sat down for a good cry. While sitting on the porch, she could see Ben pawing at the screen door. She had been out for most of the morning, and he was probably missing her. As she was making her way to the front door, she heard a voice behind her say, "How does your garden grow, old woman?" She turned sharply to see Paddy Mack grinning from ear to ear. She said nothing as she opened the door and went inside to see what Ben wanted.

The following Sunday morning, she heard something outside her kitchen window. She looked out and saw Paddy Mack and four of his friends sitting on the fence. She could see where one of the boys had removed three of the wooden slats so they could crawl in and out of her backyard. Her heart sank when she saw the damaged fence. Knowing that the weight of all the kids could collapse the fence, she asked them very politely if they would get off the fence. "I am afraid the fence is going to fall," she told them. They ignored her like they didn't hear her at all. They sat there for a few minutes, then Paddy Mack jumped down. The other boys followed suit. Elsie considered not going to church that morning, but she really hated to miss Sunday school class. She enjoyed the group so much. It was what she considered a wonderful way to start the week. She said a prayer as she put on her Sunday best, one of her dark navy-blue suits with matching shoes. After church she went to lunch with several of the ladies. She was having such a good time she almost forgot about the boys sitting on her fence that morning. When she got home, she saw a firetruck sitting in front of her house. Shirley, who didn't go to church that morning, was standing on the front lawn, talking to the firemen. Someone had set her grass on fire. Most of the yard was burned black. A policeman was also there looking the place over.

"I have a good idea who did this," Elsie told the young policeman. "We are having some problems with a group of boys in the neighborhood," she said. Elsie told the policeman about the boys who had sat on her back fence and the damage they had already done. The policeman was listening very intently to what the elderly women were telling him.

"Did you see who set the fire to the yard?" the policeman asked as he looked around the house. Shirley told him that she had been home that morning but did not see them actually setting it. Elsie told him that she was at church all morning. Even if no one had witnessed who set the fire, Elsie was hoping the policeman would take her more seriously and go talked to the parents.

"Well, if you did not see who set the fire, then I cannot go accusing anyone." He acted like he felt sorry that he could not arrest them. Then he spoke up very quickly. "If you can find someone who actually witnessed them doing it, then I can take some action!" He told Elsie how sorry he was that the kids were acting up. "They are just seeking attention. Just ignore them if you can. You know how it is! Boys will be boys," he told her. Elsie felt like throwing up her hands and screaming! It would be a different story if it was his yard! After he left, Elsie felt helpless. Why couldn't anyone see how deviant this kid was. She knew from observation that Paddy Mack was the leader of the pack. Without him, the other kids would settle down. She had seen a lot of mean boys in her time as a teacher, but she had never run into anyone as brazen as Paddy Mack! She was angry with the policeman as he drove off.

How could he ignore such brazen behavior! Elsie stayed close to the house for the next several days, watching guard over the entire neighborhood. Finally, things calmed down again.

Weeks had passed since the incident, and now school was out. Elsie felt she and the neighborhood had been blessed with no recent uprising out of Paddy. Maybe the firetruck and the policemen had put a little fear into him. Deep down, she still felt uneasy. Vacation time was the time that kids acted up more since they had all that free time on their hands. Maybe he would get interested in some other part of town and give her a rest. She and Ben still sat on the front porch every night, and they had not seen hide nor hair of Paddy and his friends. She had bragged to Shirley that she thought he might have learned a lesson, then the doorbell rang! It was Paddy Mack wanting to know if he could mow her backyard since the front yard did not have any grass growing.

"Too bad about the fire burning your front yard!" He looked down at the burned grass and grinned his evil grin. The thought of him being on her premises made her sick to her stomach. He had called her names, destroyed her flower garden, and burned her yard to a crisp, and he still had the nerve to ask her for a job. This kid was a psycho!

"No, thank you," she said. "I have a man who mows my yard." She refused ever so politely.

He gave her a hateful look, then said, "I bet you do, old woman." He turned and stormed off!

She wasted no time to going next door to tell Shirley. She knew she had made him mad, and she shivered at what he might do next. "I hope you told him no," Shirley responded. Her anger had soared as well.

"Of course, I told him no, and I have this feeling that he is going to strike again." Both women looked crestfallen as they walked around the yard thinking of what measures they could take.

Elsie was usually right when it came to unruly teenagers. Some say she could read their mind. She certainly had picked up vibes from Paddy's last visit. She felt uneasy, especially at night. She did not put anything past this devil of a boy. She always made sure her doors and windows were locked. She double-checked her doors at night, making sure they were dead bolted. Her motto was, "Don't give him any opportunity." As she doubled-checked her property at night, she wondered what had happened to her nice quiet neighborhood. Then time passed, and no bad behavior had occurred from the mean boys. She felt like she had everything under control until early one morning she let Ben out to do his morning run. Ben would roam around the backyard and sometimes lie on a chair that had a bright red cushion. It was Elsie's favorite chair and Ben's favorite chair also. He would stay outside for about an hour or so, then he would be scratching at the door to come back in.

That morning, she had lost track of time talking on the phone to a friend. She went to the back yard to look for him, but he was nowhere in sight. She went from backyard to front yard calling his name. Ben did not respond. She went quickly over to Shirley's house to see if Ben had decided to climb the fence and perhaps was roaming around her place. At first glance, Shirley could tell that her friend was getting panicky. She had that troubled look on her face.

"Now don't get so panicky," Shirley told her. "Cats will be cats, and you know how they like to roam, especially tomcats."

Elsie knew that cats would be cats, but she had this feeling that something was clearly wrong! Ben had never done this before. Shirley went back into the house to put on her shoes. The two women walked all around both houses and looked up and down the streets and into several neighbors' yards. No sign of Ben. He had just disappeared.

"What could have happened to him?" Elsie said through tears. Deep in the back of her mind, she was thinking of Paddy Mack. If so, what could she do? His parents would not even admit that their son could do such a thing, and the police would not listen. They wanted a witness, and she could not come up with one.

That night she sat on the back porch watching for the cat. As she sat there, anger began to well up in her. She was angry at so many people, especially herself, for not being able to handle the likes of Paddy Mack. She was a teacher, and discipline had been part of her expertise. Suddenly a thought struck her. She would offer a reward for Ben. She would make it such a great offer that Paddy might show his hand. She sat thinking and thinking. The more she thought about the reward, the better she liked it. It would work. It just had to work!

She did not sleep that night. She got out paper and black markers and began making posters. All she could think of was her cat. Was he badly hurt? Was he lying somewhere half dead?

The next morning, with help from Shirley, they finished up with the posters. Shirley's eyes about popped out of her head when she saw the amount of the reward. "You mean $100, don't you?"

"No, I mean $1,000," Elsie replied. "I have devised a perfect plan. Just you wait and see!"

The two elderly women put on their walking shoes and posted the signs all over the neighborhood. They put them on light poles, fences, and local business places that were close by. They were no sooner back home when the doorbell started ringing. One little girl with soft blonde hair had a black cat in her arms. "Is this Ben?" she asked. "I don't want any money! I just want your cat to be found."

Elsie gave her a hug and told her it was not Ben. The little girl told Elsie that she would keep looking. A host of people ran the doorbell that day. Some had black cats and other people more questions about the missing one.

"He means more than anything else in the world to me!" Elsie now had tears in her eyes thinking about her dear Ben.

"You will pay, even if he turns up dead?" He spoke without emotion.

"Yes," she said, "I will pay even if he is dead! I want to bury him in my flower garden." She clutched her chest as she spoke so softly.

Paddy's eyes lit back up again. "I think I can find your cat. You know I go hunting with my dad all the time, and I am a good tracker. I will go hunting for him in the morning. I bet that it won't take me long for me to find him." He swallowed hard, dreaming about all the money that he going to get. "When can I expect the $1,000 if I find him?"

"I will give it to you immediately," she assured him.

Paddy looked down at the ground. "He may be dead, you know."

"I know," Shirley told him. He turned and walked away from the door and out into the street. He walked a few feet, then turned around and looked at her again. She could tell his brain was squirming. She knew that he would retrieve the cat after dark that evening. Returning to the living room, Elsie slowly sipped her cup of tea, thinking about what should be done with the idiot that had killed her precious Ben. After a few minutes of casual conversation, Elsie told Shirley, "It's been a long day. I need to head to bed and get some rest."

Shirley got up and said, "I understand. It is close to my bedtime also. I will drop by and check on you in the morning." Elsie walked her to the door. "Thanks for being my best friend. I love you." Shirley left, and Elsie closed the door.

Elsie started the process of cleaning up the house and winding down for the evening. She turned out all the lights in the front of the house. She wanted Paddy Mack to think that she was going to bed.

Instead of pajamas, Elsie put on some jeans and a shirt. She wanted to be ready when her night visitor came into the back yard! Elsie turned out the last light in the bedroom and moved into the back of the house. Clutching a flashlight, Elsie sat down in a chair next to the back door. After waiting quietly in the dark room for a few minutes, she heard the side gate to the backyard open and Paddy Mack creep into the backyard. The teenager walked slowly across the backyard to the cellar. Elsie watched as he slowly pried open the heavy metal door to the cellar and made his way down the stairs to the floor of the cellar. Elsie smiled as he fumbled around, searching for the light switch. Elsie had unscrewed the lightbulb to make sure that it would not come on while he was in the cellar. Elsie slowly got out of her chair and moved out into the backyard. Elsie walked quickly across the yard and approached the cellar from the far side. Reaching down, Elsie grabbed the metal door with all her strength and quickly slammed the door to the cellar shut. Elsie snapped the lock shut on the door and placed a metal rod in the latch, thereby preventing it from being opened by any person inside the cellar.

The cellar was made of solid concrete and virtually soundproof. That little devil, Paddy Mack, could scream his head off. No one would be able to hear him. It was time for him to spend some time in hell and reflect on the evil things that he had done to Elsie, especially the killing of her precious baby, Ben! How long should she keep him locked in the cellar? Overnight? Twenty-four hours? A week? A month? A year? Maybe, forever? For the first time in several months, Elsie would get a good night's rest, knowing that the little devil would not be bothering her again!

THE PREACHER
FROM HELL

T he church of Great Faith in Bridgeport was getting a new minister. It had been decades since the retiring old Mr. Wiggins had briskly walked through the church house doors selling his preaching skills to the small congregation. His job interview had consisted of a well-rounded sermon about loving thy neighbor and being thy brother's keeper. At that time his voice had been strong and convincing, his sermons cutting right to the chase, and there was no doubt that the road to heaven was narrow and the road to hell was broad The small congregation sat with heavy hearts each service, feeling that God was sitting up there taking notes of all the things they did wrong, and if he wasn't, then his servant Christie Woodson was. Christie was a petite little stay-at-home mom with lots of spare time on her hands. After she sent her two kids to school, she spent the rest of the day meddling into other people's business. Christie was a gossipmonger who kept the congregation up to date on the transgressions of all its wayward members. She even went as far as taking her camera along to snap pictures. She drove by Pauline Gray's every Friday night to see if Gloria Tilley's husband was there. Sometimes he was. After snapping a picture of his car, in her driveway, she would run to the minister's house with her proof. The next Sunday the congregation could expect a sermon on the evil of adultery. Pauline Gray knew the sermons were for her, and they were not well received. She would sit stone faced looking down at the floor, wondering how much more of Christie Woodson's med-dling she could endure. Pauline became so outraged that she left the church, trying to find one not so judgmental. Pauline Gray wasn't Christie Woodson's only target by any means. She also had Ruth Ann Watkins under the radar. All it took was one time to see Ruth Ann coming out of Guy's Liquor at Christmastime with what looked like a good supply of booze. From then on, she went through Ruth Ann Watkins's garbage after Ruth Ann went to work. Christie's latest victim was a middle-aged man named Fred Carter, who had recently joined the church. Fred was overweight and had a bad complexion. Along with him being so unattractive, Fred seemed to sweat all the time. In subzero weather. Christie said he was probably an ex-gangster and was hiding under the cover of the church. No one knew any-thing about Fred for sure except he did sweat profusely all the time.

The only people that escaped Christie Woodson's vicious tongue was Sue Wiggins, the minister's wife, and Nella Ross, the church secretary. The three women went to lunch quite frequently but not by choice. They tried to distance themselves from Christie without success. She would show up at lunchtime and force her pres-ence upon them. She always had some hot gossip to share that made both Nella and Sue uncomfortable. One day during lunch, Christie let it be known that the church was wondering when Sue's husband, Mr. Wiggins, was going to retire. Sue Wiggins was well aware that her husband was getting on in years and slowing down considerably. Sue wanted more than anyone else for her husband to retire, but she knew he was not ready to give up his much-loved job. When Sue got Nella alone, she asked her if she had noticed that her husband was having a hard time doing his job. Nella told her that she had noticed Mr. Wiggins falling asleep right after lunch and that he sometimes forgot to return phone calls or make scheduled meetings. Yet Nella was very fond of old Mr. Wiggins, and she did not want to see her go. They got along beautifully.

Nella felt the church would never find anyone as devoted and hardworking as Roy Wiggins. He had been the pillar of the church and the community. He was the only boss she ever had, and she felt a bit insecure when she heard talk of his retirement. She wished that Christie had not made such a rude comment during lunch that day about Mr. Wiggins's retirement. Christie could be ruthless when she wanted to be. She definitely needed to be more considerate of others feelings. The last six months of Mr. Wiggins's employment, most church members wondered if he was going to make it through another sermon. He was forgetting his sermons and had resorted to reading them. He had trouble walking up the three steps that led to the pulpit. His knees ached from arthritis, and sometimes he could hardly get out of his chair. The members knew that he was not capa-ble of doing the job any longer. After much agonizing over all the hints they had dropped on him about retirement, he still wasn't pick-ing up on it. Poor Sue was, and it was an embarrassment to her. She told them to just go ahead and tell him he needed to retire because that was the only way he was going to quit. So they called him in one Saturday morning and told him they thought he had done a marvelous job for many years but it was time for him to take life easy. He fought it at first, telling them he was just run down and needed a good vacation. But he could see the look on their faces, and he knew they meant business. He apologized for them having to beg him to leave. After an ill-received retirement party, the Wigginses packed up and left Bridgeport to live near their daughter and grandchildren in a small rural town called Little Springs, Texas.

The church began immediately taking applications for a new minister. Since the median age of members was over fifty years old, they decided to go with a younger and more liberal preacher. The church had lost a lot of its younger members to other churches due to old Mr. Wiggins's fire-and-brimstone preaching. After multiple interviews of seemingly devoted men, both young and not so young, they decided on a dynamic man named Christopher Daniels. After hearing him preach about the mercy of God, members begin to feel like they were heaven bound again. There was no doubt with this new interpretation of the Bible that heaven could be attained by anyone who repented and tried to stay faithful. He reminded them over and over that Jesus came to save, not destroy. This was music to their scorched ears. The entire church felt they so blessed to have him come their way. Christopher Daniels was a brilliant speaker and motivator. He had the ability to convince people that their success was in their own hands because God had given them a special talent, and it was theirs to reach out and accept. All they just needed to do was to pray and find out what it was. He was more than convincing when he told them the good news. He stood tall and confident when he delivered these messages to the members. His good looks along with his charming personality made him popular not only with the church members but with people all over town.

In fact, not one bad word was said about Bridgeport's new minister, Christopher Daniels. Daniels, with his amazing talent as a spiritual leader, was lifting up the church to new heights. Membership began to grow. The pews were filled from the back to the front with no empty spaces in between. People who had sat on the back pews for years were moving closer to the front. Collections plates were piled high with donations from cheerful givers. It looked like some debts incurred long ago could be paid off much sooner than expected. The church coffers were overflowing for the first time ever. No one would have ever believed that kind of money could be pulled from the pockets of its members.

Nella Ross, being the church secretary, had the job of making bank deposits every Monday morning. Some Mondays it was depressing to see the measly amount taken in. Sometimes she felt insecure about her job there. Would the church be able to keep a full-time secretary on the payroll? The elders had discussed it with her before, sending her into panic. Christie Woodson felt it her obligation to let Nella know that it had been seriously considered. On that Monday morning three months after the new minister had come on board, she could not believe the good fortune that had descended upon the church. The elders had counted the money three times in disbelief. With big smiles on their faces, they handed it over to Nella to deposit in the First National Bank of Bridgeport The teller at the bank seemed shocked at the large amount of bills that was pulled from the bank bags. She rolled her eyes up at the ceiling and told Nella that the church must be doing all the right things and then she handed her back a receipt for the deposit.

The biggest contributor of the church was an elderly woman in her early seventies. Her late husband had owned a restaurant in town along with a string of rental properties. He died suddenly of a heart attack, leaving her millions of dollars in the bank as well as property that was generously producing. The widow's name was Madelyn Reece, and she drove a white Mercedes to church and all over the town of Bridgeport. Unlike her late husband, she was not a friendly person. She did not have the gift of gab. She had few friends and seemed a bit odd, never fitting in any place. Other women in the church sensed her loneliness. They invited her to many events but finally gave up because she seemed hopelessly out of reach. Nella was concerned about Mrs. Reece, who acted so ill at ease at practically every service. She believed that the new minister might be able to help her since he had such a remarkable way of drawing people in. Maybe he could make Madelyn feel more connected and involved. Mrs. Reece's contributions to the church showed that she cared about people and wanted to help. She was a faithful member even though she sat alone most of the time. Madelyn was still a beautiful woman. She kept her pale blonde hair cut short and always in a very becoming style.

She wore expensive designer clothes. She loved the color white! Her Mercedes was white, most of her clothing was white, and most of her furniture was in white. She still had a youthful-looking shape for a woman in her seventies. Her legs were shapely and tanned from weekly trips to the spa. Her walk seemed uppity to most church members, but Nella knew that she was not arrogant. She was just an odd duck. Old Mr. Wiggins had thought Madelyn to be stuck up because of her wealth. He spent very little time trying to talk to her. His wife, Sue, had knocked herself out trying to get Madelyn out of her shell! Unfortunately, she had made no headway.

Sue Wiggins, the former minister's wife, was a friendly and loving person who was not the least bit pretentious. She dressed modestly and wore very little makeup. She truly believed that the way a person lived their life was the best sermon they could ever preach. She was dearly loved by everyone. Even the gossips at church left Sue Wiggins alone but often criticized her husband. They believed him to be too rigid. Nella enjoyed a close friendship with Sue Wiggins and was probably her closest friend. They shopped and went to lunch quite often. If someone was causing a problem at church, it was Sue Wiggins that intervened and smooth over ruffled feelings. Everyone, that is, with the exception of Madelyn Reece.

Now that the new minister, Chris Daniels, was on the scene, Nella believed he might be the one to fill Sue's shoes. Nella spoke to the new minister about it, and he agreed that he thought Mrs. Reece was insecure despite her enormous wealth and in need of spiritual guidance. Chris agreed to go with Nella to pay Mrs. Reece a home visit. Surely, it couldn't hurt.

They both expected a cold shoulder when they knocked on the door early that Monday morning. Would she invite them in? She appeared at the door with a frown on her face, but the minute she saw Christopher Daniel, she gleefully invited them into her extravagant home. The house was really something to see. The furniture, all pearly white, looked like no one had ever touched it, let alone sat on it. Madelyn pointed to the sofa that was also pristine white. It made Nella nervous to take a seat. Madelyn immediately offered them coffee and began making conversation as if they were her best friends. Nella could not believe her eyes. Nella knew that it was Chris Daniels that had put a sparkle in Madelyn's eyes. He had that kind of effect on people and certainly this wealthy widow. Madelyn began talking about her deceased husband, something she had never done before. Before the visit ended, Madelyn invited Chris Daniels out to dinner. She wanted to take him to her late husband's restaurant, Mr. R's Steakhouse. The restaurant had been bought by a man that kept the same name because the restaurant was so popular.

Nella was delighted that the visit had gone better than expected, but she was a little bit concerned about Madelyn's interest in the new minister. He was young and very good-looking. Definitely, a man that most woman would go for! It seemed that Madelyn was not the only one with stars in her eyes. She noticed also that Christie Woodson had lost some weight and was dressing sexier. Christie had never been able to lose weight before the new minister came on board. During the conversation at Madelyn's house, Chris Daniels said something that caught Nella's attention. When Madelyn asked him about the last place where he worked, he said the Church of the Firstborn in Logan, Texas. Nella remembered distinctly that Reverend Daniels told her that his last place of employment was in Middleton, Texas. This struck her as being odd. Why would he lie? She thought about it all the way on their drive back home. There was something that didn't gel with his stories. She glanced over at him across the seat of the car, and he seemed to be in deep concentration. Nella had picked Chris up from his home that morning, and he was not going back to the office with her. She felt relieved that she was dropping him off. This could give her some time to go back to the office and snoop in his personal files. She pulled the car into his driveway. He said goodbye, acting so relaxed and confident that she felt a little bit ashamed of her suspicion. Was she looking for flaws in the new minister's character? She hoped for the church's sake, she would not find any.

As much as she tried to accept the new minister, there was just something about him that did not seem honest. She could not ignore the nagging voice that told her something was wrong. His accepting the job and willing to work with such a small congregation didn't seem to fit his style. He was flamboyant and polished. Great church material! Actually, Chris Daniels made her feel insecure about her position at the church. She felt beneath his style—he was drop-dead handsome, and she was heavy and unattractive. She wished that old Mr. Wiggins was back! She started to think about all the money the church was bringing in! That was a good thing especially for her concerning security in her job. She no longer had to worry about going part-time. She had to admit Chris had his good points! He was confident without being arrogant. It was Chris Daniels that mowed Marge Coker's yard when she fell and hurt her leg. This was something old Mr. Wiggins would never have done. In fact, Mr. Wiggins didn't like the woman. He thought she talked too loudly and was too aggressive. Mr. Wiggins had nicknamed her Large Marge. She found out about the name, and it took Sue Wiggins to straighten it out. Marge took an instant liking to Chris Daniels. Marge was so grateful for him cutting her grass that she began baking cookies and cake and bringing them to the office. Chris always invited Nella into his office to share the delicious desserts. He could be so considerate of her, she felt guilty about being so negative about him. Once back to work, Nella headed for the file cabinet that sat in the corner of his office.

She would take a better look at the résumé of the man that was working miracles with membership and filling up the collection plates. She could not help wondering what the motive was for him being there. Why would he select such a small church like Bridgeport to work for? She thought about how handsome and charming Chris was. Big rich churches would jump at the chance to hire him. He was a man that drew people to him like a magnet He didn't fit into the slow pace of Bridgeport. Most people there were middle income with the exception of a few like Madelyn Reese. Looking at his résumé, she saw that he was forty-seven years old. He had graduated from the Good Harvest School of preaching in Blair, Texas. He had listed four previous places of employment: churches in New Hope, Middleton, Logan, and Little Springs, where the Wiggins had moved. His references were impressive. Every church seemed saddened by his departure. She read the résumé a second time. His reason for leaving each church was that he enjoyed being an evangelist and building up small churches. He was certainly doing just that at Bridgeport. She closed the file and put it back in the cabinet. She wasn't supposed to be snooping in personal files, and for the last twenty years, she'd had no reason to. Mr. Wiggins's life was an open book. She wished she could say the same about Mr. Daniels. She felt the elders had hired him too quickly because he was so good at selling himself. They would be furious if they knew she was snooping. She would be fired if they found out. She was treading deep waters and she felt nervous.

The next few days Chris and Nella talked about the big change in Madelyn Reece. "She just needed convincing that people care about her and not her money," Chris told her. She had to admit that whatever had happened, Chris had done a good job in making her feel like a cherished member. Madelyn had become friendly with the other women in church, inviting them to her home for Bible study. Most of all, she invited Chris Daniels over. Nella hoped that Madelyn was not getting personally involved with all the attention he was lavishing on her. He was much too young for the elderly woman's affection, yet he was spending a lot of time at her house. Nella wondered if Chris Daniels was asking her for money behind everyone's back? One day while Madelyn was visiting the church, she went straight to Chris's office and shut the door. Nella thought she heard arguing. Suddenly Madelyn burst out the door, acting upset about something. She left immediately. Then Chris appeared in the doorway and gave Nella some new names and addresses to add to the church directory. He appeared to be in a good mood and showed no signs of anything unpleasant taking place. He complimented Nella on her good work and disappeared back into his office. Before he shut the door, he told Nella he would be taking all his calls directly. Nella was grateful for his help. Since he had become minister, the calls had tripled. Answering the phone directly was something Mr. Wiggins would never do.

Another thing that Nella was grateful for and that was Chris did not keep track of how long she took for lunch. He got his own coffee and sorted out a lot of the mail. One morning while helping her with the mail, he said, "People worry so much about things that never happen." She wondered if Chris saw how insecure she was and was trying to make her feel better. She tried to ignore all the little red flags that were flying high since he could be so considerate at times. Once standing right outside his door by the copy machine, she heard him using vulgar language. He did not know she was there. She quickly left so he would not see her. Nella, in all her years as the church secretary, had never heard old Mr. Wiggins use bad language. She felt at a loss for what to do. If she told anyone, would they believe her? She wondered why Christie Woodson had not picked up on some of his bad behavior. Was Christie like the rest of the church, blind to his faults because he was overhauling the church? She went back to her desk to get a good grip on herself. The phone rang, and it was Sue Wiggins. Sue wanted to know how things were going since she had not heard from her for a while. The sound of Sue's voice was so comforting that before Sue could make a complete sentence Nella was making arrangement to pay her a visit.

"I have something very confidential that I want to talk over with you," Nella said. Hearing the tone of Nella's voice made Sue worry.

"What is it, Nella?" After Sue swore never to tell a soul, Nella told her what she had overhead by the copy machine and how Madelyn Reece had stormed out of the office after a private conversation in Chris's office. The first thing that came to Sue's mind was that the new minister might be asking Madelyn for money or large donations. Both women shared the same view after a long visit. Nella told Sue that she still wanted to come visit her. "I am going to make a copy of his résumé and bring it with me so you can see. Try to remember everything he told us that day he came to look over the church." Sue remembered it well. She had been in her husband's office, and he had just left to go to Safeway with a shopping list to get some things for the church. Sue heard talking in the front office, and it was a man's voice. She understood that he was there to make inquiry about the minister's position that had been advertised.

When she entered the outer office, she saw a tall dark handsome man talking to Nella. He was dressed in a dark gray suit with a striped black-and-white tie. As Sue entered the room, his attention went to her as if she was the most important person in the world. As he continued to talk, Sue could see that Nella was puzzled like herself. He looked more like an executive of some big company rather than a minister at a small church. Nella had seen many applicants in the last few weeks but nothing like this Chris Daniels, who was so confident and so full of himself. After he left, Sue told Nella that there was no way he would accept such a meager salary and work with such a small church. He would look them over and head for greener pastures.

They both thought the elders and deacons would find him out of their reach and go for someone more down to earth. Things did not turn out as Sue had predicted. After a thirty-minute meeting with Chris Daniels, the elders were confident they had the right man for the job. Nella sat at her desk trying to concentrate as they sat behind closed doors. When they emerged all smiles and shaking hands, Nella knew her new boss had just been hired.

Sue told Nella that next Friday would be fine to visit. After cautioning her young friend to be very careful about her detective work, she asked her to spend the night. "No need to spend your money on a hotel," Sue told her. After hanging up the phone, Nella made two copies of Chris's résumé. She was on her way back to her desk when she heard someone come in the front door. She tucked the résumé inside a folder that she was holding just in case something like this happened. She prayed it wasn't Chris. She was relieved when she saw it was Bob Edwards, one of the elders. He wanted to see Chris about the upcoming revival. Nella, with the résumé held close to her bosom, told Mr. Edward that Chis was at home. After he left, she felt some satisfaction that she had been courageous enough to take the first step. If this new minister was up to no good, it was up to her to bring it out in the open.

She took off the following Friday morning for Little Springs. It was almost an hour's drive. This was her first visit to see the Wigginses. The house was small, with only two bedrooms and one bath. But it had been well cared for. After the move, the Wigginses had bought some new furniture, which was long overdue. Sue had gotten rid of the big sectional couch and replaced it with a smaller sofa and love seat. Mr. Wiggins gave Nella a hug, telling her how nice it was to see her again. After joining in the conversation for about thirty minutes, Mr. Wiggins excused himself and told the two women to go have lunch. They ended up lingering over coffee at a nearby Mexican restaurant. Nella was doing all the talking, trying to fill Sue in on every little detail. Sue's nose was stuck in the résumé, reaffirming to Nella that Chris Daniels had told them conflicting stories. After putting the résumé aside, Sue told Nella that she had done some snooping of her own. It seemed that an elderly woman named Loretta Springer, age 69, had fallen down a flight of stairs in her home. Her family thought it suspicious and wanted the police to look into it. The family had suspicions about another family member. After a lengthy investigation, the police had ruled it an accident. Then Sue said, "Mrs. Springer was a wealthy widow and a member of the church where Chris Daniels preached."

After lunch, the two women decided to do more investigating. They went to the library and looked up mysterious deaths in the towns where Chris had worked. Nella pulled out a little notebook where she had written down the towns and the dates. They would have to be very discreet about combing through the old newspaper clippings because someone at the library might figure out what they were doing. He made friends everywhere, so they would need to be very careful.

"What time period did Chris work in Little Springs?" Sue asked. Nella, looking back in her notebook, said that he had listed 1990 to 1993. After searching about twenty minutes, they came across an article that read, "Family thinks elderly woman's death looks suspicious." The article confirmed that Loretta Springer had died June 9, 1993. That was the year the Chris Daniels had resigned from his position at the church in Little Springs. Next, they pulled up an article about a woman named Janice Norton, age 57, in Logan, Texas, that had fallen to her death from a cliff while hiking alone. Ms. Norton was an avid hiker that went on frequent hiking trips with friends. Her family thought her death suspicious since Mrs. Norton never went hiking alone. This was her first and foremost safety rule. The family could not understand why she would go alone and didn't believe that she did. They noticed the date was September 14, 1989. They looked back at the notebook. Reverend Daniels conducted her services. He had been employed as the minister at the True Gospel Church in Logan. At the top of the article was a picture of Janice Norton. She was a very attractive woman with dark hair and a sweet smile. The picture gave Nella a chill.

"I've had all I can stand for one day," Nella told Sue. The two women left the library feeling nauseous.

Nella drove back to Bridgeport more than upset the following day. There were two elderly women who had died mysteriously and in an untimely manner. And the preacher at each church had been Christopher Daniels. Was she in danger herself working alone with him so much of the time? Maybe she should tell Christie Woodson! But Sue had warned her against it. "Christie has a big mouth, and she will spread the news like wildfire. We need to be very careful because we are dealing with a dangerous man!"

Nella felt numb.

Once back at work, Nella wondered if Chris knew about her snooping in his files and that she was looking into his past. She trembled at the thought of her mission ahead. If he found out, he would surely do something terrible to her also. No one at church would suspect him. She was grateful that she had told her findings to Sue Wiggins. She no longer drank the coffee Chris Daniels brought to her desk. She pretended to sip it, then dumped it in the large plant by her desk. She no longer ate any dessert that Large Marge brought. It would be too easy for him to slip in a dose of poison. Her excuse for turning it down was that she was on a diet.

She wondered if he believed her. Reverend Daniels would wink at her and tell her in a charming way that there would just be more of her to love! She prayed he wasn't picking up on her anxieties. Her nights were now filled with nightmares. She wondered if he had any former secretaries that were missing. Nella was working on the revival meeting plans when Bob Edwards came rushing into the office. His face was a white as a ghost. Madelyn Reece had been found dead in her bed that morning.

It looked like natural causes. Reverend Daniels, hearing the news, came rushing into the front office. He was supposed to pay Madelyn a visit that morning, but she had called him the night before complaining of feeling sick. She believed she was coming down with a bad cold. Chris had her name written on his calendar to visit at ten o'clock that morning but instead had coffee with another minister since she was under the weather. Little by little the office filled up with shocked members who couldn't believe she was gone.

The next week was hectic with Madelyn's funeral. The only family member she had left was a cousin in Denver, Colorado, who felt she had died of natural causes. He did not need her money and was agreeable that the bulk of her estate go to the church. The Wigginses attended the funeral and sat beside Nella with grim faces. Nella sat tearfully on the pew, feeling more fear than grief. After the services, Sue pulled Nella into the office and told her that they must go immediately to the police. He had killed at least three women, and there could be more out there that no one knew about. He had to be stopped.

"He must be a serial killer," Sue told Nella.

Poor Nella! She was completely beside herself. After all, it was her job was on the line, and she had to live in Bridgeport. What was she to do? Sometimes she felt so sure that he did it, and then at times, she felt that they were jumping to conclusions. Maybe these elderly women had died accidentally. Madelyn's autopsy report was yet to be revealed by the police. Maybe they should wait until the cause was reported, then they could go to the police. After much arguing back and forth, Sue agreed to wait until the cause of death was confirmed to go to the police. But it was very dangerous to wait too long.

The next few weeks were pure hell. Nella watched every move the young preacher made. He showed no signs of being upset or nervous about anything. But she did notice that he was keeping his office locked and that he was spending more time than usual at the office. Why did he feel it necessary to keep the door locked? Did he have something that he was trying to hide? She recalled the morning that Madelyn had left his office upset and he had pretended that nothing had happened. Why? She tried to focus on her work, but the whys kept coming. It was on a Thursday morning that Christie Woodson called to tell Nella that Madelyn Reece had died from an overdose of sleeping pills. Nella's heart began to race. He was getting away with murder again!

The first woman fell down the stairs. The second woman had a hiking accident. Then the third woman died of an over dose of sleeping pills. She had to admit he was clever. He was choosing ways to made it look so real. She had to stop him! She remembered she still had a key to old Mr. Wiggins's office. She scrummaged though her desk until she found what she thought was an extra set of keys. One was to the preacher's office, and the other was to his desk. She took the keys and made her way to Reverend Daniel's office. She pushed on the door and found it locked. Maybe he had left the door unlocked on purpose. Every move he made gave her a shiver.

She made her way to the desk and unlocked the middle drawer on the second try. The first thing she came across was a bank statement to an out-of-town bank. Her mouth fell open when she saw the large deposits that were being made to his account. Among them was his meager monthly salary from the church. She grabbed up the bank statement and ran to the copier. She made two copies, then ran back into his office and put the bank statement back the way she thought it should be. Her heart was beating rapidly. She then locked the middle drawer and scurried to lock the office door. She was too late. She turned around to find Chris Daniels standing at the copy machine with the bank statements in his hands.

"Do you need these statements for something, Nella?" His eyes were full of anger! "I guess that I pegged you wrong, girl! I didn't give you credit for being this smart!"

Nella began to back up into the corner of the hallway. He had caught her at her game. She began to reel from fright as he moved closer to her. He removed his necktie and began wrapping the ends around his hands. Nella felt her back against the wall, and she began to slide down toward the floor. He showed no mercy in his angry eyes. She felt the necktie go around her neck. She heard a voice in the distance, saying, "Don't wait too long before you go to the police!" Without a doubt, she knew she had! Chris Daniels was right about one thing—most people worried about things that never happened, but then again, some people were right on the dot with their concerns but waited too late to do something about it. This was true for poor Nella Ross. He had actually given her so many clues along the way. She'd seen the handwriting on the wall but could not bring herself to act fast enough. She had too many doubts and worried about what others would think of her. Chris Daniels had women all figured out. He counted on their insecurities. With his abilities, he would have little trouble in making up a story of how he found his poor dead secretary. The only thing that bothered him at this time was the trips Nella had been making to see her friend, the ex-preacher's wife. But this was his specialty, his expertise—fooling people. He knew the minute Sue Wiggins had pulled Nella aside at the funeral of Madelyn Reese that they were on to something. He had taken care of Nella, and she was no longer a problem. Now all the preacher from hell had to do was find a way to get to Sue Wiggins!

CEMETERY FLOWERS

S usan Baker loved the quaint-looking old house that was just the right distance from the next-door neighbor, one block away. It was far enough away to have some peace and quiet but close enough not to feel isolated from the rest of the world. The old house had been empty for some time, and the owner wanted desperately to get rid of it. A huge For Sale sign hung in the front yard. The house wasn't in bad condition. It just had a foreboding look. The town cemetery was located directly behind the house. The property itself was impressive, with a yard full of flowery shrubs. A huge hydrangea bush hugged the eastside of the house. Next to the front porch was a showy patch of pink hibiscus. The house still held charm even though it was quite unusual. It definitely had personality. Its large windows went all the way to the floor, spilling volumes of sunlight throughout the rooms. Two Bradford pear trees stood majestic in front yard. The trees gave more than adequate shade far into the afternoon when the summer heat was at its peak. After thinking it over carefully, Susan decided to make an offer on the house. She could envision herself sitting, in the early morning hours, on the circular porch, having her coffee. There was nothing about the place that she would change. She was fine with the old cemetery that backed up to her fence, with tombstones so close she could reach out and touch them. That was probably the reason the house had sat on the market for a long time. Not many people would relish the idea of dead people being so close to their back door. When the realtor pointed this out, she told him that dead people were the least of her worries. "It is the living that you have to keep an eye on!" She meant every word! In the past, she had tolerated more than a few disrespectful neighbors. The last one was a family whose teenage kid was a Peeping Tom! She had seen him at her window all times of the night. A very scary-looking kid with bushy eyebrows and a pimply face. The devil himself couldn't have been more evil-looking. She began looking for a place to move where there no children or weird teenagers. The quicker she could move, the better!

Finding this house had been a blessing. It was certainly within her price range. The owner had taken the first offer without hesitation. He handed over the house key quickly, happy that he had gotten rid of a heavy burden. The neighborhood would be perfect for her. There was a park nearby with a walking trail. Four blocks down the street, there was a grocery store, a hair salon, and a coffee shop. She could walk to any of them at her convenience. Oh, what nice walks she could take on sunny days. The location was perfect in every way, and she hoped the neighbors would be nice people. She would take her time making friends and getting to know the right people. Buying the property had been smooth sailing. Now came the hard part: packing. She had accumulated a mass of things, especially books and magazines. Now was a good time to get rid of some of the junk that she no longer needed or used. She sorted through her things and decided what she wanted to donate. She called Goodwill. She should have done this long ago. After a strained back and sore legs from moving a mountain of stuff, she settled in her new home, enjoying the pink hibiscus and the purple hydrangea in the front yard.

The unpacking could be done later when she felt stronger. As time went by, Susan got her stuff unpacked and starting spending a good part of each day on her back porch, watching the frequent funerals that happened almost daily. She hoped no one would notice that she had become a spectator. She did not want to be considered some kind of weirdo! So far, no one had paid any attention to her gawking. Sometimes, if the flowers were especially beautiful, Susan would wait until dark and sneak into the graveyard, taking some of the flowers, being careful not to take too many and be too obvious. She rationalized that the flowers would last much longer in a vase of cool water rather than the hot ground in the cemetery. This was not really stealing! She considered herself a woman of good morals, values, and character. She gave to those that were needy and had volunteered her services at the food bank. Susan donated to Goodwill and the Salvation Army. She respected the dead. When she collected the flowers, she made it a point not to step on any graves. How much more respectful could she be? She hoped every one of them had gone onto a better place. Susan had not met the neighbors as yet. Not personally. They had only acknowledged her with a friendly wave. So far, she had seen only the wife briefly. From the first day, they seemed rather distant, maybe with good reason. Susan understood perfectly. She was careful herself about getting too chummy with people she didn't know. It would take time to gain their trust and likewise. Because she hadn't made any friends since her move to the new place, Susan decided that she would join a large church that was within walking distance of her house. It was an immense building with a large white steeple. She would have preferred a smaller one, like the one she was accustomed to attending. The large church would be fine for now. In time, she would get to know them. Attending church was a must for her! Her mom went to church every Sunday.

Her first visit was a good one. The people sang beautiful hymns, their voice blending into perfect harmony that gave her spiritual uplifting. It was good to be in church again! Susan was deeply moved. She had never heard voices that lovely. It couldn't have been more beautiful if the angels were singing themselves. The minister gave a touching sermon about keeping the commandments of God. He quoted the Ten Commandments as the rules to live by, and this would ensure a well-lived and righteous life. Susan felt that she had kept them all with the exception of telling a little white lie now and then to keep from hurting someone's feelings. Then there was the income tax thing! It was like a white lie! Not really considered to be a sin. Everybody cheated on their taxes. Susan had cheated on her income taxes for years! She could not possibly meet the tax burden heaped upon her. She would have nothing left for living expenses. What else could she do? She concluded that it was not all that bad and certainly nothing to be concerned about. It was an understanding among good people that it was acceptable to tell white lies and cheat on income taxes.

Upon leaving the church that Sunday morning, several members greeted her with words of encouragement to come again. She left that day trying to remember names and faces. She had never been good with that. It would take time to get to know them individually.

Susan was drawn to the minister immediately! He was a sweet old man named Jim Hollister, who walked with a limp, using a cane. His wife, a slender woman much taller than her husband, stood by his side, greeting people as they filed out one of the front doors of the church. More people than she could possibly remember made it a point to greet her. Before she left the church that Sunday, she requested a copy of the church directory. It would help her put names with faces. One of the ushers told her that the directories were "on order." They would make sure she received a copy when they arrived. For the time being, she would need to rely on her memory.

One Monday night about seven o'clock, Susan heard an unexpected knock on the front door. It was late October and already dark at that early hour. It was a gloomy evening, and she was totally surprised that someone would venture out on such a dark rainy night. Her visitor was a tall man wearing pants that was much too short for his long legs. His hair was gray and neatly combed. He was dressed in a dark suit with a dingy white shirt. Other than being too small, it looked like his Sunday best. She suspected that he was a member of the nice church she had found and he had come to pay her a friendly visit. The right thing to do was to invite the gentleman inside her home and let him know she was pleased with his godly intentions.

He introduced himself as Homer Phillips and made a comment about the weather being so rainy. He took long strides as he made his way across the room to the sofa. Being a woman of good manners, she asked Mr. Phillips if he would like a cup of tea.

"Yes, I would," he answered politely. "This is a great night for a cup of hot tea. I like some Earl Grey if you have it." Looking dour, he said, "I take two lump of sugar and just a tad of cream."

After a pleasant conversation about politics and how they were ruining the country, Mr. Phillips finished his cup of tea. He told her that it was getting late and he had to be going. He thanked her for her hospitality, then left promptly at 8:00 p.m. As he walked out the door, Homer told her how beautiful her floral arrangement of daylilies looked. She had taken the daylilies from the graveyard the night before.

What a nice man! I have found a wonderful church, she thought.

The next night after Susie had finished her dinner of roast chicken and freshly baked bread, she heard a knock at the door. This time, it was a petite elderly lady in a bright green dress that almost dragged the floor. Her hair was pulled high in a bun that sat on top of her small head. She stood no more the five feet tall. She looked thin and frail. She too appeared to be wearing her Sunday best. Her face had an angelic look to it when she smiled. She introduced herself as Chloe Watson. The two women were soon engaged in a very pleasant conversation about the community. They talked about what stores to shop in and the best places to dine. Noticing the flowers, Mrs. Watson complimented her on a lovely flower arrangement that sat on her coffee table. Susan had hoped that Ms. Watson didn't notice that she was blushing at the mention of the flowers. She quickly told her guest the irises had come from a local flower shop. As soon as the lie slipped from her lips, she regretted it.

The lie had not been deliberate lie! It was an act of self-defense to save her reputation. She couldn't let her church friends know about her visits to the cemetery after dark. Trying to change the subject, Susan asked Mrs. Watson if she would like some tea to warm herself on such a cold night. Ms. Watson accepted the offer, telling her that she would like a cup of Earl Grey tea, if she had it, "with two lumps of sugar and a just tad of cream." The visit continued to be very enjoyable. At 8:00 p.m., Ms. Watson told Susan that she must go. She set her empty cup on the table beside the bouquet of irises. "I sure love the flowers. They add such a nice warm touch to the room," she said. Mrs. Watson opened the door and walked out into the cool night air. "Have a good evening. Thanks for the tea."

After her guest's departure, Susan felt a sting of guilt for having told a lie, but the guilt did not stop her from going to the cemetery after dark and collecting the best of the flowers. She loved flowers with their wonderful fragrance. Flowers made her happy! What could it possibly hurt to take a few that would soon be scattered in the wind? The flowers lifted her spirit and was good for her well-being, she told herself. Even though she enjoyed the visitors, she felt something odd about them! Why did they come and go like they were on a tight schedule? The room felt so cold and drafty once they left. She would stoke the fire and think of how friendly they seemed, yet their visits were unsettling. These visits troubled her to some extent. Maybe it was just her imagination! She would talk to

Brother Hollister about her visitors. Maybe go to his house and have dinner as his sweet wife had suggested.

The strange visits continue on into the fall. One or two visitors came each week. Each visitor was always so cheerful and wanting to know of her well-being. She still thought it odd that each one made inquiries about her bouquet of fresh flowers. She reminded herself that nice people make nice remarks. They were just making conversation, she hoped.

As time passed, Susan no longer felt guilty about the lies she told about her fresh flowers. They were necessary! Otherwise, she would not be telling them. The visitors had always accepted her stories. Besides, they were now her friends. Slowly her conscience eased. She felt quite comfortable taking flowers from the cemetery when the opportunity was there. She had been taking them for quite some time, and no one had ever said anything about missing flowers. Even her friends told her that they enjoyed the flowers as much as she did.

It was on a Wednesday night. The day had been cool, with sprinkles of sunshine—a warm day for November. The funeral that day had been someone of great importance. The procession of car seemed endless! People in new cars! Women in mink coats with fashionably dressed men on their arms. Susan sat hidden behind the curtain as she looked on. She had never seen such a crowd of people. Maybe it was the funeral of a former mayor or public official. So many people had shown up to show their respects. She would check the newspaper. She was anxious for dark to descend upon the graveyard. Surely, the flowers would be magnificent for such a celebrity. Night came, and she made a quick trip to the cemetery as soon as she felt it was safe. She was not disappointed with what she found. She scooped up at least two dozen red roses, hurried back home, and had barely got them arranged in a vase when she heard a knock at the door. She opened it to find a woman standing there. She looked at the clock. It was seven o'clock. The woman introduced herself as Thelma Nichols. The woman's eyes went straight to the red roses. Her eyes were admiring their rich, vibrant color. Susan, being a woman of good manners, invited the woman in. The guest was dressed in light-colored clothing with a dark cape around her thin shoulders. Susan asked her guest if she would like a cup of hot tea.

She gladly accepted. "Yes, I have tea about this time every night. I prefer Earl Grey if you have it."

"How do you take your tea?" Susan asked.

The visitor quickly told her, "With two lumps of sugar and a tad of cream." The lady talked about her many travels in faraway places as she sipped the hot tea slowly. "This is a perfect cup of tea." Her compliments to the hostess were gracious. When the cup was empty, she sat the cup down on the coffee table. Susan noticed that her hands were as white as the cup itself. "Oh, it's 8:00 p.m., and I must be going!" She pulled her cape tightly around her shoulders to brace herself from the cool night air.

She left exactly at eight o'clock. Susan felt more than puzzled about her visitors. She couldn't remember seeing any of them at church. Not any of their faces looked familiar! Being so perplexed, she had left a note with Brother Hollister, making inquiry about the people who were coming to her door so often. The minister did not respond to her request. She knew he was busy for his congregation was large.

Soon the chill of the fall air turned to brutal cold! It was now the dead of winter. The funerals kept coming. Susan watched from the large window that faced the cemetery. The weather was frigid. She could not sit on the back porch. The cold wind had a terrible sting, but this did not stop her from gathering the flowers under the cover of darkness. Life was good. She had recently made friends with the neighbor that lived down the street. They turned out to be very good neighbors. They mostly kept to themselves and minded their own business.

It was on a late December night. The snow had stopped, and the whole world looked like a winter wonderland. Definitely, it was a night to stay indoors, read a good book, and enjoy the warmth of the fire. She had just blown out the last candle and was settling in for a good night's sleep when a knock came at the door.

"Who could this be on such a frightful night?" She knew she must answer the door or die of curiosity. When she opened the door, there stood old Reverend Hollister. His face looked so grim!

"How are you this cold evening?" Brother Hollister asked. He looked half frozen as he stood there in her doorway with snow covering his coat and knitted cap.

She knew he had not paid a social call at this time of night to merely ask that simple question.

"Please come in," she said, knowing there had to be a good reason for his untimely visit. The snow had started coming down hard again. "Please wrap yourself warmly and come with me," he said. "I have something to show you!"

Puzzled, Susan Baker grabbed her heavy coat and began to following the minister out into the deep snow. There were at least four inches of snow covering the ground, Reverend Hollister led her around the house and back into the cemetery.

"You have asked me who all your visitors were. The time has come to show you," he said.

She followed him through the graveyard gate, holding her coat tightly around her. She had never felt such bitter cold. They fought against the icy wind as they made their way into the graveyard. She knew the graveyard well but never bothered to look at the names on the tombstone. It would make it too personal. She felt better not knowing who they were. Brother Hollister stopped at a grave with a rather odd marker. The old minister cleared his throat and stood at a grave. "Here is where Homer Phillips resides," he said as he pointed to a grave that looked as if it had been there forever. "He was killed when our bank was robbed fifteen years ago!"

He then proceeded to the next grave. "Here is Chloe Watson, and next to her is her sister, Bessie Hazelwood. All these people were beloved members of our congregation who have gone on to their reward in heaven! And over here is Thelma Nichols. She was our city manager for years. She was killed in an auto accident with a drunk driver! The whole town showed up for her funeral." He brushed at his eyes as the snow continued to fall. Susan immediately knew her funeral was the one with the large crowd of people. Her flowers were the deep red roses that now sat on her coffee table.

Susan stood there feeling like a child that had been caught in some terrible misdeed! Maybe she would be arrested and go to jail. She began to cry. This wasn't happening to her! This must be a dream! Something was so wrong here. She reached out to touch the minister, running her fingers across his hand, trying to figure out if he was flesh and blood. She could feel nothing! He suddenly turned and walked toward another grave. "And over here"—he cleared his throat twice—"is my grave!" He pointed to a crumbling tombstone void of any decor. She slowly read the name—Rev. James Hollister. She felt her body shaking from fear. How had she been so blind to the strange church? All that mattered was that they had accepted her at face value. Now the truth was out for all the people to know and see. Somehow, she found her voice.

"I don't know what to tell you, Reverend, except, please forgive me and please ask God to forgive me. I have done a terrible thing, and I am so terribly sorry." She went on talking as if she was begging for her life. "I didn't feel like it was stealing, and the flowers were going to waste!" She looked down at the grave, wishing that she was the one that was buried beneath the cold snow.

Brother Hollister seemed to be forcing a smile. She reached out for his hand, but he did not accept. Instead, he spoke sternly to her. "Sister Baker, the people who brought the flowers to the graves of their love ones meant for them to have the flowers. It is their way of taking care of them and keeping them forever in their hearts and mind." He paused for a minute. "How do you know what people feel that have passed away?"

Susan was crushed by the elderly man's question.

"I am so sorry," she said. "I now see that I was wrong! I wish that I could change this!" She was now trembling from both fear and the cold.

"You can," Brother Hollister told her. "Stop stealing the flowers!"

The word *stealing* burned her to the core. She was no longer a respected person. The words hurt more than if he had been throwing stones at her.

"Yes," she said. "I will, I will!" She watched as Brother Hollister turned and disappeared into the darkness.

Susan slowly walked back to her house reeling from the brutal cold. Its teeth cut like steel against her face, wet from tears. A strange sensation was overtaking her body, mind, and soul! Where was she? Was she alive or dead? Was she in heaven or hell? She sensed that she had been the victim of a violent crime! She sensed that she had been killed in a bank robbery recently. Was the new church her place in heaven or hell? Maybe now she would be condemned and sent to live in hell!

THE THIRTIETH
CLASS REUNION

I was so excited about our upcoming thirtieth class reunion that I could hardly sleep at night. There were so many things I wanted to accomplish before the big night. I wanted to lose at least fifteen pounds before I tackled anything else. I would get a great hairstyle, buy a smashing new designer outfit, and drive my sister's Lexus to the reunion. I wondered how my other old classmates would look. I hoped they had aged right along with me. Big hips, some gray hair, body wrinkles, and slow-moving! I must admit I hoped no one would be too successful, too famous, or too rich! I would be jealous! I just didn't want to look like a loser! My crash diet the last month had been green salads and roast chicken! I was so sick of them I thought that I would die. I lost only seven pounds, but my clothes did feel a little bit looser.

When I arrived at the convention center where we were to have our meeting, I saw lots of parked cars, so it looked like a good turnout. I felt nervous as I parked my sister's white Lexus some distance away from the next car. She'd told me to be careful. I observed a red Mercedes and wondered who it belonged to. I suspected that it belonged to Cory Thompson. He was tall, good-looking, and sort of reminded me of Cary Grant. Cory had been voted the most likely to succeed. I had completely forgotten about him until I saw the car. I hoped he would be there.

I made my way through a small group that were hugging each other and acting happy to be reunited again. I saw many of my old schoolmates, but a few faces looked unfamiliar. It was the first reunion I had attended but not the first that our class had held. I had missed the last one due to the birth of a grandchild. I recognized Emma Williams from the start. She looked gorgeous with her long red hair and slender legs. She had been voted the prettiest girl in class. As I approached her, she said my name, and I felt good at being recognized so quickly. Maybe I hadn't aged so much. We sat down at the nearest chairs available, and she began to pull out pictures of her grandchildren. All beautiful children just like their grandmother. She asked me to see pictures of mine. It never occurred to me to bring pictures of my grandchildren, which made me feel very shallow at the moment and not a very good grandmother.

She had a handful of pictures, and I was trying to act interested when we heard a commotion toward the back of the building. Walking toward the commotion, we became aware of a gathering of people down toward the women's restroom. We could tell something out of the ordinary had happened by the way people were clustered around the area. Then we heard someone say that a dead body had been found in the bathroom and it could the scene of a murder! I was shocked! Most everyone had their cell phone out and were making calls, telling their friends and family that something terrible had happened! A uniformed police officer came out and gave a loud order: "Everyone stay right where you are! No one is permitted to leave the building!"

I saw the police standing up next to the restroom, and I walked up closer to get a better look. I aggressively passed the people that had been pushed to the side. With curiosity killing me, I peeked inside, and I could see a woman lying on the floor. I had no idea who she was! After a few minutes, I found out it was Kim Rogers, the bully of Roosevelt High! My mind was racing at how such a thing could have happened. I am not talking about her being murdered but the nerve she had in coming to the reunion in the first place. I wasn't even sure if she was even invited. Nobody liked her! I couldn't imagine anyone wanting her there. We had never forgotten how cruel she was! She was hated by a lot of people including myself. Kim had made a lot of peoples miserable the whole four years we were in high school. Most of the kids she tormented were from the country and poor kids. Maybe we looked like country hicks to Kim Rogers, but she had no reason to pick on us! She was a city kid with a dad that owned a car dealership and was on the school board. No one could do anything about the bullying. I did my best to stay out of her way. Somehow, she found me no matter how far away from her I tried to stay. She was always in my face, making me look like a coward. Maybe I was? Kim was a big girl that towered over me. She played girls' basketball, and I could see how tough she was. I did not want to tangle with her. She outweighed me by at least twenty-five pounds. Despite being such a tomboy, Kim Rogers was very pretty without any makeup. She had light blonde hair that curled in ringlets when she emerged from the shower after gym classes. The ringlets made her face only sweeter. She had bright blue eyes and a delightful smile that hid her true character in a very charming fashion. A devil in disguise! It was terrifying to have her set her sights on me! I felt like a trembling mouse being chased by a gigantic tomcat everywhere on the school grounds! Her laughter and voice were etched in my dreams at night. I took gym class for only one year to stay clear of her.

I watched as the police officers started gathering information about the murder victim. An officer was talking to Jack James, who had done most of the planning for the reunion. He was waving his hands up in the air, and he looked like he was giving them plenty of information. I hoped not about me. Everyone knew the trouble she had heaped upon me. I felt my knees giving way, and I propped myself against the wall for a few minutes to keep from falling. There I remained for a few minutes, hoping no one would notice how I was shaking so badly.

I was walking away when the one of the policemen called my name. I cringed at the thought of being questioned about someone I disliked so much. Yes, I hated the girl! Yes, she had bullied me to the breaking point! Yes, I wanted to murder her, but I could not do that! I did not try to hide my contempt for Kim Rogers! I was not a good liar. Yet I knew many other classmates hated her just as much as I did. Probably forty to fifty students in our class hated her!

Especially a girl named Merle Myers. I remember the day Merle enrolled at Roosevelt High. She was a pathetic-looking girl with tacky clothes and long dishwater-blonde hair. Her face was covered with acne, and she had a large round stomach that looked like it could topple her over. We all thought she was pregnant, but she was not. She was grossly overweight along with being a poor country kid. The minute Kim Rogers laid eyes on Merle, she began making fun of Merle's clothes and her fat stomach! I must admit I felt so relieved that Kim was off me and on to someone else. However, I felt so sorry for Merle, and I tried to befriend her by inviting her into my group of friends. She turned out to be a lot of fun with a good sense of humor. She soon fit right in with my circle of friends. We were simply the poor kids from the sticks! The city kids thought that we were nothing but a bunch of nerds.

I told the police officer everything I knew. That I had just arrived and the only person I had talked to was Emma Williams. I hoped I didn't appear too nervous. Next, the police talked to Merle Myers, who looked completely different than she did in high school. She was slim with a clear complexion and dressed very fashionably. She walked with an air of confidence. She seemed arrogant while answering their questions! I began to wonder about her! Why had she come to our class reunion?

It seemed fitting that old Kim had been murdered in the restroom. Her mind was always in the toilet with her vile language! I wondered how she had been killed! Was she dunked in the toilet until she had drowned? I circled around back to the restroom and walked up to the door and looked into the restroom. I managed to get a good look at Kim's body despite the yellow tape marking off the crime scene. Kim was sprawled on the floor. There was blood splattered around on the walls and the floor. She must have put up quite a fight! A thick puddle of blood had pooled under her neck. It was a gruesome scene! I almost wished I hadn't looked! I said *almost*! I stepped a little closer to the body and saw that her hair had ringlets like it did after gym class. Her head definitely looked wet. I quickly moved back and began talking to Jack James, who looked in complete shock. He was taking the crime very hard. I thought I saw him looking at my hands as if he expected combat wounds. I held my hands in plain sight so that everyone could see that I had no scratches. I felt that all eyes were on me. I was very paranoid at the moment! After what seemed like an eternity, we were told that we could leave the building. We would all be contacted at a later date, and the police would continue with their investigation at the crime scene. It was strange that no person had said how she died. Was she shot? Was she killed with a knife? Based on the blood on the floor, I assumed a knife was the murder weapon. No one had mentioned hearing the sound of a gunshot!

As I was leaving the building, I bumped into Merle again. She looked at me, yelling my name. Evidently, because of all the commotion, she had not seen me earlier even though I had seen her. Merle wrapped her arms around me and gave me about the biggest hug I have ever had. She had incredible strength and practically lifted me off the ground.

"I've thought of you often," she said. "I remember how badly that Kim Rogers treated both you and me! No one would come to our rescue, not even the teachers."

I could detect the emotions she was feeling thinking about our days of being bullied by Kim. Then I remembered the incident that happened in our high school restroom. It was right after lunch, and the bell had rung. Merle and I made a quick dash to the restroom, having only a minute to get to math class. We had no idea that Kim Rogers was behind us. Suddenly, Kim had Merle by the hair, and she was dragging her into a stall. She pulled her over to the stool and was pushing her face down like she was going to dunk her face-first in the dirty toilet bowl that had not been flushed. After a terrible struggle, Merle finally got free of her hold. Kim's friends had gathered in the restroom to witness the humiliating assault. They crowded around us, laughing and making fun of both of us! I hated myself for not jumping in and helping Merle. For some reason, I just froze! After it happened, I wished a million times that I could do that day over. That had happened so many years ago, but it was still vivid in my mind! We never reported the incident. We were too scared, knowing that the school would do nothing about it. Now thirty years later, that incident played out again in my mind.

Merle looked at me with a lot of compassion in her eyes. I just stood there staring at her and how good she looked. We walked together to the parking lot. Merle stopped at the Mercedes and fumbled for her car keys.

I was amazed when she told me she had become a physical therapist and had her own clinic in Houston. She pulled a business card from her expensive leather bag and handed it to me. "If you ever need a friend, I am there for you!"

I knew she meant it! I was so happy for her. Now she had become wealthy. I smiled at her as she opened the car door and seated herself behind the wheel. One foot was still outside the car as she continued our conversation. As she lifted her foot, I observed a smear of blood on the sole of her shoe. I held the business card tight in my hand as if it were a brick of gold. I told her goodbye and waved to her as she drove off in the bright red Mercedes.

As I walked back to my borrowed Lexus, my mind was going haywire! My mind played out scenes of revenge by Merle. So much hatred that had been repressed for many years! Maybe all that hatred had finally been released. A volcano that had finally erupted. I could see Kim Roger's face in a dirty commode before her throat was cut. That would explain the ringlets in her hair. Never in a million years would I have thought our thirtieth class reunion would turn out like this! The scene of a cold-blooded murder! I looked down at Merle's business card. Could it be that she was trying to tell me that everything was going to be all right? She had made it to the top! She had money! She was a good friend! I felt that she would help me any way that she could.

A second thought entered my mind—Kim Rogers was dead! Did Merle kill Kim, finally getting revenge for Kim's acts of bullying her more than thirty years ago? Is there poetic justice in the world? I guess that time would tell. If she did it, I hoped that she would get away with it! If anybody deserved to die, it was Kim Rogers! While there were a lot of suspects that could have committed the murder, Merle had the best motive—revenge! A large group had showed up for the class reunion. There were probably thirty to forty suspects who had a motive to kill her. I left the reunion with a big smile on my face. I was probably the only person in the world that knew who had committed the murder! I sensed that Merle was going to get away with it!

A MOSCOW MULE

T he weather outside was so frightful that Caroline Kinsey decided to take the bus to work instead of driving. Why not leave the driving to someone else when a blizzard had been predicted as a one hundred percent sure thing? She walked over to the window and peeked through the blinds. Snowflakes were already swirling through the air like giant cotton balls. She glanced quickly at the clock, which screamed at her that she was running late. The thought of going outside in such brutal weather made her feel a bit panicky. What if the bus didn't run? She would have to explain to mean old Dr. Henderson why she hadn't shown up for work on time. She had heard all the rumors about him being so strict about work schedules. He didn't put up with excuses! She had never met Dr. Henderson! She didn't want to! Caroline stumbled to the kitchen thinking how blissful it would be to have the day off. She made coffee and put two slices of bread in the toaster. She made her way past the warm bed that had been so difficult to crawl out of this cold morning. She headed for the bathroom, knowing she had only a few minutes to get ready. Caroline splashed cold water on her face. The water was so cold it gave her a jolt! She proceeded to wash the sleep out of her eyes. Finally, she could see. She peeled off her flannel nightgown and laid it across a chair that she used as a catchall for discarded clothes. Today, she would wear blue jeans and a Christmas sweater. Maybe that would brighten up her day. She threw on a hint of foundation, then added a gob of black mascara to her eyelashes. Now she looked halfway alive. Caroline would have to eat on the run. She ran back to the kitchen to sack up her breakfast. She grabbed a piece of heavily buttered toast and filled her thermos with two cups of black coffee from her new coffee maker. If not for Aunt Florine, she would not have been able to afford the new coffee maker. Her aunt Florine always sent money for Christmas. Auntie was elderly and found it too difficult to shop for her family. Her checks were so generous Caroline watched the mail with anticipation. She'd found the coffee maker at Walmart a week before she received Aunt Florine's money. The coffeepot was bright red and had been the perfect gift for Christmas. Afraid that it wouldn't be there when she returned, Caroline hid it behind a mound of other coffeepots, hoping it would still be there when she got her money. She found it exactly where she had hidden it. Caroline grabbed the coffee maker and rushed to the register and paid for it! The beautiful red coffee maker was now perched on her countertop, looking as festive as her Christmas tree. Caroline put four strips of bacon in the microwave and grabbed a sandwich bag to put them in. As the bacon cooked, she ran to the closet hoping to find a coat that one might wear to the North Pole. She rummaged through the closet wondering how she had come to own such a horrible collection of coats! Most of them were the Salvation Army store!

Digging deep into the closet, she stumbled on a pair of old rubber boots that looked like something that had been worn in combat duty. They would work!

She was running so late, and she had to find something fast. She needed her job, and she didn't want the wrath of Dr. Henderson coming down on her. It would be too embarrassing. She finally found a black wool coat that was stained with food and had never been cleaned. The old coat was missing the two top buttons. She remembered buying the coat at the Salvation Army store when the city was having such a cold snap. After getting it home, she took a better look at the coat and vowed she would never wear it. The coat looked hideous! The plunge in temperature made her change her mind. Ugly or not, the old coat would keep her warm! She quickly put it on and took a last look at herself in the mirror. She cringed at how dreadfully tacky the coat made her look. It reminded her of the coats that the bell ringers wore as they stood beside the collection pots collecting money for the needy. She wished she was a bell ringer for the day. It would explain the coat. However, the coat was very heavy, and it would keep her from freezing to death while she waited for the bus.

She wrapped a soft knitted scarf around her neck and set out for the bus stop. Maybe the scarf would make up for the horrible-looking coat. She felt like a trooper as she marched against the fierce wind that blew her and her Goodwill coat down the street. The weatherman had been right on the dot this time. Huge snowflakes were coming down fast and furious, which gave a magical storybook setting for Christmas Eve. It should have been a time for happiness and celebration. Instead, here she was trudging through arctic weather.

I'm in the wrong line of work, she thought as she pulled her scarf tighter up around her freezing nose. Most people had the option of taking the day off or working only four hours on Christmas Eve. It was not that way at Crestview Medical Center. Since accidents and health problems don't take a holiday, neither did some of the employees at Crestview. Maybe she could understand if she was a nurse or a key person that had to be on duty, but Caroline was a lowly admitting clerk. The nurses could have easily handled the admitting in ER for that one day, but Dr. Henderson thought otherwise. So here she was following orders from the old jerk. Since she was the last employee hired in the admitting office, she was the first to get the schedule from hell. It was gut wrenching enough working on Christmas Eve, but she also was scheduled to work Christmas Day. It didn't matter to anyone that she had made plans to be with her family. She intended to spend Christmas Eve wrapping the rest of her gifts that still were unwrapped in the bottom of her closet. Now she would be missing out on all the fun, pecan pie, and everything else. She was feeling like a criminal who could not be home with family for Christmas.

Maybe she should have passed up this crummy job at Crestview and taken the teacher's assistant position that had been offered to her at the same time. Considering all things, she decided on taking the job at the hospital in hopes that she might meet a handsome young doctor, fall in love, and live happily ever after. Working holidays wasn't in the picture at the time of her decision. Now here she was standing on the street corner freezing to death! She could have cared less about her dreams of meeting a handsome doctor. All she wanted was a seat on a nice warm bus. She stomped her feet every few minutes to keep her toes from falling off. Finally, she saw the bus coming up the street, and she breathed a sigh of relief.

The bus came to a rolling stop at the corner of Meeker Street. The bus driver quickly opened the door to the shivering young lady who couldn't get out of the cold fast enough. The bus was exactly on schedule even though her hands and feet felt frozen. She noticed there were few cars on the street that morning, probably only people who had to work.

"Smart people find a way to stay home," she said under her breath. She embraced the warm air as it surrounded her. She loosened the scarf from around her nose so she could breathe. She had plenty of seats to choose from in the nearly empty bus. She sat down near the front and took off her gloves and unwrapped her buttered toast and bacon. She tried to sip the hot coffee, but the bus was too bouncy, and she was afraid she would burn herself. She looked up and saw the bus driver staring at her in the mirror. He had probably picked upon her sour demeanor. She recognized him immediately as the friendly bus driver. He always had sometime nice to say to everyone that was a regular rider. He was all smiles that morning, and it irritated Caroline to see anyone else so content. She tried to ignore him, but he was looking directly at her in the mirror. As he made a sharp corner turn, he jokingly said, "Something smelled awfully good, and it would be nice if she would share!"

She tried to acknowledge his humor with a halfway laugh, but it didn't seem genuine. She was definitely an unhappy camper.

"Someone is a scrooge at this Christmastime of the year," the bus driver said, poking fun at her sour face.

The two ladies that were seated behind her began to laugh and made comments that she couldn't quite make out. She was in no mood for levity! She tried to eat her breakfast in spite of their ribbing. She wondered whether the bus ride ever be over. She looked out through the steamed-up glass to see the huge hospital building coming into view. The bus slid on the ice-covered street as it came to a stop. She was elated to get off the bus at the Medical Center and leave the good cheer to the driver and the other riders. Knowing she was in a sour mood, they yelled, "Merry Christmas" as she walked away. She had to control herself to keep from yelling something profane back at them. She felt they were making fun of her!

She pushed through the heavy revolving door leading into the hospital ER area. The place seemed almost empty. Just like the bus! She passed a policeman as she made her way to the admission desk, which would be her working post for the next eight hours.

"Good morning, miss," the officer said. He was trying to sound cheerful. "So you are one of the lucky people who get to work today?"

He was seated at a podium by the front entrance and was still wearing a heavy jacket as the air was frigid near the front.

"Hope we have a quiet day," she said back as she settled in her chair and prepared herself for who knew what.

"Are you working Christmas day also?" the policeman asked.

"Yes, I am. I had to cancel my plans because Dr. Henderson's favorite employee, Sabrina 'Cute Butt,' did not want to come in today. She agreed to work Christmas for me since I swapped out Thanksgivings so that she could go out of town with her boyfriend. Now here I am, working while that witch is enjoying Christmas on my day off!"

The policeman could detect a tone of anger in her voice. He knew the great inconvenience of working terrible hours. He had also made sacrifices in being away from his family during the holidays. The policeman smiled at her. "I really don't know Dr. Henderson that well, but it sounds like you got a raw deal." The officer was trying his best to show her that he understood her dilemma. "I heard some of the other nurses complain about him. He is a real stickler when it comes to work! Now you didn't hear me say that," the cop said and gave an even bigger grin.

"No, I didn't hear a thing," she replied. She was glad that the cop was agreeing with her. His humor was beginning to work a little magic.

Caroline settled back in her chair as she began to lighten up a little for the first time that day. She had a feeling the day would be long and drawn out, so she'd stuck a paperback in her purse before she left for work. She hoped it would stay quiet so she could finish it. She looked up every few minutes and found the policeman watching her. It made her feel like she was sloughing off, so she put her book down and made conversation with him about the holidays. She didn't want him to think she was a slacker and goofing off at work. She did find him interesting and nice to talk to. The policeman disappeared around noon for lunch, and Caroline had pitiful few people that came her way. Everything was low key. The staffing was light. She made small talk with nurses and other hospital personnel that stopped for a minute to wish her a merry Christmas. After lunch,

Caroline admitted two people into the emergency room. The first one, a two-year old child, had a broken arm in a nasty fall at home while playing. The second one, an older man, had suffered a head injury due to a motorcycle accident.

After admitting the motorcycle man, she went back to reading her book. The day dragged on. Finally, 5:00 p.m. came and went. Her evening shift replacement had not shown up to relieve her! Caroline stewed as she read her book and watched the clock at the same time. The girl was now almost an hour late, and no one seemed to notice except Caroline. Where was Dr. Henderson when she needed him? Finally, the replacement, a girl named Maggie, came dragging in. She came through the ER entrance covered in melting snow. Maggie apologized profoundly. Caroline made small talk with her, trying to keep from giving her an earful about her tardiness. Both stood there for the next few minutes complaining about working on the before Christmas.

Caroline was weary from the dull day at work. She grabbed her stuff and made her way out into the street. She had already missed the 5:30 bus! Now it was time for the last bus of the day. She hoped it would be on time. If it was not on time, she would freeze to death. As she stood waiting for the bus, a growing sense of anger smothered her. How unfair life was to her! Dr. Henderson had let his favorite girl, Sabrina, pull this stunt of taking off work on the day before Christmas.

She kept looking at her watch and pulling her scarf tighter around her frozen face. The bus was already fifteen minutes late! Her toes and fingers were beginning to get numb. She looked up and down the street, praying the bus would come. She saw more traffic than anticipated, but it was moving at a painfully slow pace. Maybe the bus was stuck in the middle of the slow-moving traffic? She began rubbing her hands together to keep them warm. The snowfall was growing heavier, and she began to worry about hyperthermia! She had never experienced such cold. Maybe the bus wasn't coming at all? Maybe she should call a cab? She had some money left over from Aunt Florine's check. She pulled out her cell phone, but her fingers were so numb she could not punch in any numbers. Realizing that she had to get shelter somewhere, she walked up the street to the Double Tree Hotel. She made her way into the lobby and sat down in a corner as far away from the door as possible. Caroline sat there breathing in the warm air. She watched people come and go in the beautifully decorated lobby. She stared up at the biggest Christmas tree she had ever seen. Santa and his reindeers were in the far end of the lobby with dozens of packages in his sleigh.

After a few minutes, she began to feel up to tackling the cold wind again. She was getting her phone out to call for a cab when she noticed a cozy-looking little bar in the far corner near the Santa display. It was almost out of view from where she sat. She put her phone back in her purse and walked over toward the bar. She thought, *Maybe a drink will warm me up!*

She could hear talking and laughter from inside the bar. It was good to know that someone was having a good time. As Caroline entered the bar, she saw three men sitting up by the bartender. A television overhead was turned to the news, with a weatherman giving the latest report, which was bad! More snow over the next twenty-four hours. A warm drink sounded better all the time. After all, it was Christmas Eve. A good stiff drink might help combat her growing anger. She ran her eyes down the drink menu carefully. She decided on having a drink called the Moscow Mule. Ordinarily, she would have ordered some hot buttered rum. She felt the three men watching her, which made her uncomfortable. Caroline walked up to the bar and ordered the drink.

"Give me a Moscow Mule. Make it a double" she told the bartender!

The three men huddled at the bar, raised their glasses in a toast to the word *double*. Now they had decided to have a little fun with her! They weren't going to allow this moment pass by without a comment. "Has the little lady had a hard day?" the dark-haired man asked. The other two men joined in, having the time of their life. She tried to act like she was amused with their humor, hoping they would settle down. It was obvious they were well on their way to becoming drunk, if they were not already there. The last thing she needed after a boring day at work was to listen to three drunk old men! She turned her attention to the bartender, watching as he concocted her drink order.

"Have you ever had a Moscow Mule?" the dark-haired man asked before he emptied what was left in his glass.

She said "No, I have not!"

The old men began to laugh, thinking it was something hilarious. "You know why they call it a mule, don't you, little lady?" They were now being obnoxious, acting more like schoolboys than grown men. "It has such a kick to it they have to serve it in a copper mug! If they didn't, it would break the glass!" They all roared with laughter at being so clever.

The bartender rolled his eyes as he set the drink in front of her. He pointed to a table in the far corner of the bar. She could have privacy there. She seated herself and began sipping the strong drink. She was glad she had ordered a double shot. Since she would be taking a cab home, she didn't need to concern herself with limits. She had consumed about half the drink when a bald-headed man approached her table. He was wearing a dark suit with a white shirt and striped red tie. He was probably a businessman stopping for a drink before going home. He wasn't what she would call good-looking, but at least he wasn't drunk. He was smiling at her as he approached.

"Are you alone? Are you expecting someone?" he asked.

"Yes," she said, "I am expecting Vladimir Putin, but I don't think he is going to show." After such a terrible day, she was being rude intentionally. Why should she care about his feelings? He was probably looking for a lonely woman, and she wasn't in the mood for a joker!

She had consumed enough of the drink to get a buzz. The drink gave her a little more personality and nerve. Ordinarily, she wouldn't be so mouthy to a stranger, but this was a strange bar. She had to be careful!

"Mind if I join you?" he meekly asked. "You look a little down this evening."

"Well," she responded, "maybe I am little down, but I had a hard day, and I have to work all day tomorrow."

He could tell she was very unhappy with her circumstances. He motioned for the bartender to bring his drink over to her table. "Where do you work?" he asked.

She took a long sip from her drink and then said, "Crestview Medical Center!"

"Oh, you are one of those people who don't get a holiday?" As he said it, the bartender brought two more drinks to the table. The bartender pointed to the three loud men and told her that they were buying "a round for the little lady and her friend." The bald man raised his glass to thank the men that had been so generous. He then turned back to Caroline. "Why are you drinking alone at Christmastime?"

She was surprised that he would ask her such a personal question. She wanted to tell him that it was none of his business, but she stopped short. She felt it was good to have someone to listen. "I have an SOB for a boss," she said. "His name is Dr. Henderson. Good old Dr. Henderson! I have never seen him, but I hear he is an old devil!" It felt good to be trashing him! "I wish he were here right now. I would tell him just what I think of him."

"Just be glad you have job," the bald man said. "You know a lot of people are out of work in this economy." The man sounded serious and was making a good argument.

She placed her head in her hands to think about what he said. It made sense. She wasn't sure if it was the Moscow Mule or him that was making her calm down. All of a sudden, she didn't feel the need to vent any longer.

"You know," she said to the bald-headed man, "I need to change my attitude for gratitude. Maybe we should talk about something more pleasant," she said. Suddenly, she felt happy! "It is Christmastime! Let us talk about our best Christmas ever," she stated. He was more than agreeable to get her out of her funk. "Do you know that my best Christmas ever was the Christmas we moved into this old farmhouse? Daddy had lost his job, and we didn't have much money. A nice minister told us about the house. We could live there free until Daddy found a job! It was on a Christmas Eve just like this one. Blizzard and all!" She was feeling very tipsy, and her voice sounded strange. She didn't mind that she was making it up as she went. It sounded good to her. She went on with her fabrication. "The old house was cold, with only a fireplace to keep us warm. To keep from freezing, we kept the fireplace going all night long. The next morning, the whole country side was glistening in ice and snow. It was so beautiful!

"Our Christmas dinner was hot dogs and marshmallows that we heated up in the fireplace," she said. "Mama bought gifts for all the kids from a thrift store! I got a little doll. Mother spent the rest of the day making a dress for my doll." Caroline looked very content as she finished the story. "I believe that was my best Christmas ever." She was now smiling. "What was your best Christmas ever?" she asked.

He took a long drink, then paused for a moment. Finally, he said, "I think it was the Christmas I spend with my wife and daughter. We took a cruise to Alaska. They were so excited about seeing the whales. We had never been to Alaska. All of us had a great time! Especially Nell, my little six-year old daughter. We asked her what she liked best about the trip, and she said she liked the chili. After that, my wife had to made her bowls of chili, but they never turned out like on the cruise ship." His smile suddenly turned into a sad look. The following year, my wife and daughter were killed in a traffic accident! Their car was hit by a drunk driver." He was now the one with the long face.

Suddenly, Caroline felt ashamed of herself for having been so rude to him. "I am sorry for being such a jerk," she said. "I hope that I have not depressed you."

"No, you haven't," he said, his voice perking up a bit. "It does help to talk about it. If they were still here, we would be opening our Christmas gifts about this time! I hope that I haven't depressed you," he said, reaching out and touching her hand. They both sat at the table listening to the wind howl outside.

"Well," she said, "I have to go. The time has really gotten away from me. I think the last bus has run, so I will need to call a cab." She began gathering up her purse and her tote bag.

"I think you will be in for a long wait with this weather," he said. Not wanting her to leave so quickly, he asked her to have another drink. She stood up and apologized again for her rude behavior, extending her hand. She introduced herself to him, "I am Caroline Kinsey. I am so glad I came here tonight."

The bald man stood up and Caroline noticed immediately how short he was, and she wished she had not made such a nasty comment about short men.

"I got a great idea," he said. "How would you like to have hot dogs and roasted marshmallows for dinner tonight at my house? It is Christmas Eve. I have got a fireplace, and I can assure you it is safe to use. We can stop by the store on the way home. I must confess that I don't have any marshmallows."

"Well, I don't know if that would be a good idea," she said. She felt a little bit odd. She really liked him. She wanted so much to go home with him and sit by the fireplace. It didn't matter that he was short or bald. He was so nice to talk to. She didn't know what to do.

It really wasn't a good idea. "I don't know you, and this is a bar," she said with reluctance. She was beginning to feel bad because she felt that he was just a lonely as she was. "You haven't even told me your name," she said.

"Well, I didn't introduce myself at first because I didn't think it was the right time," he replied.

Oh boy, she thought. *He is about to reveal his true self. That he is married! That he has a wife and several kids.*

"Please don't think that I am being aggressive or forward. I did tell you that I work for Crestview Hospital! Here is my ID." He pulled back his suit coat, revealing a name tag that read, "Dr. Henderson."

Caroline could feel her face grow as red as a beet! She gasped for air! She was totally speechless!

THE REAL ESTATE
OFFICE MURDERS

T he real estate office was located directly across the street from the Highland Cemetery. With its green lawn and cast-iron fences, the cemetery sprawled a good two blocks on the east side of Fort Sill Boulevard. Gracie noticed the cemetery the day she interviewed for the part-time job at Fowler's real estate office. The realtor mainly needed someone to answer the phone when things got hectic and maybe help out with some other clerical work. The real estate office was old, a large wooden frame building. It was a well-maintained office with freshly painted walls and very expensive-looking furniture. She believed it would be a nice place to work. She saw a desk that had been cleared of all clutter on top. Only a black phone sitting on top of a phone directory and Rolodex file remained. The desk had a vacant look to it. Like a home after someone has moved out. She figured it would be hers if she was hired for the job. The interview was short and sweet. A few questions about her typing and computer skills. Did she know how to use a computer? Did she know how to cut and paste? Did she like working with the public? She had all her generic answers rehearsed from previous interviews. She answered a few questions that didn't make a lot of sense to her, such as, does your family mind if you work late some evenings? This made her wonder if Mr. Fowler had some sort of hanky-panky in mind. The weirdest question of all was the one about the cemetery. Did working close to a cemetery bother her? It seemed to be an important question to him since he saved it for last. According to Mr. Fowler, the last two employees had quit their job because of strange happenings that couldn't be explained. "Graveyards, after dark, have strange effects on some people," he told her. He asked her if she believed in ghosts. He emphasized the question because it had been a problem in the past. He ended the interview by saying that the two employees who quit were "a couple of nuts!" Of all the questions she anticipated, the graveyard thing was not one of them. She didn't believe in ghosts or evil spirits returning to haunt the living. She didn't give the question any thought. She could see where it might be a problem if someone let their imagination run wild. The one about working late did trouble her a little. The office was located in a rather seedy part of town, with a string of bars down the street.

She asked him how late, and he told her that working late was only necessary at the first of the month when all the rent payments were due. She told him that her family would not mind. She didn't bother to tell them she did not have any family in town, only a sister in Los Angeles and another in San Francisco, and she hadn't seen either in over two years. They were not close to each other. Money was tight! This was the reason she was taking a part-time job.

She liked Mr. Fowler at first sight. He was impeccably dressed in a light gray suit with a blue shirt and blue striped tie. He seemed like a nice person with a warm friendly smile. It wasn't until she had accepted the job and reported to work that she met his right-hand assistant, a girl named Precious Jones. As she would later learn, she was anything but precious! Ms. Jones was a tall willowy blonde who was drop-dead gorgeous, and she was going to take all the perks that came with being beautiful. Standing there in the doorway of Mr. Fowler's office, she looked more like a fashion model than a secretary of a small real estate office. Her golden blonde hair hung down around her slender shoulders. One side of her hair was flung over her right side. The other side hung in cascading curls down her back.

Precious was wearing a white blouse with black dots to match her black pleated skirt. One look at Precious told Gracie that Mr. Fowler would not be interested in chasing a mousy girl like herself when he had this beauty to cavort with.

Gracie did not know anything about the personal life of her boss. She wanted to keep it that way! She scolded herself for thinking bad thoughts about Mr. Fowler and Ms. Jones. That was their business, not hers! Anyway, she had her own problems to worry about. It had been a while since Gracie had been employed, and she didn't know all that much about computers. She had not been completely honest with Mr. Fowler when she told him she could cut and paste. She hadn't the slightest idea. However, she did have good telephone skills, and she was good with the public. She reminded herself that this was only a part-time job and she should not get too bent out of shape. What did he expect anyway for such little salary? Mr. Fowler told Gracie that Ms. Jones would train her on everything she needed to know. She would be expected to run the office herself when he and Ms. Jones had to be out of the town. From the first day, Gracie felt that Ms. Jones was going to be difficult to deal with. She was harsh with Gracie when she asked a question about office procedures or real estate issues. Her response: "I thought we had already covered that!" She had no patience with Gracie and was not giving her enough time to grasp office procedures. She was jumping from one thing to another, expecting Gracie to catch every detail instantly. Gracie wanted to think that Precious was jealous of her. After observing Ms. Jones for a few days, she knew that was not the case.

It was no contest between them. Precious Jones had both brains and looks. It seemed there was nothing about computers that Ms. Jones didn't know. Gracie reminded herself that she was there to work only, and it would take some time to get everything down pat. She had not entered a beauty contest. Competition should not be an issue, and she was not going to allow it to be. She should concentrate on doing a good job, and things would work out. Mr. Fowler made it clear that Precious was in charge when he was out of the office. At first, they both were somewhat nice and polite to Gracie. As time passed, the new wore off. So did their politeness! Requests became demands, and they wanted it done quickly and without any room for error. It seemed they did nothing but bark orders. Do this now! Do that! She wished they would have told her she would be their maid when she signed on. Ms. Jones did little to help out! She would sometimes sit and read a book, or she would have long phone conversation with male friends. Gracie was micromanaged daily by Mr. Fowler, but Ms. Jones's laziness went unnoticed by her boss. Precious could do no wrong! Now that Gracie had been shown the ropes, as Precious put it, she was expected to do the job quickly and accurately. Gracie not only had to manage the front desk, which could be extremely busy at the first of the month, she also had to take all the phone calls and screen them. If it was raining, they would send her out in the rain to get them sandwiches for lunch. She had to vacuum the floors and dust the furniture since the office didn't have a custodian. Most days, Gracie felt pretty miserable working more like a maid than a clerk. Even though she was miserable, she concluded that she could put up with them until the end of the year, when she would have enough money in the bank to look for another job!

She had to admit the time was going fast. Every dollar that she earned went into the bank. The small check that she received from her deceased husband's retirement was adequate to meet her monthly bills with little left over. It would be good to have money in the bank for things like traveling and buying some new clothes.

Summer had vanished, and fall was in the air. Brown and gold leaves were blowing in the wind, and the temperature had dropped substantially. The dog days of summer were gone, taking the hot sticky days with it. Precious had spent the day decorating the office for Halloween, which she said was one of her favorite holidays. She had no interest in the trivial grind of the daily work. Evidently, Precious was there for purposes other than office work. Today, she was hanging witches from the ceiling. She decorated the reception area with jack-o'-lantern string lights and black cats. She decided that the office needed more decorations. She sent Gracie to Walmart to buy some pumpkins. After hauling the six heavy pumpkins from the car to the office, Gracie as exhausted. When Mr. Fowler returned from his lunch, he told Precious how festive the office looked and that she had done a great job!

Mr. Fowler was a lot like Precious, arrogant and conceited. Gracie felt like a third-class citizen with their belittling and put-downs. They were so ungrateful for all that she did. She hated the way Mr. Fowler looked at Precious when she walked around the office. She hated the way Precious would talk down to her. In fact, she hated her job! The one thing that made the job bearable was that Precious was absent much of the time.

Sometimes when business was slow, Gracie would sit and watch a funeral possession snake through the cemetery. By looking at the make of the cars, it told a story about the deceased. Rich people had rich friends. It was not unusual to see more than one funeral a day taking place. She had grown accustomed to it and sometimes did not notice the funerals at all. Today had been a busy day. It was the first of the month, and people were coming into the office to pay their rent. Most tenants paid with checks. Some people paid with cash. She kept two bank bags under the counter. One was for checks, the other for cash. Today, Mr. Fowler had instructed her to hide any sum over $500 in cash under the sofa in the break room. Why didn't he want the money taken to the bank? One could hold down the office while the other went to the bank. She thought this was strange instructions from her boss, but it was his money, and if that what he wanted, then it was okay with her. She didn't think much about the office being robbed, but Mr. Fowler wanted to take all necessary precautions. She was seldom left by alone on the first of the month. There were too many tenants coming in and paying the rent. Precious was not any help! Her only purpose was to record the money and keep the books. Sometimes, Gracie wondered if Precious was keeping some money stashed for herself! Today was different! Mr. Fowler was out of town, attending a wedding in another town. He would not be back for two days. Early in the morning, Precious had called the office to tell Gracie that she was not coming in today. She would have the day to herself! A day of peace and quiet! Thank goodness!

Gracie sensed that Precious was up to something, but there was little she could do about it. Mr. Fowler, no doubt, expected her to take care of business today and do it efficiently. Otherwise, why would he give her the job? The morning had been fast paced. A steady stream of tenants were coming in to pay their rent. Gracie ate a quick sandwich while taking payments, eating while standing.

At about 1:00 p.m., a man carrying a leather briefcase walked into the office. He was wearing jeans with a gray T-shirt that said, "World's Greatest Grandfather!" He looked nothing like a grandpa with his hair pulled back into a ponytail and tattoos covering every visible part of his body. He laid the briefcase on the counter and asked to see Doug Fowler. The way he spoke made Gracie nervous! The man was a scuzzy-looking character that seemed to be in a bit of a hurry. Mr. Fowler had said nothing about expecting a visitor. He usually told her if he was expecting anyone along with in-depth instructions on what to tell them. She advised the grumpy-looking man that Mr. Fowler was not available, that he was attending a wedding out of town. He seemed upset that he was not available. The man opened the briefcase and began taking large sums of money out.

The final total was the sum of $100,000! Gracie had never seen so much cash in her life, and it shocked her down to her toes! Who was this man, and why was he here? The top of the counter was literally covered with the cash that he had pulled out of the briefcase. She stood speechless before him, thinking that this was some kind of joke! Nothing like this had ever happened before. Before she could speak, he said, "My name is John Smith. Fowler knows who I am!" Then he asked, "Is Precious Jones here today?"

Again, Gracie told him that she was the only one in the office. He closed the briefcase and began walking away when she managed to say "I need to give you a receipt." He turned around and looked at her for a few seconds, knowing how bewildered she must be. "No, I don't need a paper trail! Just tell Fowler that I dropped the money off! Make sure that you tell her too!" He pointed his dirty-looking finger at the office belonging to Precious and walked out the door. After he was gone, she quickly ran to the door and locked it. She placed the Closed for Lunch sign on the door and ran back into the breakroom with the money.

What was all this cash for? It must be drug money, she thought. Maybe some kind of mob money that was being paid to Mr. Fowler? What should she do? Should she close the office and run to the bank? But Fowler had instructed her to hide any large sum of money under the couch. Surely Mr. Fowler wasn't expecting something like this! Why was he out of town! As Gracie was stuffing it under the sofa, she heard knocking on the door. With the money out of sight, she ran back to the front office. Customers were still arriving to pay their rent money. The steady stream of people kept up the rest of day. The more she thought of the moneyman, the more terrified she became! This had to be some kind of bad deal coming down! Maybe Mr. Fowler and Precious were involved in some sort of criminal activity? This whole thing did not make any sense! Maybe she should just say to hell with the whole thing and quit her job without notice. After all, it was her life at stake. The afternoon seemed to drag on forever! Any minute, she expected the mob and a hail of gunfire!

Finally, it was closing time. Gracie felt so relieved to lock up the office and get the hell out of there before something happened! She had been instructed to close promptly at six o'clock especially when there was money in the office. Gracie was thoroughly surprised that Precious had not shown up at the last minute to grab all the rent money and deny that she had taken the day off. If she had the slightest inkling that something so out of the ordinary had happened, like the moneyman, she would have been down there before closing time. Gracie glanced outside at the darkness. The streets were empty with the exception of her car parked out front. It gave her a feeling of isolation even though the pawnshop next door stayed open until 8:00 p.m. She didn't like the man that owned it. She thought him to be disrespectful. Gracie had been in the pawnshop a couple of time looking at bracelets, and the owner had been rude to her. He had even lied about her being over at the pawnshop on company time. Gracie glanced back at the clock. It was after 600 p.m.

She locked the front door, checking it twice to make sure it was locked. She flipped on the closed sign. She then went to the back to retrieve the money. She would take it home tonight and then bring it back in the morning. If she took it to the bank, it would leave a paper trail! That old man had said he didn't want that. It would be Fowler's problem! She found a box in the closet that was full of Christmas decorations. She emptied the box, pulled the money out from under the sofa, and loaded it in the box. She covered the money with newspaper and a few magazines. She was headed back to her desk to turn out all the lights when she saw a young woman coming toward the office. How could this be? She was sure that she had locked the front door. Gracie took the box full of money back to her desk and set it down. Maybe this girl had something to do with the moneyman. She noticed the girl was very thin, rail thin. Her face had pockmarks, and her eyes were colorless and without expression. She resembled a zombie more than anything else. Her mind was whirling as she scoped out the strange-looking stranger. It just didn't make sense. The woman pounded on the front door.

"Is anyone there?" she asked.

Gracie, looking out the front window, said, "What do you want?"

"I need to pay my rent," she replied. Gracie opened the door and let the woman enter the office. The woman reached in her pocket and pulled out a wad of cash. "My name is Jane Smith, and my rent is $500. I live in the Raintree Apartment, number 1313." The zombielike girl counted out five one-hundred-dollar bills. Grace tried to locate her account but could not find any property that the real estate office managed at that address. Maybe she was at the wrong office, Gracie thought. The girl began to talk softly, "Aren't you scared of the graveyard being so close?" she asked.

Gracie, trying to keep her wits about her, answered her question. She was having a hard time staying focused. The zombielike girl continued speaking in a soft voice. "Well, I-I live not far from here, and I never walk by the graveyard after dark if I can help it! I've seen things out there that I don't understand! I work nights," she said, pointing toward the string of bars about two blocks away. She smiled, showing her ugly, decaying teeth! She ran her bony hand through what was left of her thinning hair. Gracie thought that the woman was scary-looking!

The woman looked very distraught as she explained how she had ended up working in a bar." I got fired from my nursing job. They thought that I was doing drugs," she said. "They called me a drug addict!" She laughed and ran her fingers through her hair again. "So I had to take the job in the bar! "I know what it's like to work a job where you are treated badly," she stated. She looked at Gracie with a touch of sadness in her eyes.

Grace wondered if her dislike for her job was showing that much. How could the girl possibly know what was going on? Gracie wrote out the receipt, even though she could not find the property the girl was talking about. When Mr. Fowler got back to the office, he could straighten it out. The woman started to walk away, then turned around and asked if Gracie had any coffee. It had been a long time since she had coffee. She looked so pitiful that Gracie could not bring herself to say no. She hurried back to the break room to see if any coffee was left. The coffeepot was on, with some coffee in it. Gracie poured a cupful and hurried back to the front area and handed the cup of coffee to the woman. The girl's bony hands shook as she accepted the drink. She put the cup to her quivering lips and took a deep drink. There was something so creepy about the girl's demeanor that Gracie wished she would hurry up and drink the coffee. Time was of the essence! Gracie needed to get home with the $100,000 before some robber busted into the office. As far as Gracie knew, the office had never been robbed. But there was always that possibility if someone thought there was cash inside.

"Well, it's getting late, and I have to lock up," Gracie told the woman. "My boss does not like for me to stay open later than our normal hours." No sooner had Gracie gotten the words out of her mouth than Precious Jones came bursting through the front door like a whirlwind! The minute she saw the pitiful creature sitting on the couch, she began to roll her eyes. "I need to see you in the break room now," she barked at Gracie. They no sooner had gotten to the back than Precious began to rant and rave about the office still being open.

"Why is that witch sitting on the couch?" she asked. "Have you lost your mind!" she barked. "What will people think when they see the likes of her sitting in our office? I cannot believe you gave her coffee." When Precious was angry, she spoke much too loudly. Other people's feelings didn't matter! Gracie walked away, going back in the front office. She looked up, and the woman was gone! There was no doubt the poor girl had been insulted! Precious pranced back to the front office in her three-inch heels, relieved to see that the girl was gone. Precious went into her office and closed the door. She wasted no time in making a call to Mr. Fowler.

About fifteen minutes later, she came out of the office and told Gracie, "Mr. Fowler wants to see you tonight!" She added, "He is headed home now. I told him what a mess you have made of everything. He wants us both to stay until he gets here. He wants to make sure that all the rent receipts match the money taken in."

Gracie had the feeling that she was going to be fired. Maybe she should just up and quit. Why hang around and take verbal abuse from Mr. Fowler? Her thoughts went back to the big stash of money in the box on her desk!

Precious had no clue what was in the box. If she turned over the money to Precious, she had no doubt that Precious would tell Mr. Fowler that she had been the one to collect it. After thinking about it for a moment, Gracie placed the box in her desk and sat down at her desk. She would not tell anybody about the box and the $100,000 sitting inside it. Gracie and Precious stared at each other with growing contempt, waiting for Mr. Fowler to show up. The silence was shattered by the phone ringing.

"Get the phone," Precious barked.

Gracie picked up the phone. The call was from a Mrs. Price. She was complaining about roaches in her apartment. She was asking for an exterminator. Gracie was writing down the address when she heard someone knocking on the front door. It was the pawnshop owner from next door. He sounded excited as he entered the office. The man told Precious that someone had slashed all of the tires on her new car. Precious darted out the door in a quick run with the pawnshop man behind her. After a few seconds, Gracie heard a scream. Precious came running back into the office, using curse words that Gracie had never heard in an office before. Precious got on the phone and called the police. She demanded that an officer come out to the office. She paced the floor till a patrol car pulled up in front of the office. Precious went out to meet him. The officer who took the complaint seemed a lot more interested in Precious than he did making out a report.

"No," Precious said. She couldn't imagine who would do such a thing. No, she didn't have any enemies. No, she didn't have a jealous boyfriend that would commit such a crime.

Gracie wondered if the officer was really listening to what Precious was saying. As the officer wrote out the report, his eyes were drinking it all in. The phone rang again. It was Mr. Fowler wanting to talk to Precious. Gracie motioned for her to come back in the office. Precious ripped the phone out of Gracie's hand. She began crying and telling Mr. Fowler what someone had done to her car. During her sobs, she could tell that Mr. Fowler was interrupting her. Fowler was telling her something that Gracie could not hear. After Precious hung up the phone, Precious turned to Gracie and told Gracie flat out, "You are fired! Mr. Fowler said we cannot afford to have such a screwed-up mess at the office. You are allowing riffraff and drug addicts to hang around the office!"

Gracie felt tears stinging her eyes from all that she had been through that day. Her nerves were shot! First, the man with the money! Then the zombie woman! What was going on? Suddenly, she recalled the remarks that Mr. Fowler had made about former employees at the office being afraid! What were the strange happenings they were talking about?

Precious barked at Gracie, "Pack your things up and get out!"

Gracie started crying as she got her stuff together, putting most of them in her purse. She picked up the box containing the money and her jacket that was hanging over the back of her chair on her shoulders to protect herself in the night air. Precious watched every move she made, like a cat watching a mouse. She leaned back in her chair and said so sarcastically, "I hope the receipts match up with the money you have taken in today. If not, you may have some explaining to do!"

Precious then got out of her chair and followed Gracie to the door. "I hope you have learned something important from this job experience, something valuable that you are taking with you," she said! "Goodbye," she said as Gracie walked out the door. Precious smiled as she slammed the door to the real estate office shut.

The pawnshop man had sat there grinning at what had just taken place. It was like they were poking fun at her for being fired and rubbing it in her face! As Gracie walked to her car and got in it, she thought about the wild day that she had just experienced! The crazy people! She now understood what Fowler was talking about with regard to the other employees who had quit! Gracie was now so grateful that she had not given the moneyman any receipt for the $100,000. There was no money trail! Maybe Mr. Fowler would think that Precious had stolen the money? Maybe Precious and the pawnshop man had something going on? What about the $100,000? Was it drug money? Was it for some criminal activity that Fowler was involved in? Why didn't Fowler want it deposited in the bank? Was he trying to avoid an audit by the Internal Revenue Service? If the money was something illegal, then Fowler could not afford to make a complaint or file a police report! A lot of questions? No real answers! Gracie decided that she was not going to worry about it.

Gracie was backing out of the parking space when she saw the moneyman coming up the street. The man was walking toward the office in a big hurry. It was him! She recognized the ponytail and the T-shirt. She knew that the moneyman was mad! He pulled out a gun as he started to open the front door to the real estate office. Gracie sensed that there was going to be murders committed in the office. Gracie was not going to hang around and become another murder victim! She burned rubber out of the parking lot. Precious and the pawnshop man could deal with the old man! She was sure it was not going to be pretty sight! Precious and the pawnshop owner deserved whatever happened to them! Explaining what happened to the missing $100,000 would be impossible! As Gracie drove away, she suddenly smiled, thinking that it was time to travel! Maybe an island in the South Pacific? Or a Mexican cruise? She could think of a lot of places she would like to go!

THE MOTHER
FROM HELL

I am so sorry that I ever listened to my cruel and heartless mother. Little by little, she bullied me into becoming a massage therapist, something I never wanted to do. The truth be known, I was afraid of her for several years. She got her bluff in on me the year I graduated from Reno City High School. I knew she meant business when she told me that I would be on my own if I didn't get my license as a massage therapist. In other words, if I didn't do as she wanted, I would be left homeless! It was a very scary thought of being forced to move out and having to pay rent and all other living expenses by myself. Mother knew I had other dreams, but this did not matter to her. My dream was to get a degree in agriculture. I wanted to do some farming and own my own cattle ranch. I wanted to be known as the J. R. Ewing of Reno City!

It hurt me to bend to her wishes. I think I know how she hatched the therapist thing. She owned a building downtown Reno City which had sat vacant for almost five years. She wanted to rent it to someone who would restore it. Mom kept harping on the subject until I changed my mind in order to survive. The old building would be my inheritance someday. Repairing the old building might not be such a bad idea after all. The property was valuable since it sat in the middle of downtown Reno City. The First National Bank was on one side, and Bowman's shoe store was on the other side. The shoe store had been there for over twenty-five years and was still going strong. The idea of being a massage therapist had some appeal. The program was just a few months compared to four years in college to get my degree in agriculture. It was not too difficult to get a license and then I could be my own boss. How sweet that sounded to my bruised ego! Finally, I went to Smith College and got my training and state certification as a massage therapist. I set up shop in a small corner office of Mom's old building. Going to a surplus furniture auction, I bought a message table and ten chairs. I had on old friend, Jack Stoner, created and paint a large sign: Griffin Moriarty-Message Therapist, which I hung in the front window. It seemed like forever before I got my first customer. Actually, it was only a couple of days. My first customer, Cynthia Wolf, walked in the door. She was a hairdresser who wanted to ease the tension in her neck and shoulders due to standing on her feet and working on a person's hair all day. She was an older woman who had seen my sign and decided to give me a try. When she walked in the office, she looked at me with surprise!

Cynthia explained, "I thought that you were a woman based on the sign outside, 'Griffin Moriarty.'"

I replied, "I thought the name Griffin would explain to the public what gender I am."

We talked for a few minutes before I explained to her the process under which I would perform a massage. She could undress in the bathroom, put on a soft robe, and come out and lie on the massage table.

When she was ready, I came out and slowly massaged her neck, shoulders, and back for a period of twenty-five minutes. When I was done, Cynthia was completely relaxed. She put her clothes back on and returned to the room.

I said, "That will be $20 please."

Cynthia smiled and reached in her purse and pulled out a $20 bill. Plus, another $5 for a tip!

"Great job," she said. "I will recommend you to all of my lady customers that come into the hair salon!"

I smiled as she left the office. My immediate thought, *This may not be such a bad job after all!*

Over the next three months, my daily customers increased from two or three a day to as many as ten per day. Amazingly, the business that I'd hated to start was now generating up to $1,000 per week. With each passing week, I became very fond of all the ladies that were my massage clients.

The only female I couldn't stand was my mother. I had always been ashamed of how she looked. Her hair was long and stringy. I don't think that she washed it more than once a year. Somedays, she didn't bother to comb it. She stood five feet, eleven inches, an inch taller them me. She never wore dresses, just old T-shirts and faded blue jeans. She never owned makeup of any kind. After I started my massage therapy business, I bought her some Avon makeup, just trying to help her look better. My mother ended up throwing it in the trash, claiming that it made her skin break out! After many attempts to please her, I finally gave up! She was impossible!

I was doing pretty well with my massage therapy business. Over a period of twelve months, I socked away over $10,000! The first year I made around $40,000. I was able to purchase a small farm north of town. The property consists of twenty acres and an old farmhouse with a barn. It was my dream! Going out there every evening relieved all the stress from a long day at work. My day usually started around 9:00 a.m. and lasted until 6:00 p.m. I had acquired the reputation of being a good therapist, thanks to Cynthia. She referred all her lady customers to me. Some of the ladies were in their thirties and forties and easy to deal with. The ones I liked least were the elderly women. They wanted to talk about all kinds of stuff that was not related to services that I gave to them. For example, I was asked to explain the behavior of boyfriends and crazy husbands! Sometimes, I felt more like a mental health counselor! Elderly women in their sixties and seventies were the most difficult ones to deal with. They wanted to stay past their thirty minutes to talk! And talk! And talk! Time was money to me! I had to maintain a strict schedule in order to make the most money! Gradually, they would offer more than the usual fee for a half hour in order to talk to me. Eventually, I was charging each of them up to $100 per hour! They would pay in order to stay and talk with me about their personal issues.

The more successful I became, the more hatred I had toward my mother. The massage therapy business was thriving, and my mother started demanding more money! At first, she wanted to raise the rent on my office space in her old building. I agreed to increase the rent by $100 per month. Then she started demanding a rent increase of $300 per month. At first, I had no choice but to pay it. When she started demanding a rent increase by $500 per month, I said, "Enough!" I started looking for a new location for my business. I was not taking it anymore. I was through being her whipping boy! Within a couple of weeks, I had located a new office in a new business park that was just being constructed on the north end of town. The new office location would be closer to my farm acreage. When the new office was ready to move into, I gave my mother a written notice that I was moving at the end of the month and that she would have to find a new tenant. The next week, I started moving my office equipment and files to the new office. Mother showed up while I was moving and started yelling, screaming, and making an ass out of herself in front of the moving company employees! It was total chaos! Finally, the police were called, and she was escorted off the premises.

My mother certainly felt that she was losing control over my life. No longer able to influence my actions at home or in the business world, her behavior become more erratic! When she was taken to jail for disturbing the peace, she had to hire an attorney to try to get the charges dropped. The lawyer started calling me at my business and home, wanting me to sign a sworn statement that she was not causing any problems and that the criminal charges should be dropped. She also sued me in small-claims court, claiming that I owed her several months of rent after moving out of her building. I refused to drop the charges or pay her any more rent money. Her small-claims action was thrown out of court due to insufficient evidence. A few months later, the judge convicted her of disorderly conduct, giving her probation time of one year. The hostility continued to escalate—threatening phone calls at home late at night, picketing in from of my office, carrying a sign saying that I was a lousy massage therapist! She was crazy, and she was driving me crazy! I had to hire a lawyer to get a restraining order against her. The judge quickly granted the restraining order after listening to her ranting and raving in court about what an ungrateful son that I turned out to be after she had raised me for almost twenty years. The court order prohibited her from having any contact with me, both at home and at my business. Within a few weeks, she started committing acts of vandalism toward me, throwing rocks through windows at my home and business. While I was working with patients at my office one day, she took a steel metal object and busted out the car windows on all sides of my car. How could she be stopped? What happens if she kept doing these crazy things?

What does a person do when their mother refused to accept a child as they are and simply let go? What should I do? I started researching those questions at the local library, looking at criminal justice materials. I was shocked to find out on the average, there are five homicides every week in America where a child kills their parent. That amounts to over 250 homicides each year where the child kills one or both parents. With regard to what happens to the kids that kills a parent, I discovered that only about a hundred per year are arrested or prosecuted for the murder. Children that are prosecuted tend to receive more lenient punishment if the child can show evidence of child abuse, sexual abuse, domestic violence, or a drug/alcohol atmosphere at home. The most practicable solution would be to kill her! That would the best solution!

I began to make plans on how to get rid of my mother! How should I do it? How could I get away with it? Being a massage therapist, I knew that I had strong hands. I could strangle her with my hands! There will be no blood! I could wrap her body in blanket and transport her out to my farm. Where would I bury her? In the barn? I thought. The barn would be the perfect place. I could take my time digging a hole, and I would not have to worry about someone seeing me. It took four evenings of hard digging to get the hole big enough to hold her large body. The next question I had to resolve was, When do I kill her? Do I kill her in the morning? Do I kill her at night? When would be the best time to kill her? I decided that it would be best to kill her early in the morning. I could put her body in the trunk of my car and go to work like it was a normal day at work. I would leave after work and make my usual trip out to the farm after work. After dark, I could take the body out of the trunk and bury her in the large hole that I had dug in the barn. No one would be the wiser. I knew this would not be easy.

After weighing the possibilities, I decided the best strategy was to meet her in a private place after dark. I extended an olive branch to her by dropping a note in her mailbox, advising her that I had some money for her. The offer of money would motivate her to meet with me with no questions asked. The note specified a time and location to meet, with instructions to bring the note with her. We meet two days later in dark parking lot of an old grocery store that had been closed down for several years. I arrived thirty minutes early and parked in the back of the parking lot next to the old building.

Twenty minutes later, she drove up in her old Ford car. Seeing her pull into the parking lot, I flashed my headlights on and off to indicate my location. She drove up beside my car and rolled down her car window. She asked, "I got your note. What's the deal?"

My response: "I got a $1,000 for you! Come and get in my car!"

She slowly got out of her car and walked around and took a seat in my car. "Show me the money," she demanded immediately!

Pausing for a moment, I reached in my coat pocket and pulled out a bank envelope full of $20 bills. I held the envelope out in from of her, teasing her. "Before I give you the money, give me the note that I dropped into your mailbox," I demanded. She paused for a second and then pulled the note out of her shirt pocket. I handed her the money, and she gave me the note. She grabbed the envelope and started counting the money. I checked the note to verify that it was the note. The note was the only incriminating evidence that could be used against me.

I don't remember the exact moment that my hands went around her neck. My mind was spinning out of control. I grabbed her enormous neck and began to squeeze. She resisted, trying to get away from me. My strong hands were too much for her to handle. After a couple of minutes, she lost consciousness and slumped over in my front seat. I continued to squeeze her neck with all my might. I heard her gasping for air amid my tightened grip on her. I kept squeezing until she stopped moving. Then all was quiet! She lay very calm and very dead in the passenger's seat of my car. For the first time in a long time, I felt calm and relaxed.

What should I do with her body? Go bury it in my barn? If the police came looking, that would be one of the first places that they would look. I sat there with her dead body in my car for several minutes, trying to figure out what to do. Finally, it suddenly dawned on me. Getting out of my car, I retrieved an old blanket out of the trunk of my car. Going around the other side of the car, I opened the door and covered her body with the blanket. I searched her pocket and retrieved her car keys. I went around to her car and started it with her keys. With the motor running, I moved around and dragged her body from my car and placed her in the passenger side of her old

Ford car. Getting into the driver's side, I put her car in gear and drove out of town. Driving out south on the old state highway, I searched for a large curve in the road. I finally found the spot! I pulled off the side of the road. Getting out of the car, I looked around to make sure that there were no other cars in the vicinity. Seeing nothing, I got in the passenger's side of the car, slowly pushing her dead body behind the steering wheel. I backed the car up several dozen yards and put the car into drive, placing a heavy rock on to the gas pedal. The car jerked and then suddenly started moving forward, picking up speed as it went. I jumped from the car just in time to see the car going off the road and down the hill. The car hit a large boulder and exploded in flames at the bottom of the hill. Any evidence of a murder had just been destroyed in the car fire. I slowly dusted myself off and started walking back into town. I had to retrieve my car. For the first time in a long time, I smiled! I walked back into town. I retrieved my car. I smiled! For the first time in twenty years, I got a good night's rest!

NOSY NEIGHBORS

T he night had been long, filled with loud thunderstorms that lasted all night and into the early morning hours. The storm had finally moved on and then nothing but soft rain continued with a soothing sound that made me want to sleep forever. I had to make myself get out of bed that morning even though I felt I could do with a few more hours of sleep. The rain had made the morning cool and sweet. I simply could not lie in bed all day because I had planned on planting a lilac bush that I bought at the nursery three days before. It still was on the patio blooming with beautiful purple flowers that gave new life to my dull backyard. I tried planting it the same day I bought it, but the ground was much too hard. Determined to plant the large shrub, I dug into the hard soil that was fighting me every step of the way and making big blisters on my hands. I was getting nowhere, so I put the garden hoe back into the garage and went for the water hose to soak it down for a while. I should have done this in the first place. While the parched earth was soaking, I lounged in a cushioned chair. Mrs. Shipley, my next-door neighbor, stuck her head over the fence when she realized I was sitting there. She wanted to know if I had seen our neighbor Mrs. Whitlock, who lived on the other side of me. I tried to recall when I had last seen her. To the best of my memory, I had not seen her in over a week. I hadn't realized it had been that long since I had seen Ms. Whitlock because I had been putting in a lot of extra hours at work. The last time I recall seeing her was at the mailboxes. We had chatted for a few minutes, then we both went inside. The heat had been intense, and standing there talking was not the most pleasant thing to do. At that time, she'd looked fine and in good spirits. Now I was concerned about her since Mrs. Shipley hadn't seen her recently. Mrs. Shipley, whom I call Victoria, said she had knocked on Mrs. Whitlock's door and there was no answer. She was sure that everything was fine, but it would be a good idea for us to look in on her just in case she had become ill or taken a fall. Since I lived right next door to Mrs. Whitlock, I would be the most likely one to see her coming and going.

I suddenly felt a lump in my throat since I had promised her nephew that I would faithfully keep an eye on her. I had his cell phone number written on my kitchen cabinet door. I had done a pretty good job on keeping watch over her until I started working a lot of overtime. I told Victoria that I was working extra hours, and she agreed to help look out for her. Mrs. Whitlock had taken a fall about a year ago. Nothing too serious but her nephew worried about her. He wanted her to move to a senior living center, but she refused to even think about it. In her own words, she was fine and did not to be placed in a nursing home. Mrs. Whitlock didn't see herself as getting older, just better. At age 79, she was still feisty and on the go all the time. She took excellent care of herself with trips to the gym and the makeup counter at Macy's. She never would reveal her age to anyone. After worrying about her all day one Sunday, I broke down and called her nephew. I came right out and asked her age.

He was silent for a moment, then he told me that she was seventy-nine. I was shocked! However, looking at her wrinkled hands told me she was probably a lot older than she looked. As we talked over the fence that morning, Mrs. Shipley said the weatherman had predicted heavy rain for the night and it might be a lot easier to plant my lilac bush after the hard rain. After looking at my blistered hands again, I decided to wait another day and let nature soften the ground. I set the plant back under the covered patio for protection from the sun. Another day on the patio would not be fatal to the blooms on the lilac bush. I visited a few more minutes with Mrs. Shipley and then decided to take the morning off and go into town to do some shopping. My plans were mostly to do grocery shopping. I was practically out of everything since I was putting in so many extra hours at work and not getting anything else accomplished. Before I left the backyard, I promised Mrs. Shipley that I would check on Mrs. Whitlock face-to-face. If she didn't answer the door, I would call her nephew to see if he knew where she was. Maybe she had gone to visit him. If she did, that would be a good two-hour drive. Most likely she would be spending the night.

I took a quick shower and dressed into a pair of jeans and a short-sleeved shirt to make myself more comfortable for the July heat. The morning was slipping by, and I didn't want to waste it on fixing breakfast. I could grab a cup of coffee and a sweet roll at the shopping center. I ran a round brush through my short brown hair and put on a tad of foundation and mascara. Before I left the house, I picked up a little blue book that I used to write telephone numbers for family and friends. I was never one to remember telephone numbers. I had called Mrs. Whitlock many times before, but I still couldn't remember her number. Maybe she wasn't the only one having problems! I dialed her number to let her know that I wanted to check on her and that I was on my way over. I let the phone ring six times. There was no answer! Maybe she was in the shower. I was almost to her door when I turned around and went back home. I would stall a few minutes to give her time to finish what she was doing. Occasionally, she would not answer the door if she wasn't expecting anyone, but it was unlike her to not answer her phone. Unpleasant scenes began to enter my mind. I cringed to think of her lying helpless on the floor with a broken hip. I reminded myself that I was jumping to conclusions for a number of things might be keeping her from answering the phone. After waiting twenty minutes, I grabbed my purse once again along with a large canvas tote that I usually took with me for grocery shopping. I locked my front door and headed across the yard toward Mrs. Whitlock's house for the second time that morning. As I crossed the yard, I could see that her car was not in the driveway, but that wasn't unusual. She only parked her car in the driveway when she was making trips back and forth out to lunch with friends, shopping or whatever.

Before I went to her door, I checked her mailbox. It was brimming full! I stepped back, feeling a little surprised at the volume of mail. It looked like it had not been picked up in over a week. Maybe something was wrong? I retrieved the mail and went quickly to the door. Feelings of anxiety crowded my mind as I rang the doorbell, expecting the worst possible thing.

No answer! I then knocked on the door so hard it hurt my blistered fingers. I was about to return home to call her nephew when I saw movement in the house. Peeking through the window, I caught a glimpse of her bright pink robe that I had given her for her last birthday. Pink was her favorite color. She opened the door with a big smile on her face as if she didn't have a care in the world. She never looked happier or healthier. I stepped inside her immaculate house and saw an overnight bag sitting on the floor by an armchair. At first, I was so relieved to see her and that she was okay, I forgot my frustrations.

"Where have you been, my dear lady? We have been so worried about you!" I was very concerned! I am sure I must have sounded condescending to the elderly lady. She looked a little sheepish, knowing she had disappeared without telling anyone.

"I stayed the night with the girls in town" she said. Her blue eyes were bright, and she looked excited. "We went to the theater downtown, and everything ended so late, we ended up spending the night. We decided that it would be a lot of fun to stay in a hotel. That made us gals feel like college girls again. We didn't have dinner to around midnight." She clasped her wrinkled hands and exclaimed, "It felt so good to stay out late!"

I scolded her a bit for not telling anyone where she was. I then gave her a big bear hug to let her know that I loved her and was only concerned about her well-being. She offered me a cup of coffee, and I took her up on it, realizing I had not had my coffee that morning. Along with coffee, we had homemade cinnamon rolls that she had made from scratch. Between bites of sweet rolls, she chattered about seeing the play *Chicago* with her two good friends, Sara and Olive. She told me I should go see it. She then asked me something that she had never asked me before: "Do you have a boyfriend?" I thought that was a strange question to be asking me. Maybe she was trying to tell me that if I could pry into her private life, then she could pry in mine. I giggled as I told her that I was still looking for the perfect man. She smiled and said, "Don't wait too long!" Before leaving, I asked her if she needed anything from the supermarket. She said she had already done her weekly shopping. I knew she was a very independent woman, so I was not surprised at her answer. As I drove to the shopping center, I wondered why her mailbox was so full of mail and why she hadn't bothered to get it in several days. That was very strange! I used to see her getting her mail every day.

Remembering that I had not let Victoria know that she was all right, I looked for a place to pull over and call her to let her know that we had worried in vain. Mrs. Shipley answered on the second ring. I let her know that Mrs. Whitlock's absence was due to a night on the town with her two best friends. I told Victoria about finding the mailbox full of mail, and she agreed that this was out of character for Mrs. Whitlock. We agreed that maybe we needed to watch her more closely or let her nephew know that she was becoming more forgetful.

As I pulled into the shopping center, the sun had become brutal, and I was having trouble with the glare. The temperature felt like it might be in triple digit numbers. I parked under what little shade I could find under a small group of trees. I rummaged through the glove compartment, trying to find my sunglasses. I found mostly receipts and an old wallet I forgot I had. I also found a twenty-dollar bill that I had tucked inside. I happily made my way to a little shop that sold sunglass along with costume jewelry. I had no sooner entered the shop when I ran smack into Sara Billingsley, one of the women that had accompanied my neighbor to the theater. Sara was just as feisty as Mrs. Whitlock but not as fastidious about her looks. Sara recognized me immediately as the neighbor that lived next door to her good friend. We exchanged greetings, and I asked her how she liked the play *Chicago*. She stopped shopping for a minute and just stared at me and said, "Why do you ask? I have never seen it."

I cringed. I felt like a fool! I said, "I thought you saw it with my neighbor, Mrs. Whitlock!"

Her response: "You must be confused! I haven't seen her in several weeks." She stood there smiling at me, giving me time to get my foot out of my mouth. "Good to see you," she said as she headed toward the clearance section in the back of the store.

I felt like a total idiot as I walked back to the rack of sunglasses. I found a pair of designer sunglasses that were far too expensive but bought them anyway. I just wanted to snag a pair of sunglasses and get on to the grocery store before it got too hot. I was not feeling so well since I knew that Mrs. Whitlock had deliberately lied to me. I was wondering why.

It rained that night just as Mrs. Shipley said it would. That morning I got out of bed and changed into my work clothes. I want to get the lilac bush planted once and for all. I was tired of seeing it sitting on my back porch yelling, "Plant me." I grabbed the garden hoe and began digging. The rain had softened the ground into pure magic for planting. In no time, I had a hole big enough to plant the large flowering plant. The planting was easy, but the mud was something else. I was knee-deep in mud when I heard Mrs. Whitlock come out on her back patio. At first, I thought she was talking to me, and I almost answered her over the fence. Then I realized she was talking on her cell phone. I was totally shocked that she knew how to use one!

I knew she wasn't computer savvy, so I figured she didn't care for a cell phone either. Maybe her nephew had bought it for her and taught her how to use it. Peeking through the fence, I could see her plainly. I watched her as she walked across her patio. I thought that she appeared to be looking in the direction of my backyard. I hoped she hadn't seen me. If she did, she might go back in the house for privacy. I sensed that she was looking in my direction, which made me a bit nervous. I stopped moving and stayed very still. I did not want her to know that I was listening to her phone conversation. I crouched closer to the ground, which made it easier for me to peek through the bottom of the fence at her. After a few minutes of pacing, she took a seat on the patio and was completely focused on who she was talking to on the phone. Her voice sounded excited again like it did that morning when she told me the story about her night on the town with the girls. I heard her calling someone "sweetie" and telling them that "no one is ever too old to find true love again." I concluded that she was talking to her nephew Nick. She had mentioned something the other day about Nick meeting this woman at work and how he was very impressed with her. As far as I knew, Nick had never been married, and according to what she said, her nephew was very lonely after being dumped by a former girlfriend. I heard her say, "Talk to you later," then she disappeared around the side of her house.

I had the lilac bush practically finished, so I went quietly back into the house to digest her conversation with whoever she was speaking to and figure out why she had not been getting her mail! I wanted desperately to call up Victoria Shipley and repeat what I had just heard. She would know what to make of it. I considered Victoria one of the smartest women I knew, and I felt she would come up with a good answer. She had a knack for figuring these things out. She was a no-nonsense type of person who used a lot of good common sense. I picked up the phone to call Victoria but put it down quickly. She was a good Christian woman, and she might think this was gossip. And come to think of it, that was what it was—pure gossip. I felt ashamed of myself for being such a busybody. Surely, I was prying too much into Mrs. Whitlock's private life and making too much out of nothing. After all, Mrs. Whitlock was a grown woman, and if she chose to cavort around all night, that was her business and none of my business. I decided to keep my big mouth shut and not tell a soul. I felt a tad of success being able to pass up the temptation of gossip after putting the phone down. I would keep a watchful eye on Mrs. Whitlock per Nick's instructions. If she seemed to be getting more confused, I would tell her nephew and let him handle it. I watched her like a hawk for the next couple of days without her knowing, I hoped. I saw nothing unusual about the elderly woman.

I invited her over for coffee, and she kept repeating the story about going to the play with her friends Sara and Olive. It was good to see that she was okay physically, but I knew she was lying to me because she didn't want me to know what was going on. I knew that she had not been to see the play with her friends. Sara had told me so! Maybe I should let her know that I had talked to Sara and that I knew her story was fabricated. I was more confused now than ever. I had never known Mrs. Whitlock to deliberately lie to me, so there had to be a good reason. If she had a cell phone, then maybe she had internet service also. Questions began to pop up in my mind. Had she met some man online? Elderly women did it all the time because they were lonely. Was this really what was happening to poor old Mrs. Whitlock, who was trying to hang on to her youth? She was truly a good person that had helped a lot of people. She had a heart of gold, and she deserved to be surrounded with good friends. Maybe I could get her to confide in myself or Victoria. I had a feeling that she was keeping a dark secret, and someone who cared about her needed to know. It was exhausting for me to think about it. I had to let it go!

I truly hoped that she was not getting herself into a mess. It was obvious that she had money. She lived in a beautiful home, had a luxury car, and owned some pieces of jewelry that were very expensive-looking! She would be an easy target for some predator that was looking for a lonely widow to scam. I anguished over calling Nick. I didn't know how he would take it. He might come immediately and confront her. She was dear to him, and he was very protective of his favorite aunt. I also knew that if I told him, she would be furious with me for meddling in her business. I now wished I hadn't promised her nephew that I would keep an eye on her. I was going to end up losing a good friend, but I had to think of her well-being. I tried to remind myself that it wasn't up to me to determine what was best for the elderly woman. That was up to her family.

I tried to be extremely observant the next few weeks, but work had become overtime almost every day. I came home so exhausted that I was too tired to cook. I stopped by fast-food restaurant or heated up frozen dinners. I then fell into my recliner to watch television until it was time to go to bed. I was watching the ten o'clock news one night when they had a special report on several elderly women who had been scammed out of their life savings by a very charming younger man. It caught my attention, and I thought about it far into the night after I had gone to bed. I knew that something was occupying Mrs. Whitlock's time because she was not visiting with me or Victoria nearly as much. I told myself it could be because Victoria had been out of town a lot lately, spending time with her ailing daughter, and I was working so much overtime. We were the ones that had not been available for visits.

It was toward the end of the week when Victoria paid me a visit to let me know that her daughter was doing a lot better. She also said that she thought Mrs. Whitlock was acting strange. I asked her what she meant by strange, and she said that she had gone over to visit Mrs. Whitlock, and she'd acted as if she didn't want any company. This was very strange. She adored company, and Mrs. Whitlock could talk your ear off with her endless stories. Victoria told me that her mailbox was full again, and she hardly ever saw her outside anymore. I was relieved when Victoria told me that she had called Nick and had a talk with him. He agreed to come down in the next few weeks to find out what was going on with her. He thought it might be time to check into getting her into assisted living. He dreaded the thought. Nick asked that we remain observant and let him know immediately if any big changes or red flags were going up. He thought she might be slowing down a bit, and that was to be expected due to her age. I did not completely agree with Nick. I wished he would come see for himself that something was out of order.

Being concerned about what Victoria had told me about Mrs. Shipley not wanting any company, I decided I would pay her a visit and see how she reacted to me. Maybe she hadn't felt well that day. I had baked some banana nut bread that morning. I wrapped up several slices to take to her. She took a lot of time answering the door, and when she saw me, she looked very annoyed!

"I don't need nosy neighbors spying on me," she said in a very nasty tone.

In all the time I had known her, she had never been rude. I began to feel uncomfortable that I had gone over to see her.

"I just wanted to say good morning and bring you some fresh-baked banana bread," I replied.

She quickly took the bread in both hands, but she did not invite me in. She stood at the door, looking very agitated. I sensed she thought I had been spying on her again. The truth was, I was! She told me that she was busy and that she would talk to me later on in the week. She practically shut the door in my face. It was clear that she was letting me know that she did not appreciate my visit.

"I understand," I told her as nicely as I could. I turned and left as quietly as I came. I felt just like a big pest as I walked across her yard. I had to mind my own business! It had been a long hot day, too hot to water the yard until after sundown. It was a Sunday afternoon, and I had had a busy morning at church services, then a luncheon followed. I didn't get home until after two o'clock. Feeling tired I took a long leisurely nap, then read for several hours. I did not need to cook that evening. I had brought leftovers home from the luncheon. After sundown I went into the backyard to water the lilac bush, which looked like it was having a hard time with the sweltering heat. As I stood there drenching the bush, I heard a man's voice coming from Mrs. Whitlock's patio. I looked through the cracks in the fence and saw a tall slender man standing there. From what I could tell, he was a much younger man!

He looked much younger than Mrs. Whitlock. He had on beige walking shorts and a white polo shirt. He legs looked lean and tanned. His hair was dark, and from what I could make out, he was very attractive. I heard him talking to someone on phone. It sounded like a business deal. I heard him say what a great opportunity it was! I couldn't imagine why he would be on her back porch talking of a business deal. I continued watering the plant with my ears tuned into every word I could catch. Maybe I was too cautious and even a little bit jealous. He was a very handsome man. But red flags kept going up and up and up. Surely, she had met this younger man somehow, and it was not going to turn out good for her. I went straight to the phone to call Nick. Realizing how angry Mrs. Whitlock would be, I hesitated as I dialed his number. Then I hung up before it rang a second time. I prayed he would not call back. My mind began to whirl. She was still an attractive woman, but not that attractive to interest a man his age. He looked young enough to be her son. I felt stuck between a rock and a hard place. Maybe I shouldn't have hung up the phone. I sat down and thumbed through a mail-order catalog, trying to figure out what to do. I didn't want to see a nice person like Mrs. Whitlock scammed out of her life's savings. The longer I thought about his phone conversation, the more apprehensive I became. I decided I would wait until dark, then sneak to the side of her house. I could peek through the window and see what was going on. If he was still there, then something had to be going on. It would not be a problem to get to her side window to get a good look. If I wanted to go into the backyard for some reason, it would not be difficult either because she left the gate unlocked so the yard man could mow and water her backyard. I paced the floor until around ten thirty. The news was over, so I dressed into dark clothing so I would not be seen so easily. Before I left on my spy mission, I checked to see if her lights were on in the yard. I could see that the backyard was all lit up, but the side was dark, which would be good for me. I practically ran across my yard and around to her side window.

For once, I was glad that she did not have a dog. The side of her house was totally dark, and I had to walk very careful not to bump into something. I positioned myself at the window and crunched down. I had a good view of the living room. I looked in, and there they sat on the floral sofa. It was a ridiculous sight. The good-looking man was stripped down to his shorts! Mrs. Whitlock was wearing some outrageous see-through nightgown! I gasped from shock! They began kissing, and he ran his hands over her shoulder, caressing her and holding her close. I don't know how long I stayed glued to the window looking at the sickening sight. Suddenly, I felt something behind me! I turned around and saw the biggest policeman that I had ever seen in my life towering over me. He did not look happy.

"What do you think you are doing?" he asked me. He then shined a flashlight in my face, which blinded me completely.

The lights in every room came on. I heard some rumbling around in the house. Mrs. Whitlock came outside to see what was going on. The policeman marched me around to the front door so that he could talk to Mrs. Whitlock. Whoever the mystery man was in her house, he did not come outside. I wondered why not. I tried to talk but was having difficulty. I was terrified that I was going to be arrested on the spot for being a Peeping Tom. Mrs. Whitlock told him that I was her nosy neighbor. He asked her if she wanted to press charges against me. She had on a housecoat now that made her look like she was just lounging leisurely around the house. She stood there for a few minutes. Finally, she said to the overgrown policeman, "Let it go this time."

He nodded his head and marched me back toward my house.

I felt so relieved that I wasn't being carted off to jail. As the policeman walked me back home, I tried to explain to him that I was only trying to check on an elderly neighbor because she had been acting so strange. I think he bought my story. He told me that if I thought she was not capable of taking care of herself, then I should call some family member or call social services.

"You could get shot peeping in someone's window so late at night," he added. "This was a poor way to check on her! Leave her alone and don't bother her. If I get another call out here, you could end up going to jail!"

With that warning, he got into his patrol car and drove off. I ended up calling Nick because I felt so foolish. Mrs. Whitlock got to him before I could make the call. He was not the least bit friendly with me, and he told me that he did not need me to look in on his aunt any longer. He would make other arrangements to have his aunt looked after. I took it to mean he thought I was some kind of a nut. I went to bed that night feeling shaken to the core. I felt scalding angry and very foolish! I was only trying to help watch after a neighbor! And what did it get me for trying to be helpful? I got a severe lecture and scolding from the police, along with almost getting arrested. I concluded that she could take care of her own ungrateful self! I was done worrying about her and her welfare. I concluded that I needed to take a vacation until all this blew over. I knew I was being ridiculed for my actions. Maybe it was time to go visit my sister and do some sightseeing. She wanted us to take a trip to Yosemite and spend some time together. It would be good for me to get away for a while. A change of scenery would be good for my sanity and my ego.

The next morning, I called my sister and made arrangements to take the trip to Yosemite with her. Before I left for my trip, I told Victoria that I would be gone for over a week. I was sure the gossip had reached her about my peeping through Mrs. Whitlock window. She gave me a big hug and said, "Have fun!"

It was fun to pack for the trip. I packed exactly as my sister instructed me. "Roll up your clothes to prevent wrinkles and save space." It turned out to be the best packing advice ever. I had room for the things I would buy on the trip. We ended up having a ball! We explored hiking trail that went on for several miles. We saw fantastic waterfalls and wildlife everywhere. I lost ten pounds with all the walking. The sequoia trees were unbelievable huge and breathtaking. We did more hiking than anything else. In fact, I thought the soles of my shoes would wear out. We even did an event that was out of character for me—ride mules! The riding trails were glorious. I was having so much fun I did not want to leave all the shops, restaurants, and fabulous activities. And too, I only had myself to look after. I hope all the gossip was dying down about my escapade with the police. This trip had already been healing.

I felt like I had revived myself completely with the wonderful trip. The days went by much too fast, and soon I was on my way back home. I had a glass of wine on the plane and fell asleep and didn't even know when the plane landed. I got back from my trip late in the evening. Our plane was delayed due to a thunderstorm. It was good to be home. The yard had been without water for over ten days, and it was turning brown. There was still enough daylight to water my backyard along with the lilac bush. Mrs. Shipley had offered to water it, but I knew she had all she could do with watering her own and running back and forth to her daughter's house. I took my luggage to one of the spare bedrooms and set it on the floor. I didn't feel all that tired, so I decided to give the backyard some water. It was much more important that I water the backyard instead of unpacking. I opened the drapes to let in some light. I immediately went to the backyard to do a quick spray of water.

I was standing by the lilac bush when I smelled a terrible odor. I had never smelled anything so foul. I couldn't tell exactly where it was coming from. The wind was blowing harder with a promise of rain. My nostrils stung from the horrible smell. The best I could tell the putrid smell was coming from Mrs. Whitlock's place. I peeked through the fence and could see the back door was ajar. I laid down the water hose and turned off the faucet. My curiosity was getting the best of me like the night when I almost got arrested. I went back into the kitchen to get a sturdy wooden chair to use as a ladder. I would climb over the back fence so no nosy neighbor could see me from the side and call the police on me again. I wasn't exactly a spring chicken, but I made it over the fence without event by climbing to the top then dropping to the ground. The smell was now penetrating my nose until it was almost unbearable!

As I walked up to the door, I put one hand over my nose and pushed the door open with the other. Immediately, I saw her as I entered the house. She was sprawled out on the kitchen floor. She was wearing the same hideous nightgown that she'd worn that night. I saw movement on the floor and realized it was maggots. I let out a scream! There were mountains of them crawling in and around her body. She was lying on her stomach with her shoulders bare. There wasn't much tissue left on her shoulders. Her whole body was a sea of writhing maggots. When I realized that I was about to vomit, I ran out the back door. I don't know how I managed to get back over the fence, but I did. I attributed it to fear and adrenaline. I ran back home and called the police. I told the lady that answered the phone at the police station that I smelled something terrible coming from the next-door neighbor's house. I did not tell them that I had already been over there. I stood over the sink trying to keep from vomiting. I then made myself a glass of ice tea, hoping it would settle my stomach before the police got there. I hoped it would not be the same fat policeman. Within fifteen minutes, my doorbell rang, and it was a lady police officer. I took her into the backyard, where she could experience the terrible smell for herself. I could tell by the look on her face that she knew the smell of death! The officer radioed for another unit to assist her. When the other officer arrived, they went over to check out my neighbor's house.

Within thirty minutes, more police cars began to arrive. I saw yellow crime tape put up around the property. I knew that they would be back to question me since I am the one who reported it. I would tell them everything I knew about the stranger that I saw on her patio. I would tell them about the same man I saw on her sofa hugging her tight. I shivered to think how she had met the end. I hoped death came quickly for her. She was such a nice old lady. I wondered how her nephew Nick would feel now? He would be the one feeling foolish! As for me, I sat there thinking that I could identify the young man that had murdered her! Knowing that I could identify him, would he be coming back to kill me?

WESTERN JUSTICE

Walterine Hogg stood at the edge of Main Street anxiously awaiting the arrival of the Butterfield Overland Stage. The agent who sold her the ticket told her the stage was usually late. He told her not to worry. There could be a number of reasons why the stage was not on time. She was not worried about the stage being late, she was overwhelmed to make such a trip alone and almost penniless. The morning heat was already stifling in the small town of El Paso, Texas. The year was 1860, and El Paso was yet to become a boomtown. The railroad had yet to arrive along with the saloons, prostitutes, and gambling houses, which would create a thriving economy for El Paso in the next few years. Until the boomtown arrived, there was literally no opportunity for a young woman to find employment.

She wiped the sweat from her beautiful face with a white handkerchief and tried to be patient like the ticket man told her to be. She stood beside one suitcase. It contained all her earthy possessions, which consisted of two dresses, a pair of what she called her Sunday shoes, needles, thread, and a few pieces of jewelry that her mother swore was valuable. Pinned inside the thick layered petticoat was fifty dollars. This was all she had left after buying her ticket to San Francisco. This small amount of money included the sale of the farm along with the horses, cows, chickens, and all the farm equipment. A few weeks after her parents died suddenly from a fever, Mr. Nixon, one of the bankers in town, came to call on her and offer to buy the property. Mr. Nixon was a short bald man with the bushiest eyebrows that she had ever seen. It made him look as if his hair had fallen from the top of his head and landed right above his eyes. He peeked from under heavy brows with small beady eyes. His unattractive looks gave him the appearance of being a pettifogger. Walterine did not know about her father's indebtedness to the bank until Mr. Nixon informed her of this pending obligation. After the debt was paid in full, Walterine barely had enough money for her traveling expenses. She was told the cost of her ticket included meals and lodging at various way stations. With such a small amount of money she would need to watch every penny for such a lengthy trip. Also, she had to keep in mind how she would survive until she found employment.

She packed only what she thought she could manage. Mr. Nixon, seeing how distraught she was, offered to store her belongings at no costs until she could make other arrangements. She thanked him for his generosity, but more than likely she would not be returning to claim them. He could do with the furniture or anything else as he wished. There was no way that she could take any of the household furnishings with her since she was traveling by stage. She had no family in town that could store her belongings. It was pure anguish to walk out of the old house knowing that she was leaving it all behind.

The tightness in her chest made her feel as if she could hardly breathe. The fear of the unknown was almost paralyzing. She had no idea of what was ahead for her. She had never thought about the possibility of being homeless. And it had come so soon. She felt anger toward her parents that they had left her all alone. She wished that she had been the one to die. She had cried so many tears in the last few days that she felt totally empty. Only with divine help from above would she be able to carry on. She kept telling herself that there would be no reason for her to ever return to El Paso. She had no family and very few friends that she could count on. It would be better if she made a start somewhere else, somewhere she could get a good job and meet interesting people. She could think of no place except San Francisco. At least she had heard stories about it. She remembered when she was a very young girl, her mother would tell her stories about living there and what an exciting place it was to live. It was a place where people were going and coming all hours of the night. There was always plenty to do to keep everyone entertained. Her mother told her about dress shops where dresses could be bought ready to wear. Fancy restaurants where people wore their Sunday best! She told her about the theaters with famous actors whose only job was to perform. It was a place where it was okay to indulge and show other their prosperity. A place where it was not a sin to dance the night away! As a little girl, she would go to sleep dreaming of such a magical place.

Walterine knew her mother had never been to San Francisco. She was almost a grown woman before she realized that her mother was trying to put a spark of hope in her young daughter that there was a much better life out there than life on the prairie. She knew that her mother had never had a store-bought dress or any special party to attend. Her life had been the life of a lonely hardworking woman who had so little to show for it. She got old before her time. There had been no galas for her mother to attend in a pretty dress. She knew only the sounds of the howling wolf or the dry winds that moaned all day and all night. There were times that she wanted to scream at her mother, "Stop with the lies," but she did not have the heart to do so. The look of joy in her mother's eyes when she repeated the tall tales told Walterine that it was her mother's way of dreaming also. That was a way of coping for people who are lonely. Now Walterine felt like she was doing the same thing as her mother— dreaming and making believe that she could go to San Francisco and live happily ever after. Now the moment had come! She could no longer afford to go on with make-believe. She had to actually get started to a city of make-believe! She fought back tears of dread. Surely God knew her helpless state and he was there to guide her. Her faith was the only thing that kept her going. She believed that everything happened for a reason.

Were the stories her mother told her meant to be a guide? She needed more time to think about her future. It would be good to be traveling. She could deal with it better on the stage than sitting on a lonely farm, waiting to be evicted from the only life she knew. The distant city of San Francisco, over a thousand miles away, would take ten days of traveling by stage to get there.

At last, the stage appeared. She had seen stagecoaches before when she accompanied her parents into town to buy supplies. She had never paid much attention to them before. Now this would be her home for the next two weeks. Taking a closer look at the coach, she noticed a graceful swinging motion of the carriage instead of a jolting up and down. This would be a good thing. She had been concerned about the rough ride and wondered how she would manage it. She had heard stories of the hardships of travel. There was danger of being robbed or killed by outlaws. There would be much discomfort with the intolerable heat this time of the year. As the coach came closer, she observed it was painted a dark blue with a bright yellow undercarriage. The window in the door was glazed over. The side windows were not. There was a canvas covering above each window which could be rolled up or down depending on the weather. The interior was much nicer than she expected. There were three uphol-stered benches that looked like they could accommodate maybe eight to ten people. The stagecoach came to a stop, and the driver jumped down. He picked up her suitcase as if it were weightless and threw it haphazardly on top of the coach. It landed with such a bang that a passenger already seated inside began to complain.

"You would think they would treat our belongings with some respect," she mumbled. She was fanning herself with a large purple fan. "My dear, I hope you didn't have anything breakable!"

As Walterine stepped inside the coach, she assured the com-plaining lady that she did not. Before she could get herself seated comfortably, the stage was on its way.

"Where are you going?" a pretty lady in a green satin dress, with a hat to match, asked her.

Walterine considered the woman to be the most beautiful woman she had ever seen. Her clothing was exquisite. The lady seated next to her was dressed equally as beautiful. Seeing them suddenly made her feel shabby. They both were looking at her as if she were a dreadful sight.

"I'm going to San Francisco," Walterine said in a very timid voice, hoping to sound friendly. The last thing she wanted for such a long trip was to sit next to unfriendly people. Once seated, she straightened her dress the way she always did when she was nervous about something. Before she boarded the stage, she felt proud of the dress she had made for herself earlier that year. Now she felt shabby, considering the beautiful dresses that the other ladies wore.

"My dear," the lady in the green dress said. "Do you have any idea how long this trip is going to be? You are traveling so light!"

Walterine was too embarrassed to tell them that all she owned in the world was in that one suitcase along with fifty dollars pinned in her petticoat. She felt close to tears by the way the two women were acting. Surely, they thought she was some pitiful thing! But that didn't mean that they could berate her and make her feel bad.

She tried to straighten her dress again. She felt eyes on her, but this time it was not the two snooty women. It was a young man that was sitting across the aisle from her.

"Do you have family in San Francisco?" His voice did not have the prying tone the two women had. He was dressed in a tailored suit with a glistening white shirt. His shoes were very polished and looked expensive. They were even nicer shoes than the banker Mr. Nixon wore. He was also strikingly handsome. He laid the newspaper he was reading across his lap and introduced himself as Durston Fort. She smiled back and told him that her name was Walterine Hogg. He tipped his hat and told her that he was very happy to meet her. Walterine knew the young man was trying to rescue her from the two meddling women. His attempt didn't last long.

"Your father must have been wanting a boy when he named you Walterine," the lady in green dress said.

Walterine did not know how to respond to such rudeness. He father loved her more than anything and would not have traded her for any boy. She looked across at the young man who had just introduced himself. She wanted to answer his question about her family.

"Yes, I do have family in San Francisco." She bit her tongue, knowing it was a lie. "I have an aunt. She owns a hat shop, and I am going to work for her." Both women looked surprised. Walterine felt she could read their minds. Surely, no one would want such a shabby-looking girl as a salesclerk! It would not be good for business.

Once again, the stage coach had become silent, with only soft groans from the weary travelers. Walterine prayed that no one would ask her anymore questions about family or where she was going. The young man buried himself again behind his newspaper with the feeling that he had successfully interrupted the interrogation of the shy girl. He felt compassion for her. She seemed so intimidated by the two rich-looking women that it bothered him terribly. He doubted his intercession would last for long. They were two nosy women who seemed intent on meddling in the poor girl's life and finding out why she was traveling alone with only one suitcase.

The second man that sat beside Durston Fort was a Mr. Horace Mills. He introduced himself to Walterine but did not give any information about himself. He looked bored with the trip and kept his eyes closed as if he were asleep. Walterine doubted that anyone could sleep in such conditions.

The rough road was enough to keep anyone awake. Coupled with the heat, it would be next to impossible. She imagined Mr. Mills to be some kind of businessman, maybe a banker or cattle buyer. Whatever he was, she was sure he had money and lots of it. Of all the people on the stage, he looked the most stressed out. She wondered if the two rich women's talk had worn him out and that pretending to be asleep was his only escape from the two meddling women.

The third man was the least desirable of all. He was heavyset, with a beard that looked in need of a trim. His name was Teed Riley. He sat staring at Walterine, which gave her a very uneasy feeling. He had a long scar down the left cheek that gave him a mean look. He no doubt was a tough man. He wore a gun belt around his bulging waist. He looked mean enough to use it for whatever reason. She hoped he would not be traveling all the way to San Francisco with them. Surely, this disgusting looking man did not have any legitimate business in a town like San Francisco.

They traveled about two more hours when she caught Durston smiling at her. She smiled back, grateful for the attention he was giving her. She was used to men staring at her. Her long black hair hung damp around her face. Despite the heat and fatigue, she still looked beautiful. She rummaged through her small handbag and pulled out a soiled handkerchief to sponge her face. She was beginning to feel the effects of the terrible heat. She could not understand how Durston managed to looked so comfortable. The air had become so hot she felt like she was going to faint. She closed her eyes for a minute. Suddenly, she felt a cool area on her forehead. She opened her eyes to find Durston sponging her face with a wet cloth. A water canteen set beside him on the seat.

"I know that you are traveling a long way from home," Durston told her. "If I can be of any assistance, please let me know." At that exact moment, she felt like she had fallen in love. When he spoke, she could feel her heart racing. She hoped the other two ladies were not picking up on her feeling for him. Surely, it was showing in her face.

She felt like a ragamuffin sitting beside the two well-dressed women. She had no idea that she would be meeting someone this special as Durston on the trip. She wished that she had worn her Sunday best, but even that would not have been sufficient.

"Are your family roots in San Francisco?" the lady in green started to question Walterine again. Instead of looking at the countryside, the lady seemed to be keeping her eyes on the restless girl as if she were some sort of wretched creature that had to be watched.

"No," Walterine answered back quickly, "Just my aunt." She leaned her head back against the seat and closed her eyes. Maybe the meddling women would get a hint. Walterine did not want to talk about a town she knew nothing about or an aunt that she did not have. The stage bounced as it hit big holes in the road. Her back ached. She opened her eyes again to find Mrs. Dunn staring at her.

"Most of my family is from…" Her mind went blank. She was so frustrated that she could not think straight. She did not like to lie. In all her years, she had not found any predicament that needed lies. Since she had started this trip, it seemed that all she was doing was making up lies to keep from embarrassing herself. Guilt rushed over her like swift water. She didn't understand why she felt so guilty. Was it a crime to board a stage alone with only one suitcase?

"Well," she stammered, "I have been away for a long time, and I hardly remember anything or anyone." Her anxiety was becoming paramount. Being so nervous and shaky, she now had the attention of everyone on board including Riley. She could see the question in his evil-looking eyes: "Why would such a young woman be traveling alone and so far away?"

They all were now looking at her as if she was on trial for her life. It was evident they thought something was strange about her.

"Well, girl, you are not making a lot of sense! Are you from the north, south, east or west?" Riley spoke very loudly as he took the cigar from between his rubbery lips. He had made her business his, like the others had. She now felt cornered! They all looked at her for an answer with the exception of Durston. Why couldn't they mind their own business and leave her alone? She was not hammering them with questions. She could have cared less where they were going.

Walterine felt put upon! She felt caged and was trying to claw her way out. She was sure her lies would catch up with her sooner or later, but still her life was not their business. She could not let these prying people get the best of her. She was not a criminal! Just because she looked penniless did not give them the right to badger her. She knew she was stuck with them for the time being, so she would do her best to get along with them.

"I'm originally from the north-south," she said, not looking at anyone in particular.

"The north!" Tweed Riley bellowed. "You sound like you're from Alabama, like a farm girl!"

Walterine had no idea which direction he was talking about. She didn't know much about anything except El Paso. She felt foolish and embarrassed. She could feel her face turning red.

"We are waiting, girl," Tweed said very sarcastically. "Are you from the north, south, east, or west?"

"Well, I am actually from the north and the south!" Her voice sounded weak and pitiful! The two women and Teed Riley snickered. Durston continued to read his newspaper, and Mr. Mills kept his eyes closed.

"I think something is very wrong," the woman in green muttered. She fanned herself faster as she spoke. Everything went silent. The conversation came to a complete stop. No one said anything else. Walterine continued to look down at her clenched hands. Durston sat quietly behind his paper as if it were a fort separating him from the rest. She hoped he could come to her rescue again. This time, he did not. She wondered what he was thinking.

Travel was quiet for the next few hours. The stage had stopped several times for the passengers to relieve themselves. The three women went in one direction, the men in the opposite. The stops were short. Soon they were on their way again. The next stop of any duration was a way station. Walterine was starved, and her bones ached from sitting so long in one position. They had traveled for what seemed like an eternity when the stagecoach driver announced that they would be stopping for the night. Accommodations would be few, but it would be a chance to get a warm meal and a sponge bath before going to bed.

The way station was a scruffy old building that stood in the middle of nowhere. Walterine was delighted when the man who ran the business brought out a steaming pot of beans and ham hocks. He placed a pan of corn bread on the table beside the pot. He gave each passenger a large bowl and a spoon. Walterine was the first to dip into the pot. She had never been so hungry. She filled the bowl half full of the soupy beans, then she took a piece of corn bread. She took a large bite of the bread and found it to be completely tasteless. However, the beans and ham hocks were delicious. Before she could take her second bite, Tweed Riley was helping himself to another bowl of beans. He slurped as he ate. The two women looked horrified at the way he was eating. When the two rich women tasted the beans, they frowned as they looked at each other. The frowns soon turned to sober faces as they ate like it might be their last meal for a while. Durston and Mr. Mills sat at the far end of the table. If they were disappointed, it did not show. Bedroom accommodations were adequate but not good. Walterine had to share a room with the two rich ladies, and they both snored all night long. Walterine slept little that night and was up at the crack of dawn. She wondered whether she would have to endure ten days of sleepless nights while traveling on the stage with these ladies.

The lady who had been wearing the green dress claimed she had not slept a wink that night. She was now dressed in a light brown dress that looked equally expensive. The other lady had changed her dress to dark gray one with a white bow at the neckline. Both women were inquisitive of why Walterine had slept in her dress. She told them she had been too tired to change into her nightgown. They rolled their eyes like they had never heard the likes.

After a quick breakfast of fried eggs and sausage patties, the stage started on its way again. Walterine felt somewhat revived. The way station had indulged them with cold water from a nearby spring and had given the travelers a large supply of it. Instead of a warm bath, Walterine submerged herself in a tub of cold water that night before she went to bed. She felt refreshed for the first time since she started the trip. Durston and Mr. Mills looked refreshed also. She wished she could say the same for Tweed Riley. He was still looking his grimy, dirty self with tobacco strains running down his chin. A disgusting sight!

The stage moved at a snail's pace. The road once again seemed endless. Soon their clothes were stuck to their wet, perspiring bodies. The evenings were somewhat cooler than the day, but the mosquitoes made life miserable after sundown. The following night, everyone slept on the stage. The days came and went uneventfully. Travel was pure hell. They had been traveling four more days with two night stops. The passengers would sleep under shade trees and bathe in nearby creeks. The horses were placed under good shade trees with an abundance of water and hay. As they were boarding the stage again early that morning, she heard Durston talking favorably about the next town they were approaching. The town had hotels and restaurants and places to shop. It had saloons for the men to have a few drinks. They would be spending the night there. Mrs. Atkinson, the lady that wore the beautiful green satin dress, offered to share a room with Walterine. Walterine knew immediately that Mrs. Atkinson didn't want to hear Mrs. Dunn snore all night long. Mrs. Atkinson's excuse was that she knew Walterine had to save as much money as possible. It would be good to cut down on expenses, but Walterine wanted some privacy for the evening. Maybe she could take a long walk later and perhaps run into Durston and get to know him better. Besides, if she agreed to share a room, she knew the meddling would start up again.

The entrance to the hotel was a lovely room! Walterine was very impressed! She stood in awe taking it all in. She didn't know such a place existed. It had such elegant and extravagant furniture. A white settee with lilac pillows faced the front doorway. A vase of fresh flowers set on a long table that was over next to the window. She followed the two other ladies to check in.

Her room cost one dollar for the night, and it would be facing the street. A room to the back with less noise was two dollars. She accepted the cheaper one. She took the large metal key the hotel man gave her. This was her first time to stay in such a nice hotel. The key had the number 15 written on it. She was totally breathless as she climbed the stairs. The room was very large and far beyond any expectations. The bed had a beautiful lilac covering with two large pillows that matched the bedspread and the pillows downstairs. She sank into the softness of the bed and was asleep as soon as her head hit the pillows. She slept fitfully for about five hours.

When she awoke, she realized that she had missed dinner with the two other ladies. If they had knocked on her door, she had not heard them. She liked the window facing the street. She would be able to see what was going on. She looked down at the street below. She could hear people talking and laughing. The streets were dark with the exception of two small lamppost lights. As she looked further down the street, she could see only darkness. She glanced at the clock that sat on the nightstand by her bed. It was eleven o'clock. She was now rested, wide awake, and most of all, hungry as a horse. She wondered if any restaurants were still open at this time of night. She doubted it, but she was starving, and it would not hurt to look. She straightened her dress by running her small hands over the bodice and down the full skirt. She ran a comb through her long black hair. She didn't like the idea of being alone on the street because of all the stories she had heard on the stage. It was not a safe place for a woman to be alone. She took the large hatpin out of her suitcase and placed it in her pocket for protection. She could do a lot of damage with it if anyone tried to harm her. She wished that Durston had asked for dinner. He had not! Was she a fool to expect such an eloquent man would be calling on such a shabby woman as herself!

She closed the door gently behind her so she would not make any noise. If the two women saw her parading around at midnight, they might think she was the wrong kind of girl. She tiptoed down the stairs. She felt like she was a thief stepping so lightly on the stairs. As she walked through the door, out onto the street, she picked up her pace. She felt like a bird out of a cage.

The night air was cool, and it felt so good to be in town where business places stayed open all evening. There were few people out on the street. She walked down the sidewalk until she came to a saloon. She was starving and thirsty. Maybe she could get some meat and bread in the saloon. She was so hungry she would settle for anything. The noise was loud, and everyone inside seemed to be having good time. She knew that respectable women didn't set foot in such a place, but she was too hungry to care. She had never been in a saloon before, and this time she had to in order to eat.

She would pay a short visit to see what was going on and get something to eat and drink. As she entered the door, she prayed no one would recognize her. What would she do if one of the men travelers was inside? She looked around. All she saw were strangers. It was late, and her traveling party had more than likely already paid their respects and had gone back to the hotel for the night. Looking around the room, she spotted a table in the corner which looked like a good place to sit. Two saloon girls had already noticed her and were eyeing her mysteriously. They whispered for a moment then the girl with the curly blonde hair came over to her table.

"Do you want something, honey?" the girl asked. The blonde girl's dress was a deep crimson red. It was low cut, and it exposed a huge bosom. She tried not to show how shocked she felt.

"Yes," Walterine replied. "I will have a cold beer and a couple of those boiled eggs you have in the jar on the counter." Walterine realized how out of place she looked in her farm girl dress. The saloon girl smiled as she took the order. She began to walk away swinging her hips wildly as if she was putting on some kind of show. She made her way back to the bar, took two boiled eggs out of the pickle juice, and put them on a plate. She came back to the table with the eggs and a cold beer.

"How much do I owe you?" Walterine asked.

"It is on the house," the blonde girl said. Walterine didn't understand what she meant. She took out two quarters and tried giving it to the blonde girl.

The saloon girl gave Walterine another smile and walked back to the bar, where the other saloon girl stood, watching Walterine devour the boiled eggs. Walterine grabbed the glass of cold liquid and put it up to her mouth. She took a little sip, expecting it to taste something awful. To her surprise, it was sweet and very pleasant. She was so thirsty that she gulped it down as she stuffed her mouth full of the last boiled egg. Food and drink had never tasted so good. Now she understood why men liked the beer. As she swallowed the last morsel of food, the blonde saloon girl approached her table for the second time. All the men in the bar were now looking at the girl with the long dark hair. The saloon girls seemed to be fascinated with the innocent-looking young lady like the men.

"I'll have another beer." She licked her lips as she spoke. Walterine was still thirsty from the long day of traveling on the stage coach.

The saloon girl laughed and said, "Are you sure that you want a beer or another mug of apple cider like the one that you just consumed?"

Walterine felt her cheeks turn red! She had made a fool of herself again, not knowing the difference between apple cider and a beer. What an idiot, she was! Walterine grabbed her purse and ran out the door.

The streets were now completely empty. A skinny old man that looked as thin as a broom handle was sweeping the sidewalk. He scolded her, "The saloons are closing! You need to get yourself home, young lady, before you get into real trouble. It is not safe out here this time of night!"

Walterine began to walk fast back down the dark street. She didn't have far to go back to her hotel room, but it was late and dark. She had never been up at this time of night before. The young woman had never felt more afraid than she did now in the strange town. She began to question herself as she hurried along as to why she took the chance to venture out in the middle of the night. Certainly not a smart move on her part. She scolded herself as her steps became faster and faster. The sounds of her shoes hitting the street seemed to scream her presence for the whole world to hear. Suddenly, a dark shadowy figure appeared in the alleyway. Before she could muster a scream, huge hands were around her throat, cutting off her air. She knew she would die if she didn't do something. She remembered the hatpin in her pocket. With one free hand, she reached deep into her dress pocket and pulled out the sharp hatpin. She aimed for his chest and swung with all her might! As she plunged the pin deep into his chest, he let out a bloodcurdling scream! The man slowly let go of her. Swearing loudly, he clutched his chest and fell to the ground. Blood covered her dress and feet. Realizing that she was still holding the sharp object, she placed it back into her pocket. All she could think about was to flee to scene. She looked around to see if anyone was watching! She was shaking violently and trying to make sense of what had happened. She looked down at the large man at her feet. He lay very still. She tried to take a step forward and realized that she had lost a shoe in the fight. She reached down to pick up her shoe when she saw something lying beside it on the ground. The lamplight from the street was flickering with a soft light, giving a little visibility to the alleyway. She looked again and saw it was a large roll of money. She reached down, grabbing up her shoe and the money along with it. She then put the money in her pocket with the hatpin. She looked both ways and saw no one in sight. It was well past midnight now, and the streets were completely silent. When she entered the hotel lobby, all was quiet. The man at the front desk was still asleep and in the same position that she had seen her earlier when she left the hotel. She made her way up the stairs to room 15. She unlocked the door and collapsed into a chair that sat beside her bed. She was holding her breath to keep from crying out loud. It was so good to be behind locked doors again.

She sat silently for a minute. She pulled the roll of money out of her pocket. She had never seen so much money in all her life. "There must be hundreds of dollars," she muttered to herself. She began to count but stopped at the count of $1,000! She was just too tired to count all of it. She removed her blood-soaked dress and hid it at the bottom of her suitcase along with the money. She changed her clothes and washed her face. Falling into bed, she went right to sleep.

Morning came too quickly. She jumped out of bed and splashed her face with water. She combed her long dark hair, then pulled it back into a bun. She was ready in no time to join the other two women for a breakfast of bacon, eggs, with hot biscuits. She barely had time to eat all she wanted of the delicious food before the stage drivers was announcing it was time to board the coach. Walterine stood outside the coach as long as she could. She was the last of the travelers to climb aboard. She reclaimed her seat with the others as they settled in for another hot miserable day of traveling over the bumpy roads. The stage was pulling out of town when she heard Durston ask, "Did anyone hear about the bank being robbed last night?"

"Yes, I did hear about it," Mr. Mills said. "It is the talk of the town this morning."

Durston eagerly added, "They say that two men robbed the First National Bank in the middle of the night. Rumor is that one of the men got away, but the other was not so lucky. They think they found one of the bank robbers dead in an alley this morning."

Durston was now filling his pipe with tobacco. He puffed, and smoke began to billow up. He went on with his story. "The dead man they found in the alleyway is a bit of a mystery. The sheriff said he wasn't shot! After checking out the dead man's body, they discovered that he had died from a large puncture wound to his heart. Another thing, the sheriff said was that no money was found on him! The other bank robber must have gotten away with all the money!"

Walterine sat there listening to Durston and the others talk about the robbery. The two women claimed they heard strange noises coming from across the street.

"I didn't realize it was a robbery going on." Mrs. Atkinson's face was glowing with excitement. "Did you hear anything, my dear?" she said, looking at Walterine.

Walterine tried to swallow, and her throat never felt so dry. "No, I was so tired I didn't hear a thing."

"I wonder how he came to be killed with a sharp object. I think one of the robbers may have been meeting a woman that was in on the robbery," Mr. Mills replied.

"You may be right, probably some old saloon girl," Durston said as he took the pipe from his mouth.

Walterine started to shake again. What if someone saw the whole thing and they were just putting her through some kind of test to see if she would confess? Did everyone think that she had killed a man last night?

"I think the manner in which he died is the key to solving who's in on it," Tweed Riley said.

"I agree with you," Mr. Mills said as he crossed his short legs. This was the first time they had agreed on anything during the whole trip.

"We should all try to remember what we heard last night." Mrs. Dunn said. "I think the sheriff may want to question all of us when we get to the next town."

"I am sure they will be offering a large reward. With all the money missing from the bank, the townspeople will really be up in arms," Teed boasted. The large man with the rubbery lips and dirty-looking teeth was now grinning at Walterine as if he knew she had done something! Walterine felt herself go limp. Maybe that was why Teed Riley was traveling on the stage. Maybe he had it all planned out with another resident in town. By the way he was grinning at her, she felt that he knew something! He was sitting across from her, torturing her with his accusing smiles. She just had to get off the stage as soon as she could. Maybe she should confess in the next town and tell the truth as to what happened. Surely, the sheriff would believe her. She had not been in on any bank robbery. She had killed him in a fight for her life!

She clenched her small fists as the stage moved slowly on. Would this trip ever end? She wondered how much money she had in her suitcase. She wished they would come to another stop for the night. This time she would count all the money for sure. She did not feel poor any longer. As they traveled on, she decided to keep all the money. She had earned it. She would be a fool to turn it in and starve. Maybe this was how God was providing for her. She closed her eyes, trying to pretend she was asleep. It seemed like they had traveled a thousand more miles when the stage driver announced they were coming into Yuma. They would spend the night there. Hope welled up in her at the chance of escaping their glaring eyes. Something inside her told her that Teed Riley knew something. She just had that feeling. The stage came to a stop on the main street of Yuma. Walterine told the stage driver that she was sick and that she would not be continuing on with them. He climbed back to the top of the stage and threw her bag down. She quickly told the two women that she would not be rejoining them. She needed to rest for a few days.

"Take your time, dear," Mrs. Dunn said. "There is another stage through here in about a week. You can catch that one."

Walterine looked around for Durston and the two other men. Durston and Mr. Mills had disappeared into a saloon, but Teed Riley was standing across the street looking back at Walterine. She pretended not to notice.

She retired early that night after a brisk walk to refresh herself and look the town over. She liked what she saw. On her walk, she passed a dress shop that was had a Help Wanted sign in the window. She could buy herself a few nice dresses and decent shoes to look for work. The more she looked the town over, the more she liked it. She would apply for the job that afternoon. Getting the job would be a perfect reason for her to stay. If asked why she stayed, she would tell them that she had run out of money! She looked so shabby! Surely, no one would question her need to work.

Soon, Durston and Mr. Mills appeared out on the street. Moments later, Mrs. Atkinson and Mrs. Dunn stood beside them, fanning themselves. Everyone was there except Teed Riley. Her heart began to race. What would she do if he remained in town? Was he trying to smoke her out and get her to confess for the reward money? Or was he planning on forcing her to give him the money and keep it for himself? What would she do if he started harassing her? She smiled as she thought about the hatpin! It had saved her life once before and it could save her again. As she moved from the window and closed the curtains, the last thing she saw was a glimpse of Teed Riley. Without a doubt he would be coming for her, and without a doubt she would be ready for him!

THE MIDNITE TRAIN

She saw him walking up the tracks, and she immediately noticed his youthful stride. His pace was different than the other homeless men. Most were weathered and grizzly looking. The men would often knock on her door for a handout. Something about this man was different. Even at a distance, something told her that he was not the usual vagrant that was traveling south for the winter. He was different in that he did not have a look of dejection even though he walked as if all of yesterday's sorrows had fallen heavily upon his wide shoulders and that today's burden would not be easy. She always felt sad when she saw these calloused men with the look of gloom and doom in their faded eyes. Each and every face showed no hope of escaping their own private hell or ever climbing out of their deep pit of misery. Who were these men? And where did they come from? Did they once have family who loved them? What kind of work did they once do? Were they once successful and happy? How had they ever come to such despair? She could go on endlessly with the questions of why. Surely, they had all been men with dreams, but somehow these dreams were cut short by the paths they had taken. Here they were walking the railroad tracks with their heads bent low, asking the world for nothing more than crumbs of food. It was important to her to give them a helping hand and make them feel that someone cared. She did care! She was a woman of God! She never turned any of these people away. She had given clothes to some when she saw the rags that hung from their thin bodies. Her heart broke for them. She was lost in thought as she looked out the window at the man on the tracks.

He was quickly approaching her door in such a swift manner that she was sure his stomach was empty and he was in bad need of a nourishing meal to stifle his hunger. She smoothed her long brown hair back from her face and wished she had applied a little makeup and taken the time to put on something decent to wear. She caught a glimpse of her homely face in the mirror and frowned. Nothing about her was pretty! She had been told many times that she was plain, and she had no reason to believe otherwise. When she was in the fifth grade, Milton Gentry had made fun of her looks. She went home that day crying. After looking at herself in the mirror, she concluded that she was just like Milton Gentry described! Her face was as long and slim as a horse, with small colorless eyes. She would never forget those cruel things Gentry had said to her during recess. From then on, she kept her head down to prevent anyone from noticing what a plain Jane she was.

She had slept late that morning and was planning on a trip into town to do some shopping with her aunt Gwen. But Aunt Gwen had called the night before, telling her that she was coming down with the flu and wasn't up to doing anything. She planned to stay home and get plenty of rest. As usual, Aunt Gwen cautioned her niece about feeding these homeless men since the cold weather had arrived, which would be driving them south. Aunt Gwen would always warn her about helping those people with no purpose in their wasted lives other than to freeload off kindhearted people.

"I'm moving you away from those tracks," Aunt Gwen would tell her. "You can come live with me."

But this was Connie Jo's childhood home, and too many fond memories to turn loose of it just yet. Besides, she liked her privacy, and Aunt Gwen talked so much it was hard for her to concentrate on grading her students' work. Aunt Gwen was very protective of her only niece, and since she had no children of her own, she hovered over Connie Jo. Aunt Gwen knew that her niece had a heart of gold, but it was going to be her downfall. "One of these days, you're going to open your door to the wrong person!" Her warnings were constant. Connie was not hearing her advice and letting it in one ear and out the other. It was Connie's mission in life to share her last morsel of food with anyone in need. Aunt Gwen wondered why Connie didn't go into some type of missionary work or join the Peace Corps since helping others meant so much to her. Connie had seriously considered joining the armed forces instead of going to college. Her mother had been a teacher, and Aunt Gwen was a teacher. She wanted to follow in their footsteps and keep teaching going in the family. Since her aunt had retired, Connie thought she read too many crime books and watched too many crime shows to fill her dull days. Connie felt she had made the right decision in becoming a teacher. For the time being, she was content living in the house beside the railroad tracks and teaching her sixth-grade students at Jefferson Elementary School. School was out for the Christmas break, and she was tired of making lesson plans and grading mounds of homework. She just needed a break. She was tired of the same old routine and wanted to do something a little different, something out of the ordinary! She didn't know at the time, but today, she would be doing something totally out of character.

She stepped back from the window, not wanting him to know that she had seen him approaching. It was still early morning, and hobos usually didn't knock on her door at that time of day. She was relieved that she had noticed him before he was at her front door. At least a few minutes' notice was better than an unexpected knock on her door. He knocked softly on her door. She opened it to find a handsome face staring down at her. At a distance, she could not see how attractive he was. She noticed how smooth his face and hands looked. Definitely, he did not have the hands of a laborer. His clothes were stylish, though they could use a good washing. His shoes did not reveal much mileage on them, and they look quite expensive. He was quite a contrast to the other ragged beggars whose shoes were worn out and falling off their rough-looking feet.

"Could you spare some food in exchange for work, miss?" His voice sounded tired, and his eyes looked weary. To make matters worse, he was trembling from hunger.

"Come in," she said as she opened the door wide. This was very unusual for her to invite a vagrant into her home. She was a woman alone, and this could be very dangerous. Her thoughts went straight to Aunt Gwen. She would hit the ceiling if she ever found out. She normally did heed her aunt's warnings. Being so careful, she always made them wait outside on the porch while she prepared the food. When the food was almost ready, she would politely ask them "to go wait beside the gate," which was a safe distance from the front door. She would then set the plate of food on the end of the porch and quickly go back inside and bolt the door. No one had ever given her any trouble before. With stomachs so empty they hurt, they were most happy to comply! Only after the food was in their hands did they act like animals. After a large portion of food was devoured, a look of satisfaction would spread over their gaunt faces. She hoped their next meal would come soon and that all people would be kind to them. She would tell them that they were welcome to the food and when they were finished, to leave the empty plate on the porch. No need to knock. She did not want to open the door more than necessary. She would retrieve the empty plate after they were well on their way and the danger had passed. They left as quickly as they came as if they were headed to a planned destination. Many times, she wondered if they had a destination at all, or just wandering about like Aunt Gwen claimed.

She shuddered as this stranger walked across her living room floor. A sense of dread began to clutch at her chest. He was now inside her home, and she would have to deal with the consequences; if he turned out to be a bad one, she could be in grave danger. She was now second-guessing herself for letting this man into her home. She quickly looked him up and down. He was large and powerful looking! He had long muscular arms with a thick-looking chest that pushed at his jacket. He turned and smiled at her. She could see that he had very good teeth for a hobo.

"Please make yourself comfortable," she said as she pointed to a chair at the table. He removed his hat and soft leather jacket. He wore a tan sweater and blue jeans. Her heart warmed as he stood there like puppy waiting for his next command from her.

Maybe he would wag his tail. She giggled to herself, trying to find some sense of security in her reckless decision.

"Where do you want me to sit, miss?" he answered. She sensed he was trying to put her at ease. She motioned for him to take a seat at the kitchen table. After seating himself, he looked up at her with kind eyes. She looked away quickly, not wanting him to see the plainness of her face. Why couldn't there be something pretty about her? If so, maybe he would find a reason to linger at her home. She poured him a cup of hot coffee and set it on the table in front of him. She brushed his arm as she set it down. He sat ever so still, not saying anything as she apologized for her clumsiness. He took a deep drink before he realized the coffee was piping hot. He winced as the hot liquid burned his dry mouth. He let out a startled cry! She felt his embarrassment as soon as it happened.

Trying to make for a better moment, she said, "I can make you bacon and eggs?" The way she structured the sentence, it sounded more like a question then a statement. Then she said, "Is bacon and eggs okay with you?"

"May I see the menu?" he asked. His sudden sense of humor cracked her feelings of fear. Surely, he couldn't be all that bad. The air was definitely beginning to clear for both of them. He was friendly and charming, and she liked him very much. "That sounds great," he said, "I'll have the daily special if that is what you are referring to."

She liked his humor instantly. Life on the rails had not beaten him down. He might be a bum, but he was a charming bum.

She hurriedly got out the cast-iron skillet and crammed eight pieces of bacon into the pan. Normally, she wouldn't have fixed such a generous portion. She concluded that if he hadn't eaten in many days, he must be starving. He tapped his fingers on the table as he waited for the food to cook. He seemed edgy and desperately in need of something to eat quickly.

"How do you like your eggs?" she asked politely, trying to make him feel like a guest instead of a beggar. She was glad when he replied, "Fried." It would be easier doing fried than scrambled.

No need to pour out any hot grease from the heavy frying pan. The eight pieces of bacon had created a mountain of grease, but that would only add to the flavor to the fried eggs.

She took four eggs from the refrigerator and cracked them directly into the pan. She jumped as the hot grease splattered up her arm, causing tremendous pain. Her mind was not on what she was doing, and she had been careless. It had been a long time since she had burned herself frying eggs or anything for that matter. But this morning was different. She was nervous about having a strange man in her kitchen since she had no idea who he was. When he realized that she had burned her arm, he quickly jumped up from the table and grabbed a wet towel. He led her to the sink, where he placed her arm under cold running water. It was December, and the tap water was freezing cold.

"Is this helping?" he asked. His voice held much concern for her injury. He had his arms around her shoulders with his face so close to hers that he could have easily kissed her. Then he turned away when he noticed how closely he was holding her.

She felt instant relief when the cold water drenched her arm and hand. The water had never felt colder. Her arm began to feel numb from the cold, and she could no longer feel the pain.

She felt awkward at the mess she had made of trying to fix him breakfast. He probably thought she was acting like a silly girl when any man paid attention to her. "I'm okay," she said, trying to play down the bad burn on her arm and her carelessness.

"I will finish frying the eggs!" he said. "Please sit down and rest," he told her.

With the kitchen towel wrapped around the burn, she went over to the table and sat down. He could finish cooking his own breakfast, and he could fry the eggs his way. She watched as he stood at the stove with his back to her. It was fun to see him playing chef. The first thing he did was to turn down the fire under the skillet and moved back some.

"This is the way you handle a hot frying pan," he told her. He began weaving and jumping around like he was trying to dodge bullets. He was making her laugh, and she was enjoying it tremendously. If only her sixthgrade students could see her now! They were aware that she was not married, and they wanted to know if she had a boyfriend or had ever been married. She told them she had never been married and she didn't have any serious relationships going now. Sometimes, they acted as nosy as Aunt Gwen about her being a single woman over thirty.

It was a matter of concern to her friends if they sensed she was lonely. They wanted her to just be happy. Both her students and her aunt could be downright pests when they thought Connie was unhappy or spending too much time alone.

Connie was now overjoyed that Gwen had canceled their shopping trip that morning. Not that she was happy that her aunt had caught a nasty cold. She was weary of her aunt scolding her all the time for her acts of kindness. Her words were still ringing in her ears!

"You can't go on feeding every Tom, Dick, or Harry that appears on your doorstep."

Connie glanced up at the clock. It was almost ten o'clock in the morning, and Aunt Gwen had not called to tell her good morning or check to see if she was still alive. She hoped that her auntie wouldn't phone while the hobo was there. Or even worse, drop by without any notice if she got to feeling better. There would be no explaining to Aunt Gwen as to why she was being so foolish and entertaining some hobo who had just jumped off the midnight train. It was almost surreal watching the strange man cooking his own meal over the stove. He had grabbed one of her aprons, which was almost too small to go around his trim belly. She wished she had a chef's hat to top it off. He looked like he belonged in the kitchen more then on the railroad tracks. The eggs were almost done before she realized she needed to make toast. His clowning tactics had made her forget about the toast, her hurt arm, or her own safety.

"I'll do the toast," she said as she quickly grabbed up the last two slices of bread left in the bag. She popped them in the toaster. "I need to put bread on my shopping list." She was now talking to him like he was a long-lost friend instead of a complete stranger. It took only a minute for the bread to pop up. He took the bread from the toaster and piled it on the plate beside the bacon and eggs. She watched as he wolfed down the mountain of food. He ate without talking but kept smiling at her between bites. Somehow this man at her table did not seem like an outsider anymore. She wanted to know more about him. She wanted to know where he came from and where he was going. She noticed he no longer had the jitters from his empty stomach. The food had revived him. He looked brighter and more alive. It made her more comfortable, seeing him so content. After eating the big breakfast, the stranger insisted on washing the dishes, reminding her that her arm was too injured. He did a good job cleaning up the stove and spattered grease on the wall. She sat with the towel still wrapped around her burned arm. She loved the attention he was giving her. It made her feel special.

"Let me have a look at that burn," he asked, after putting everything away. He looked it over carefully, turning her arm from side to side. "Better put something on this, if nothing else, butter." He walked over to the icebox and took out a stick of butter. He peeled back the paper and began gliding the cold stick of butter over the blistered burn. After coating it with a thick layer, he said while still holding her hand, "I think you will live!"

Suddenly, she felt like she was head over heels in love with him and nothing else mattered. She just couldn't contain herself. She leaped out of her seat and threw her arms around him and kissed him deeply on the mouth. Her leaping upon him made him almost lose his balance. She caught him by surprise, and it took him a minute to unwrap her arms from around him and pushed her away gently. She had embarrassed them both!

"Let's sit for a little while," he said, sitting, directing her to sit down in a chair near the table. She had never done anything like this before, and she was totally humiliated. What a fool she had made of herself! She wished she could melt through the kitchen floor. She could tell she had made him very uncomfortable.

He looked over at the Christmas tree that set beside the fireplace. Connie Jo had decorated it beautifully with lots of pine cones and tinsel. "Let's finish decorating the tree," he suggested, trying to make conversation. "It could use more bright red ornaments."

"I have finished it. There are no more ornaments left," she said. He looked at the tree and agreed that it looked terrific. "You did a good job. The angel on the top is perfect," he said. "And the bubble lights look great! Bubble lights were my favorite thing as a kid" he said as he kept looking at the tree. Talking about himself as a kid made her wants to know more about him.

"What is your name?" she muttered when she realized that she was not tongue-tied anymore.

"Does it matter?" he said softly. She could tell by the way he said it that he was not being sarcastic. Maybe his humble status was the reason for this reply. Maybe he wondered why any woman would care about a wondering homeless man such as himself.

"No, it doesn't matter at all," she told him. "It is just because you don't look like the others."

"Like other homeless people?" he said with a small amount of laughter in his voice. He could tell that she was intrigued by his way he was living his life.

"Why do you do this?" she asked. "Why this bleak way of life? Do you enjoy going hungry and wandering the railroad tracks?" She wondered if he was even listening to any of her questions. He was now looking out the window as if he was lost in his own private world.

She looked down at the redness of her wounded arm. There were large blisters forming on her arm.

He reached out and touched her arm very gently. "Thank you for all the hospitality," he said. Finally, he said, "I've got to get going." He rose from the chair and picked up his leather jacket, which he had placed over one of the chairs at the end of the table. As he picked up the jacket, a large knife fell out of his pocket. It landed with a loud thump and bounced under the table. He quickly retrieved it, telling her that "it was a knife that had belonged to my father. It is a sentimental item. Actually, I keep it for protection mostly," he said. "Now before I go, miss, do you need any work done around the premises?"

She noticed that he had not asked her name or any information about her. She would have gladly told him that she was Connie Jo Barrett and that she was a sixth-grade teacher and that she was not married. She wished with all her heart that he had showed more interest in her. She felt close to tears. How could she feel so emotional about a hobo that had come down the tracks merely looking for a handout? Now his belly was full, and that was all that mattered for the moment. She didn't know why she cared, but she cared so much!

"Do you really have to go?" she asked. She gasped when she realized that these words had come out of her mouth. What was wrong with her? She was a respectable woman and a churchgoer. She felt terribly embarrassed as she tried to rephrase her statement. "I mean, it looks so cold outside. Maybe you should stay inside somewhere until the weather warms up." She could feel her face flushing hot. She was digging herself into deep hole with these comments.

"I won't freeze," he said as he walked closer to the door. He shuffled his feet as he moved across the room. He stopped at the door and looked back at her. "Are you asking me to stay the night?" he asked, rather mystified at her suggestion.

"Yes," she said, "I'm asking you to spend the night," quickly adding, "You could sleep in the barn if you like."

"You don't have a barn," he replied. He looked pleased that she had found a true sense of humor to match his own. A moment of silence ensured as he pondered what to say about her offer. Finally, he responded, "I appreciate the thought, but not this trip." He removed his hat and placed it back on his head again as if he were in deep thought. He then walked out the door. She followed him outside, stopping on the front porch as he started walking away.

"Why do you choose the rails?" she asked again. This time her voice sounded very sad as if she had to know why he chose to go cold and hungry.

"Because I like the adventure! Is that so hard to understand?" he declared. He was getting very annoyed with all her questions. She had given him a meal, but that didn't mean he had to explain his life's story to her. Realizing she was asking too many personal questions, she dropped her arms at her side. The burnt arm began to sting.

"I have a question for you," he said as he stood in the cold breeze. The wind coming out of the north was getting much colder. He looked up at the gray sky and asked, "Why did you invite me in your home? You have no idea who I am. Do you invite all homeless people into your home for a friendly meal?"

She didn't speak. She didn't know quite how to explain herself. Surely a woman of sound mind would not have done such a stupid thing. She had no more explanation of how she lived her life then he did.

"Are you sure there is nothing I can do for you?" he asked again, sounding extremely grateful for the handout. "I have one more question before I go." He began to wring his hands. "Do you live here alone?"

He was now looking deeply into her eyes. She felt it was a good sign.

"Does it matter?" she answered.

"No, it doesn't matter. Just wondering why you don't have a husband and a couple of kids."

She watched him walk away. This time, his steps were not so weary. He turned and looked back at her once again. For a minute, she thought he was coming back.

"I will be back this way again. Maybe sooner than you think," he said. "Will your door still be open to me?" he asked. The humor had disappeared from his face.

She thought a minute before she answered him. Maybe she should be a little more mysterious this time. "I don't know," she said. "It depends on how adventurous I feel! Be careful." Then she quickly closed the door as he walked back down toward the railroad tracks.

Suddenly the phone was ringing. It was Aunt Gwen telling her to watch the evening news. A woman had been found dead in her home, stabbed multiple times. According to Aunt Gwen, it was a grisly murder! Connie didn't recognize the name of the dead woman that Aunt Gwen kept repeating over and over. "She lives four miles down those tracks from you!" Aunt Gwen yelled.

Connie Jo didn't know the woman and didn't want to know. She was too busy thinking about the large knife that had fallen out of stranger's coat! He had explained it away quickly, but that was about the only thing he had bothered to explain. She wondered why.

"Now will you listen to me?" Aunt Gwen asked.

"Yes, I am listening to you, Aunt Gwen! I think you are absolutely right." After placing the receiver back in the cradle, she went quickly to the front door, making sure it was locked. She would go into town and get extra locks for the doors and sticks to put in the windows to keep them from being easily opened. She shivered as she thought about the dead woman's fate. How horrible it must have been! It could easily have been her! The poor woman was probably doing a good deed! Where did it get her? She wondered if the homeless stranger had charmed the poor murder victim in the same way as the man had charmed her? She sensed that it was the same man that she just had in her house. She wondered at what point he had decided to kill the victim. Did she say something wrong? The wind was blowing harder now, and dark clouds were forming in the winter sky. She hated the whistling sounds the wind made, especially late at night when it was so loud that it kept her awake. She thought of the night trains that passed so late in the night, making such a noise that a scream could not be heard above the roar of the passing train. She wondered if the stranger would come back to her house after dark. Now she couldn't stand the thought of being alone in her home after dark. She quickly gathered up a few things and stuffed them into an overnight bag to take to Aunt Gwen's house. She would tell Aunt Gwen that she was too scared to spend the night alone after what had happened to the poor lady down the road.

She would never confess to Aunt Gwen or anyone for that matter what a fool she had made of herself for letting a homeless man into her home! Not even the police! Everybody would all laugh at her like Milton Gentry had done in the fifth grade. Now all she wanted to do was get out of the house quickly!

With her small suitcase and purse in hand, she headed to the front door to leave the house immediately. She frantically opened the front door, and there he stood! His large frame towered over her. She began to back up as he aggressively followed her into the house.

"I came back to explain why I chose this way of life," he stated in a strange-sounding voice.

Dropping her luggage, Connie Jo looked down at his right hand and saw the long sharp knife that had fallen out of his jacket earlier. Clutching her purse, she slowly opened it up and pulled out a small caliber pistol. Seeing the gun pointed at him, the stranger started backing up toward the door. As he was reaching for the doorknob, Connie fired her pistol four times! *Bam! Bam! Bam! Bam!*

The man dropped his knife and clutched his chest. The man slumped over and slowly fell to the floor. Connie walked over and glanced down at the stranger. The man was lying facedown on the floor, slowly bleeding to death. Connie calmly put her gun back in her purse and walked over and picked up her phone and dialed 911! This serial killer had killed his last victim!

NIGHTMARE HONEYMOON

T he coming of the morning light revealed that he was dying! How could he survive? He needed medical care from a doctor. The insects knew it before she did. She looked down at him lying on the floor of the old shack. The evening before, she had made him a makeshift bed on the hard floor with a sack of flour for a pillow. He was too sick to complain about the harsh bedding. He simply closed his weary eyes and fell into a deep sleep. Sleep had overtaken his exhausted body, and she was grateful for the intervention of sleep. Then something deeper than sleep had taken over. Restful sleep had turned into the big sleep, the sleep from which no one returns. The insects were landing in a frenzy on his swollen throat and chest, telling her that he was gone! It didn't matter that he meant so much to her. The worms and death owned him regardless of what he had been or who he was. At the rate that they were swarming, his whole body would be consumed in a short time. She could not bear to look at what was happening to her young husband. How could life reduce a man so full of hope and dreams to such a dreadful state so quickly? They had been married only three months when they decided to move from Texas to Clear Creek, Kansas. It was a quick decision made without much planning and even less resources. They were starting out with practically nothing. It would take a lot of courage and determination to make it through. They were not strangers to the hardship of life. They were young and strong, and they would just stay focused. They had each other! That was all they needed for a good start.

They had been eager to start the journey, knowing each passing day brought them closer to their dreams. Nothing came easy for people on the prairie, especially those traveling. Cassie had suggested taking the stage, but Johnathan did not want to part with his horses and wagon. Johnathan was sentimental about some of his possessions, not wanting to let go of the only link he had to the past. He was sentimental that way. She realized just how sentimental her new husband was, and that was about the only thing she knew for sure about him. He was practically a stranger when they got married. He seemed like a good man, a hardworking, honest man, and that was what she was looking for. She appreciated that he was good-looking and tall with broad shoulders and green eyes that made her fall in love at first sight. He was so easy to fall in love with. His smile was genuine, but she knew so little about him. She thought it odd that he did not like to talk about himself, but she concluded the past was painful and he didn't want to relive it by stories. She enjoyed the cool evenings spent with him talking about the future.

After a week on the rough trail, Johnathan's handsome face looked haggard, and the sparkle had left his green eyes. She could tell he was feeling poorly by his flushed face. He looked under the weather, and he was moving much slower than his usual energetic self, yet he never complained! He was the one that woke up first in the early morning and the last to go to bed at night. Day in and day out, he had taken care of the heavy work, making sure she did not over exert herself. They ate canned food from fruit jars and beef jerky that Johnathan had dried from the hot Texas sun. Johnathan was totally concerned about her welfare. He was exceptionally kind to the horses, and Cassie liked that in a man. He stopped to water them often and let them eat while she napped under a cool shade tree.

The last few days, Cassie had noticed a big change in Johnathan. Chores that seemed to be easy for him were now a burden. She could tell that he was not being totally honest with her when she asked him if he was feeling sick. He didn't want his new bride to worry, so he hid the illness until he began to show signs of confusion. Yesterday, he could not remember that they were married. This was a crushing blow to Cassie! She did not know how she would manage if he became incapacitated. Now all that mattered was getting him to a doctor. Before, she had worried herself with the little things that she felt might make a big difference to him. What mattered now was that he was growing weaker each day. It no longer mattered to her that she had lied to him and told him that she was only eighteen years old. She was actually twenty-five years of age. She was five years older than Johnathan. She had been very uncomfortable with the age difference since it made her feel like an impostor and a bald-faced liar. Along with the word *liar* came the term *old woman*! Maybe he wouldn't love her after he found out her true age. It was an easy secret to conceal at the time because she didn't look a day over sixteen. Her olive skin was smooth and soft. Her figure was nice and trim, and she had curves in all the right places. The day of her wedding, she looked more like a schoolgirl than an old maid of twenty-five.

In the 1860s, women would get married at sixteen years of age. Most women had a child by the time they were eighteen years of age. Revealing her age at this time was not a good idea. Besides, there was no one to be the wiser. She had taken excellent care of herself. The passing years would maybe catch up with her, but by then she would need not concern herself. They would both be quite old and settled in their ways. One more secret that she had kept from Johnathan was the small amount of money she had hidden in her petticoat. It was money from the sale of eggs and butter that she and Aunt Jena had managed to save. They planned on using it to buy train tickets to St. Louis. They had even looked at buying tickets on the Overland Stagecoach. They would have money left over until Cassie could find a suitable job. Cassie had an adequate wardrobe for the life of a farm woman but nothing more. Maybe she could buy a new suit to look for work once they reached Aunt Sybil's. Her wardrobe consisted of three dresses. Two were housedresses, and the other was the nice soft blue dress she wore to church on Sunday. She was wearing her church dress the day she met Johnathan at Aunt Jenna's funeral. She would never forget him standing there looking at her. It was raining, and it made the day all the more miserable! Despite the shabby clothes he wore, his handsome face drew her attention. She could not stop looking at him. Something about his eyes that kept her captive. She thought her mind had already been set on meeting an educated man in St. Louis, but this ragged man, with an amusing smile and broad shoulders made her forget about St. Louis. She wanted to know him better. He was the ideal, good-looking man that every girl in town wanted to settle down with and have children. Cassie herself was a beautiful woman with long brown hair, bright blue eyes, and a perfect shaped nose that earned her the nickname "Pea Nose." Being such a beautiful woman, she could have her pick of any eligible men in the county. She had chosen to remain single until she was in her twenties.

Cassie had taken care of Aunt Jena until she died several months ago. Aunt Jena was the only family member she had ever known besides Aunt Jena's sister, who lived in St. Louis. She had never met Aunt Sybil. She only knew her through the long letters that Aunt Sybil wrote often. Aunt Sybil would beg them to come to St. Louis. After Aunt Jena's death, she felt lost and alone. She felt she no longer had a purpose in life, so when Johnathan asked her to marry him, she eagerly accepted. It didn't matter that he was practically broke like her. They could work hard and make something of their lives. They talked long in the nights about the business they would build—a general store in Clear Creek, Kansas. They would become an important part of the community and be well-respected citizens.

Within two weeks after the funeral, they went to the Reverend Winslow's house and got married. Then Johnathan moved into Aunt Jena's house with her. Johnathan was practically homeless by the time he married Cassie. His father had died, owing a loan that he could not pay. The bank took the house and the land. At that time, Cassie was not aware of Johnathan's plight. She only knew she had met the man she wanted to share her life with. She had lost Aunt Jena, and that had been devastating. Then she met Johnathan, and her life changed. Now she had a good life again.

Looking over the property that Aunt Jenna had left her, she felt there was little to gain by staying there and farming the small tract of land. It was not big enough for either farming or ranching to be prosperous. Letting go of the sagging old house, which probably would have not survived many more winters, was easy to do. They sold the chickens and the three cows to the nearest neighbor. They would use the money to buy supplies for the trip. Three months after the wedding, they packed the wagon with several sacks of flour, coffee, beans, sugar, boxes of canned fruit, and a Winchester rifle. Johnathan could use his rifle for fresh meat such as wild turkey, rabbit, and deer along the trail. They packed clothing, bed linen, and two quilts that Aunt Jena had spent one long cold winter making. Their belongings were so few they had plenty of room in the wagon to sleep at night. It took little time to pack since they were not taking furniture. After they got established, they could furnish their new home in style. Johnathan loaded his prize rifle and placed it under the wagon seat. It was the last item placed in the wagon. As Johnathan drove the wagon away from the house, Cassie turned and looked at it as long as it remained in sight. She wiped tears from her eyes, feeling that she would probably never see the house again. She had fond memories of growing up with Aunt Jena, who was always so cheerful. She thought about the garden they planted with all the ripe tomatoes, green beans, and green onions. Some evenings for supper, they had only sliced tomatoes, but they were so tasty they ate the whole platter. She thought about gathering eggs from the nests in the chicken house and how much fun it was to take them into town to sell to old Mr. Hawkins at the general store. She thought about the creamy milk in a large white churn. Cassie would churn until white butter floated to the top. They shaped the butter into big balls and took it to old Mr. Hawkin's store along with the eggs. He bought everything they brought in. Aunt Jena had taught Cassie well. She thought her how to bake bread and can vegetables from the garden. They always had plenty to eat no matter the season.

At Christmastime, they walked into the woods and cut down a cedar and decorated it with pine cones and red ribbons. Now it was all suddenly gone within the blink of an eye. Now she was a married woman with a husband to care for. In a way, it was sad! In another way, it was exciting!

The future held some promise for the young couple on a prairie honeymoon. At night lying next to him with his strong arms around her, he would tell her about a town called Clear Creek, where they would start a prosperous new life together. They would work hard, save money, and buy a store. It would be on Main Street, with the sidewalk always swept clean in front of it. It would start out small and grow bigger and better. The townspeople would tip their hats and call them Mr. Gleasen and Mrs. Gleasen. When they talked about their store on Main Street, they forgot the hardships of the days of travel to their new home. The dreams keep them moving on during the stifling heat and rugged roads that were nothing but old wagon trails. Trails so weak to their weary eyes they were barely visible. They managed to keep moving on. Cassie was always relieved when they stopped for the night. She had no idea of how far it was to Clear Creek, and she doubted that Johnathan knew himself. She often fell asleep the moment her head hit the pillow, but there were nights when she felt someone was watching. She heard noises in the night that sounded like someone walking near their crude beds. She mentioned that to Johnathan, but he only smiled, telling her that it was because she felt anxious over the trip.

Then one morning, the sky had grown dark and the air was cool, giving them some relief from the sun. Maybe they could cover a great distance under the cloudy sky. Travel was much easier with the cool breeze blowing in their faces. The horses had picked up their pace. Then after a turn in the road, a creek loomed on the horizon. They stopped and rested the horses and then found a place where the water did not look deep. They had crossed many creeks before without any trouble. This time would be different. Suddenly the horses were in distress with the swift water. It was deeper and swifter than it looked. Cassie could tell by Johnathan's face that they were in big trouble. Her young husband was fighting with all he had to keep the horses moving straight ahead and through the creek bed. The water was now flowing over the wagon bed. She panicked as she prayed with all her might that God would save what was needed the most. She closed her eyes as she hung on a sack of flour that was leaned up against the back of her seat. When she opened her eyes again, everything that had been in the wagon bed was now floating swiftly down the creek behind them. They lost everything except the clothes on their backs and one sack of flour that she hung on to for dear life. Gone were the beautiful quilts that Aunt Jena had put so much time and love into. Both she and Johnathan were soaking wet and shaking from the near-death experience. They traveled for what seemed like an eternity when they spotted an old abandoned frame house. At this point, Johnathan had taken a turn for the worse. He was now so confused he could not even remember her name. Maybe he was in shock! She got him out of the wagon, carrying him into the shack, and urged him to sit down on the floor. She used the sack of flour to make a pillow. She drew water from a well in the front yard and gave him a drink of water from a rusty old bucket hanging over the well.

She felt his forehead, and he was burning up with fever. She tore a piece of her petticoat off and soaked it in cool water and placed it across his face. She tried to comfort him as best that she could in the old house. Then she went outside and unhooked the wagon. She took the harness off the horses to give them a rest. She tied the horses under a shade tree about twenty feet from the house. She left enough slack in the rope for them to graze. She went back inside to check on Johnathan. He looked to be asleep and resting somewhat comfortably. She took a cool drink for the water bucket, then went back outside to sit on the porch to think about how she was going to get Johnathan to a doctor. Could there be a town close by? She had no idea where they were. She bowed her head and was saying another prayer when she heard a noise that sounded like someone was coming. As she turned, she saw a wagon coming up the trail. She hoped it was some nice family or someone who would help her with her sick husband and tell her where she could find a doctor. As he came closer, her heart sank. His appearance was alarming. He pulled the team of horses up beside her and tipped his hat like a gentleman. He was dirty-looking and in need of a bath. His hair was bushy and matted. Despite the fact that he was trying to act friendly, his face showed another side of him. He had mean-looking eyes which told her he could be trouble!

Trying to sound calm, she said, "My husband is sleeping in the house. He is very tired from the trip." She offered him and his horses some water. She did not want him to know that she was alone or that her husband was too sick to defend her. She had never felt so helpless in her life. Her feeling must have shown in her face. He sat looking at her as if she was something to devour like a meal.

"I think you got trouble," he said as he climbed down from the wagon. She tried to act like she didn't know what he was talking about even though her nerves were shot and her belly ached from hunger. She couldn't remember when she and Johnathan had a decent meal. She felt almost too weak to stand. The filthy peddler began walking toward her. He pointed to a weather-beaten old barn in back of the house that looked like it was about to collapse. When he smiled, he showed stained yellow teeth. "You can be nice to me, and I will be nice to you."

She did not put up a fight. She was beaten down, and she knew it. Maybe there was a slight chance he might help them. If only she could get Johnathan to a doctor. As she walked away from the house, she felt that she was going to faint. How could their dreams turn into such a nightmare?

She held back tears as she followed the peddler to the barn, where she was forced to be nice to him for the rest of the night. Before the ordeal was over, she believed she would die. Johnathan was the only thing that kept her going. She begged him during the night to go check on Johnathan. The peddler refused! He tied Cassie up with a rope while he went back to his wagon for a bottle of whiskey. When he returned, he forced her to drink a big gulp of it. Then it started all over again! His filthy hands were all over her. It seemed like an eternity before he finally fell into a drunken sleep. She too felt dizzy from all the whiskey to attempt an escape. She would wait until she was sure that he was asleep. She laid her head against the side of the barn, where she sat in the hay. Soon her eyes were heavy with sleep, being exhausted by the long day that she had endured. She fell asleep. The next thing she knew, it was morning, and the old man was ordering her to get to her feet. Fear rose in her throat as to what had happened to Johnathan during her long night of pure hell. Had he survived the night? It was doubtful!

The night was over, and a new day was dawning. She followed him back to his peddler's wagon. The sweltering heat was now mixed with the putrid smell of death. Johnathan did not survive the night! There was no reason to be scared anymore. The peddler walked back to his wagon and retrieved a bag of biscuits and a jar of honey.

"Here is your pay," he said showing no emotion at all. "This will keep you going until you get to Clear Creek." He tossed the biscuits and honey into her trembling hands. She felt like she did not have enough strength to stand until she heard the words *Clear Creek*.

"How far is it on to Clear Creek?" she managed to ask.

"Not far! Get some rest, girl. Eat some biscuits and honey and head out," the old man said. He showed no emotion for all the hell he had put her through. She stood with the sack in her hand as she watched him drive away in the wagon slowly. Her fear had turned to rage. She looked down in the bed of their wagon, which was once filled with the precious few things they owned. It was all gone—but wait, she saw something lying there. Something was lodged up under the seat. How had she missed it? She grabbed it up as if she had found gold. It was Johnathan's rifle! She didn't know if the gun was loaded, but she aimed it anyway at the moving wagon. She pulled the trigger! She saw his large body fall from the wagon. The horses stopped as if they knew something was wrong. She ran over to where he was sprawled out. Blood was seeping out of his matted hair. Half his head was blown away!

She climbed onto his wagon and turned the horses around and drove them back to the old house. She had to take care of a few things before she left. She gave water to all four horses from the well and then tied her two horses to the back of the peddler's wagon. She would not go back inside the house. Death was all around, and she needed to get to Clear Creek. Johnathan would have wanted it this way. She thought about the prayer she said as they crossed the swollen creek. "God, please save us and help us keep what is needed the most!" She looked down at the rifle that had saved her and thought, *God does answer prayers! The answer is in plain sight!*

THE HAUNTED HOUSE

William Taylor accepted the fact that he was a little different from most young men his own age. William could not imagine life without living with his mother, Bessie. His mother was his security blanket that protected him from the rest of the cruel world. William's father had abandoned them when William was just two years old. William planned on taking care of his mother for many years to come. While Bessie thought that she could take care of herself, William knew otherwise. Bessie was so lonely, the last surviving member of her family. All of Bessie's brothers and sisters had passed away many years ago. William could hear his mother crying far into the night after he went to bed. William graduated with honors from high school and had been awarded a scholarship to a nearby university. William wanted to go to off to college, but he was afraid to leave his mother alone. The thought of leaving home and going away to college were wrecking William's health. He could not go to sleep at night. The insomnia and sleepless nights were piling up. William's daily nightmares about his childhood and the old house that they lived in when he was a child. William could see a young woman's ghost emerging from the nearby pond and waving at him to come and join him and run away into the nearby woods. William would reach out for her, but he could never reach her. The young woman's name was Verna. The dreams also included images of an older man chasing after them with a shotgun. William wished that he could understand the dreams about people that he had never meet. William knew that he needed to go off to college and get an education so that he could be successful in the outside world. William wanted to be a teacher to help other kids cope with the stress of daily living.

While in high school, William had no social life, no girlfriend, and no close friends to socialize with after school. He focused on his studies and did very well on all his exams. William waited until he was nineteen years old before he passed the driver's test and obtained his driver's license. While he was very hesitant to leave home and go off to college, his mother insisted that he go ahead and move to the campus before the start of the fall semester. With classes starting the last week of August, William packed his belongings and reluctantly headed off to college.

William spent the first semester in college trying to adjust to other people living in his dorm. Finding that he could not study due to the noise made by other students, William spent his spare time in the campus library. While he was applying himself to his studies, most dorm students spent their spare time drinking beer, smoking pot, and chasing girls. William loathed his roommate, a wild farm boy who sought to set the world record for beer drinking, pot smoking, and looking for women for sex. William knew that the roommate was surely going to come to a tragic end. Magically, William made it through the first semester and was getting ready to come home when he received word that his mother had suffered a heart attack. William threw his clothes in his luggage, sensing that he may never return to school.

Immediately, after arriving back home, William dismissed the nurse attending his mother. The nurse protested, saying that his mother should have nursing care until she fully recovered. Bessie begged him to allow the nurse to remain, insisting that she was taking very good care of her. William escorted the nurse out the door.

Bessie was happy that William was home for the winter break and would not return to school until after the holidays. William enjoyed the return to the routine of getting up each morning and fixing her breakfast. After watching her eat, William would draw her bath water and make her bathe. After her bath, William would bring her into the living room to sit down in the recliner. After making sure that she was comfortable, William would take out the family Bible and read several verses from it. They would then discuss what the Bible verses meant and how they should apply to their daily lives. Bessie would rest in the recliner for an hour or so. William would then take her for a short walk around the backyard. The fresh air always made her feel better. William enjoyed assuming the duties of housekeeping, keeping the house very nice and clean. In addition to house-cleaning chores, William did all the laundry, the shopping for groceries, running to the pharmacy to get his mother's prescriptions, and taking his mother to all her doctor appointments. They would wind down the day by watching a movie and talking about old times when William was a young boy. One evening, they talked about the old house on Cemetery Road that they lived in when William was a young child. It had been several months since they had discussed the old house. William sensed that his mother thought that it was strange that he continued to have nightmares about the old house even though it had been eighteen years since they had lived in the old house. His mother insisted that they had some good times there even his father was a drunk that had run off with another woman. William had no memory of these events that happened when he was three years old.

William enjoyed his mother's stories about the old house. Bessie described the old house as the nicest house in town, located on a road on the outskirts of town. The way she described the old house, it had to be the nicest house in town. There was a large front porch which had a large wicker chair near the front door that Bessie would sit in during the afternoon while sipping cold ice tea with lemon. William sensed that he had actually met the beautiful young girl named Verna that appeared in his dreams. In his dreams, William would see Verna descending the large staircase dressed in a beautiful silver gown that indicated that she was ready to be escorted to local dance that was held at the community barn every Saturday night. Verna could sing and play the piano. She wanted to attend the Juilliard School of Music and become a critically acclaimed world-famous piano player. Verna would attend the school during the fall and spring semesters and return home to spend the warm summer months with the family.

One summer, Verna returned home to find that her father had hired a young black man to help around the ranch. The young man was a skilled laborer that took care of the yard and the livestock around the place. Verna would visit with the young man while he was working in the yard. After a few weeks, Verna and the handy man would meet in the barn and drink beer. The couple fell in love. Verna became pregnant. The young couple decided to run away together and get married. The father found out about the affair and become outraged! The old man slapped and beat Verna until she fell to the ground, becoming unconscious. The young black man, having a felony record, fled the area and ran off, knowing that he would be arrested and charged with rape and criminal homicide if he remained around the farm.

The more that they talked about the old house, the more intense the urge of William to visit the old home place and explore it himself. The holiday break passed quickly, and William decided to head back to school to start the spring semester. William packed up his personal belongings and headed out early in the morning to return to school. William decided to take a side trip to visit the old homestead. After sharing a tearful goodbye with his mother, William started down the road, promising Bessie that he would call her that evening at seven o'clock.

The side trip took about an hour to drive by the old house. The old town was slowly deteriorating, with many of the old buildings in the downtown abandoned and in a state of disrepair. Arriving in front of the old homestead, William pulled over and parked his old car. The old house was abandoned and starting to fall to the ground. William got out of his vehicle and slowly walked up to the old porch that bordered the old house. William worried that the porch would collapse when he stepped up onto it. The wood held steady as he carefully stepped up on the porch and walked carefully over to the front door, which was partially open. Pushing the door open, William stepped inside and looked at the interior of the house. There was spiderwebs and animal waste everywhere. What a mess! The house clearly had been abandoned for several years. Glancing around at the ceiling, William noted that many of the ceiling tiles had fallen down and that the birds were using the house as sanctuary, flying around in the inside of the house. Glancing around, William smiled as he saw the old winding staircase that was in many of his old dreams.

William walked over to the bottom of the staircase and looked up the steps leading to the top. William closed his eyes and visualized Verna slowly walking down the staircase toward him. William smiled. Verna had her left hand extended out to touch him. Suddenly, a dark figure of a man appeared behind her and shoved her down the staircase. William screamed as Verna tumbled down the stairs and landed at his feet. William knelt down to touch her and saw her bleeding profusely from her mouth. William took Verna and clutched her in his arms, screaming out, "No! No! Please don't leave me."

After holding her for a few minutes, William realized that she had stopped breathing and that she had passed away. Slowly, William laid her back down and looked up to the top of the stairs. The person had fled the area. William raced up the stairs and started searching for the man that was responsible for murdering Verna! The upstairs area was composed of three bedrooms and one bathroom. William carefully searched each room. Nothing in the first bedroom. Nothing in the second bedroom! The bathroom was clear. William slowed moved toward the last bedroom, sensing that the killer was hiding in there. William entered the bedroom and glanced down at the foot of the bed. Lying there at the foot of the bed was a man who appeared to be about fifty years old. Turning the man over on his back, William was shocked to discover that the man was his father!

What the hell, he thought. Mom had told him many times dad had run off with a young woman. Looking closer, William discovered that he had two bullets wound in his chest area. The body was cold and stiff! William realized that the man had been dead for several hours. Who killed him?

William pondered the question. Who had killed his father? Who had pushed Verna down the staircase and caused her death? Someone had killed two people? Further, how did the killer get away? William looked around the room, thinking, Maybe the killer was still in the house! Maybe the killer was hiding somewhere.

William walked slowly over to the closet and opened the doors. What a shock! Crouched on the floor of the closet was Bessie, his mother! Oh my god. His mother had killed his father and Verna, his girlfriend! What a shocker! William suddenly realized that his mother had killed two people and gotten away with it for almost twenty years. No wonder William had had nightmares on this for almost twenty years!

GETTING RID OF A
LOUSY HUSBAND

C arol Dunning was going on twenty years old when she met Dexter Wright. It didn't matter that he was fifteen years older than she, that he didn't have a regular job, or that her father didn't approve of him. What mattered to this young woman who had the world at her feet was that Dexter made her feel emotionally aroused and that he was someone who would appreciate her for the intellectual person she was. She needed someone her equal. He was a writer like her father, and he possessed a certain air that spoke volumes of self-confidence. She didn't know what made him tick, but she was more than willing to invest her time finding out. He wasn't typical of any of young men in her life so far. He wasn't the young man groveling at her feet trying to say things to impress her. Dexter seemed focused on what he should be doing in life. This feeling caused Carol to focus on what was important in life.

Carol was both beautiful and smart. She had the looks of a model, and her dad was rich and famous. People looked up to the Dunning family, especially her father. He was a leader in the community, and he made good things happen around him. She idolized her dad for the way he lived life. Always the winner and never the loser. He was a self-made man. If he wanted something bad enough, he made it happen. That was the way she like it! Having control and calling the shots. Some people thought him arrogant. And he was. He had talent, and he was going to pursue his passion. He wanted to write, and that was what he did. His work had become bestsellers from the beginning. No working his way from the ground up. His fans patiently awaited his next novel. Everything he touched turned to gold. Carol's mother was quite different. She didn't like that her husband didn't have a real job. She wanted him to be an accountant, someone that got a guarantee paycheck on scheduled time. Selling novels was not guaranteed. Writing was a gamble. She nagged him all the time, telling him that his good luck wouldn't last and that he would fall flat on his face and they would someday be penniless.

Carol's dad grew to detest his wife's attitude through the years. He felt he had married the wrong woman. She had no dreams, only fear of what could happen to anyone that took prosperity for granted. She flinched at every dollar he spent, warning him that his head would soon run dry of stories and then where would the family be. She was one of those people who let opportunities pass them by because of constant negative thoughts.

Carol was different from her mother, and her father doted on that. He liked the way his beautiful daughter felt she was destined to do something great or out of the usual. He taught her that she was the master of her own fate. She was a firm believer that if you didn't like the way things were, change them. She was not unhappy when her parents went their separate ways. She took her dad's side. She was a bit tired of her mother's gloom-and-doom attitude and no real appetite for what money could buy. Carol was in every sense as a material girl and a vain one at that.

Carol liked looking in the mirror at herself. She had been born beautiful and perfect. No need for the help of the surgeon's knife. The rich are always more beautiful and talented than anyone else, she thought. It was an entitlement. It's just a fact of life that everyone needed to accept. Life had handed her bushels of blessing, and she was determined to take advantage of them all. She had no time for negative thoughts like her mother. In fact, she couldn't remember any unhappy days. Money did buy happiness and popularity. She was voted the prettiest girl in her senior class. When she entered college, she was chosen as homecoming queen. Quite an honor for a freshman girl. Her life was a social whirl around campus, getting the full attention of the college's most eligible men. *Failure* was not a word in her vocabulary.

She couldn't remember ever sitting at home on a Saturday night unless she was sick. Even then she had wound up meeting Dexter Wright, the man she would spend the next six years of her life with. She remembered that night so well, now with regret. She was planning on going to a rock concert with a rather dull college student named Damon Jenkins. Damon had approached her during one of her weak moments, which was almost never, and she'd accepted a date. The poor guy was infatuated with the lovely blonde that all the guys wanted on their arm. He had continuously followed her around campus like a lovesick puppy. Everywhere she went, there he was. Her rudeness didn't shake him. He pursued her with a passion until she finally accepted this one date. She never intended on seeing him again after tonight. She had to admit he was clever with the concert tickets. She hoped he understood it was all about the rock band that was performing and not him. How stupid could he be?

Damon was not all that bad looking, just a not-so-popular guy that she considered an average Joe. She had noticed him staring at her in one of her art classes and that he had bumped into her intentionally while exiting the classroom. She thought he had some nerve to think that she would date the likes of him. She knew nothing about him except that he was too ordinary and all his friends were the same. He certainly did not hang out with the popular crowd. The more she thought about him, the more nauseous she became.

The concert never happened for them. She ended up faking a bad cold. She just couldn't be bothered with the Damon Jenkins of the world. She was high society, and why should she care about his feelings? She would try to be polite and halfway decent. Her father had taught her to be polite for her own good around the community.

Damon arrived ten minutes early looking dreadfully tacky in a pinstripe suit that looked like something out of the sixties. His shoes were polished to the hilt and as out of style as his suit. He looked pitiful, like he was going to cry when she told him that she would not be going out with him. She clutched a Kleenex in her hand and dabbed at her nose, trying to act under the weather. She gave a few sniffles to make it look more convincing. She couldn't tell if he bought the story or not.

He had no sooner left the house than the doorbell rang again. She thought for sure that it was Damon returning to reassure her that it was all right, that they could get together at a later date. As she opened the door, she braced herself for Damon's nervous babbling again. Instead of Damon, it was an older man who introduced himself as Dexter Wright. He acted as if she should know and immediately recognize the name.

There was no babbling from this competent-looking man, only a request to see her father. Ordinarily, she would have slammed the door in the face of an uninvited guest, but there was something about him that made her stand in the doorway wanting to get to know him better. She suddenly forgot about the sad young man whose heart she had just broken and sent away in rejection. The man standing at her door looked worthy of some of her time and attention.

Dexter was a tall muscular man with stringy hair that hung down around his collar. His attire was a dingy polo shirt and blue jeans. Even with the untidy hair, his face was uncommonly handsome, with piercing blue eyes against a tanned complexion. She had never seen a more beautiful human being.

"Is my father expecting you?" she asked, knowing full well that her dad was not expecting visitors. Even before he answered her question, she had invited him into her home. As he entered the room, he held out a stack of papers that he proudly proclaimed as a masterpiece just waiting to be published. She immediately accepted the manuscript as she called her father into the room. At first, her father refused to see him, dismissing the uninvited guest with a sharp tongue and telling him how rude he thought he was making such an imposition. But Dexter Wright was a clever man. He had reached his goal by entering the house and leaving his manuscript in the hands of the famous writer's daughter. He had made quite an impression on her, and he too felt the vibes. After Dexter left that evening, she would not allow her father to rest until he settled quietly in his favorite chair with the thick manuscript, promising to look at it.

After much intercession on Dexter part, Carol's father began scanning through the pages. He found nothing promising about the would-be writer. He scanned a few more chapters, then came to a conclusion there was nothing here worth the paper it was written on. Carol, who was waiting patiently for a promising review, was angered at his evaluation. Disappointed by her father's dismissal of the novel as badly written, Carol sat up the rest of the night reading the novel herself. She instantly fell in love with the two main characters who were fighting the world to be together despite the difference in their ages and social status. The plot held her captive. She wanted to be Annabella, and she felt like she was. She believed the story to be about herself and Dexter and that somehow fate had brought them together. Now that she had read his novel and was so moved by it, there was nothing else she wanted more than to be with him. Somehow this man that she had never met before tonight had written the story of her true feelings as a woman, something that no man had ever come close to.

Even with her father fervent pleadings, she packed her things and married him two weeks later. She insisted she knew him completely by reading his work, and she had no doubts that he was the one she was meant to spend her life with.

Carol's father was sickened by their marriage, yet he could not condemn his daughter's recklessness. He had made more than a few mistakes in life and felt she was a bit like him.

The apple does not fall far from the tree, he thought.

With his blessings, Dexter and Carol started life together. At first, she was blissfully happy being with him. She continued going to school while he rewrote his novel, trying to follow her father's advice. He would read his work to her, and she would feel fascinated at the fantastic work he was doing. After dinner, they would go for a walk along the lake and discuss all the great workshops he would attend that would further his career. Someday, he would be just as famous as her father. She never doubted his talent or his motives.

At first, Carol felt he was on the right track with the writing workshops even though they could be quite expensive and he had to travel so much of the time. He didn't like spending nights alone. He always came back home with great reviews of his writing that important people had given him. He continued to go on long trips, once to London. Months turned into years. Dexter continued to spend more and more time at writing workshops, but somehow his work was never published.

Despite the fact that they were living off Carol's money, Dexter never seemed to care about not bringing in any money himself. It was always the same story: he just needed the right opportunity to sell his novel. Carol was shocked one day when she found a letter of rejection from a publisher that he had claimed was interested in his work. The rejection was sharp and to the point, yet Dexter had led her on to think his reviews were promising.

Carol had finished her last year at college and had accepted a job as an art teacher at a local high school. The pay was terrible, but that was not a problem for now. She wanted to be an artist, and besides, she had money, her daddy's money. As she became more involved in her teaching position, Dexter started drinking more when he was home alone. He seemed to be drinking more than writing. When she arrived home from work, he would be sitting at the computer with a glass of scotch in his hand, pretending to be working. He would raise the glass in a gesture that meant hello. She usually ignored him whenever possible. He was far too intoxicated to carry on a good sensible conversation.

That was okay with her. It seemed they had nothing to talk about anymore. She would retreat to the kitchen to prepare the evening meal, which they ate in silence. After dinner, she would spend time alone on the patio or bring home some project from school. Life was so different now. The long walks they used to take together in the evening were no more. Sometimes, she would walk by herself down by the lake to be out of the house and out of his sight. She didn't understand why she chose the lake. She hated the lake with its muddy waters that was mysteriously dark and far too deep. She never understood the attraction of any lake. It was a filthy sewer of dirt and scum, and the thought of swimming in it make her sick. Maybe she walked on the shores because it was time consuming and time was what she was trying to kill in the evenings when alone with him. How she wished she had listened to her father's take on Dexter. Why hadn't she seen his true color? He was no more than a parasite, sucking the very life out of her. Lately, she noticed that Dexter was spending more and more of her money without consulting her. He no longer asked her before he took large sums of money out of their bank account. His latest spending spree was on a boat that he had hidden out at the lake because he knew she would not approve. A huge fight erupted when Carol found out about his costly purchase. Evidently this was a toy just for himself, and he was using her money for his own selfish needs. She boldly approached him screaming that he knew about her fear of water or anything to do with the lake. He stormed off that night telling her that she impossible just like her arrogant father. He did not return home until early morning. There was never an apology or even a hint of remorse for his irresponsible spending.

The money was going out much faster than it was coming in. Dexter was acting stranger than usual. Carol began to have serious thoughts about her marriage to this gigolo! They had been married for six years now, and Dexter had not brought in one dime. Her father had been right about Dexter. He was a loser and a fraud. He was no longer handsome to her. In fact, she felt he was repulsive, with his bloodshot eyes and fat belly that hung over his baggy shirts. He no longer cared about his appearance or what she thought of him. He had no interest in romance. A bottle of scotch was all that mattered to him.

Carol began to spend more time at work, staying late at school working. This is when she met the new art teacher, a man named Eric. Eric was a workaholic, and he too stayed late in the day to help mentor students. She was so impressed with his work that she showed one of his paintings to her father. He was impressed. One thing that she'd learned to appreciate in the last six years was her father's opinion. She cherished the kind of self-made man he was. Always in control of everything except the daughter that was so much like him. It saddened her to see his health deteriorating. He was no longer the robust man that conquered all his foes. His eyesight was failing, and he could no longer focus on anything long enough to write. Carol could see his rapid deterioration. She knew his time was short. Then she would inherit his vast fortune of several dollars. It pained her to think of sharing it with Dexter. She could not bear to think that her talented father's money would go to a bum like Dexter, who had probably never worked a day in his worthless life. She simply had to figure out a way to get rid of Dexter!

That night she lay awake thinking of a way to tell him that she had found someone else. But that wouldn't work. There would still be a divorce settlement, and he would get far more than she was willing to turn loose of. She wanted to catch him off guard in case she came up with a good plan.

Money was everything to Dexter. The more she thought about Eric, the more she detested Dexter. But she didn't want to make any rash decisions. Impulse had landed her in this mess with Dexter. Before she made a commitment with another man, she would be sure of him. She had not divulged much about herself to Eric. She knew very little about him. She liked it that way. She wondered how much the other faculty members had told Eric about her. She guessed Eric knew about her marriage to a worthless bum that was nothing more than a drunk. Her collages had encouraged her to leave him.

That night, she met Eric at an out-of-the-way pub. She did not want to be seen publicly with him. Gossip traveled fast. She wished she could turn back the clock and start all over again with Eric. He was young, ambitious, and they had the same interests. Eric knew that Carol was very miserable in her marriage. He could see it in her eyes, yet he never pushed her to talk about it. She could talk about her failing marriage when she was ready. They began to spend more and more time together.

The nights when she was out with Eric, it did her heart good to know that Dexter was home alone, drunk on his butt, wondering if she was really where she said she was. She hoped that he would not become suspicious until she was ready to act. But Dexter was not stupid, lazy but not dumb. He was now questioning her about her whereabouts. Carol, who was a master of deception, told Dexter that she had been seeing a marriage counselor. She was afraid she was losing him because she had put her job before him. Somehow her working so much had taken its toll on their marriage. She was saying the words that Dexter wanted to hear. It was all her fault.

"The counselor told me that we need to spend more time together. I love you so much, Dexter! I don't want to lose you." Carol felt dizzy from all the lies and deceptions she was telling him. "I want a romantic evening like we used to have," Carol told him with real conviction.

Dexter seemed happy that Carol was willing to work things out. The last thing he wanted was to lose his meal ticket. He began making plans with her, saying he would stop drinking so much and give her more attention. He was also to blame for their marital troubles. He immediately began to pack a picnic basket with nothing but bottles of scotch and her choice of drinks, Crown Royal. She watched as Dexter filled the basket and got out a soft blanket. He seemed sincere in what he was doing, but Carol knew it was too little too late. He'd had his chance. She knew he was not thinking about her. It was only to his benefit that he was willing to put forth some effort to make the marriage work. She was his cash cow! He had to do something to stay in her good graces. He was only buying time. He was an unpublished author with no income. He was at her mercy. Now it was time for her to make a fool of him.

Dexter wanted to go out on the lake that very night to show her that he was absolutely sincere in his pledge. He wanted it to be like it was in the beginning. Carol figured she must have him plenty worried. She gave him a kiss and told him that she had too much to do for class the next day. It was a lie, but she had to have time to make her plans. It would be better for her if they waited until Saturday night. "Planning is part of the fun," she told him. Dexter seemed a little miffed at her putting it off. He claimed he was more sincere than she was. He puttered around the house rest of the evening doing what he did best, which was nothing.

Thinking about Eric would make it easier to go home to Dexter. The rest of the day, she felt like she was in the twilight zone or on some other planet. Her classroom seemed surreal. Everything seemed out of place, even the clock on the wall. She was sure of herself in one way, then in another way, she was scared stiff. When faculty members passing her classroom and asked her what she was doing this weekend, she wanted to scream at them, "I'm getting rid of my husband." Of course, she could not do this. She hoped no one noticed she was acting weird. She told them in a calm voice that she and Dexter were going out to the lake; he had finally talked her into it. They knew her fear of the water. After they left, she wished she had kept quiet.

Finally, Saturday night was there. They were alone on the lake with the basket of booze. Dexter had been drinking heavily most of the day, so he let her have the wheel despite her protests. He told her driving a boat was just like driving a car. Driving was the least of her worries that night. She saw only a few boats in the distance, but they were nowhere near them. She was now grateful that the lake was so vast. She tried to act relaxed. The breeze was nice, and it felt good to have the wind blowing through her hair. Dexter already had a drink in his hand and a cigarette in the other. She mixed herself a Crown Royal and pretended she was drinking it. When he was looking the other way, she poured her drink into the water. She wanted to be in complete charge. For some reason, Dexter had become talkative. He wanted to know how school was going and if she had any promising students. He always wanted to talk about artists since he considered himself to be one. She told him she had a student named James Bradley whose work she felt was superb. Dexter rolled his eyes when he thought she was not looking. That was so like Dexter, making fun of her like she was a fool. Looking at him with pretend love in her eyes, she told him that discovering him had been exciting and she still felt he was a talented writer, maybe better than her dad. Of course, this was a big fabrication, but she could not have said anything more comforting to him than his work being good. The lie made her feel good also. She put her almost empty glass to her lips and took the last sip.

"Will you pour me another drink?" She stretched out her hand, but her glass was out of his reach. He rose to his feet just like she wanted to and walked over to where she sat. He was really beginning to get clumsy. On his way over with the drink, he almost fell. He handed her another drink, then poured himself another scotch. This must have been his umpteenth drink of the day.

Instead of sitting down, he fell into his chair. Again, she poured most of her drink overboard and pretended to enjoying the outing. As they talked, she noticed his speech was becoming very slurred, like it did right before he would pass out. She sat there for a few more minutes watching him fade in and out. She hoped that she had not waited too long. If he passed out, she may not be able to lift him overboard. But she had to make sure he was drunk enough to shove him overboard.

"Dexter, can you come over here?" she asked. "I think I see something very strange in the water."

Dexter blinked his eyes like he wasn't for sure if someone was talking to him. Dexter asked, "Did you say something sweetheart?"

"I said, can you come over here and help me figure out what is floating in the water next to our boat?"

Dexter tried to stand but had trouble getting his balance.

This is the perfect moment, she thought as he regained his wobbly balance and came walking over. He walked to where she was standing.

"Right here," she said. "You may have to lean a little over the side."

He did as she told him.

"I don't see anything," he mumbled. He was looking in the water, trying to see what she was talking about. "It the Loch Ness Monster," he said, trying to be cute and charming.

"It almost gone under the boat," she said. Dexter leaned further over the side. Dexter was now in a very vulnerable position.

It's now or never, she thought. It was getting too dark, and it had taken him longer to get polluted than she planned. She didn't want to be out on the lake at night by herself. She must act fast. Standing at his back, she pushed with all her strength, trying to shove him overboard. Dexter slumped and fell over the side of the boat into the murky lake water. Dexter tried to grab on to the side of the boat. She reached over and smashed his hands, and Dexter lost his grip on the side of the boat. Slowly, Dexter fell backward into the dark water and disappeared from sight.

Being rid of Dexter, Carol was now free to enjoy life that she dreamed about all her life. Carol had all of her dad's money and a man, Eric, that would give her all the love and attention that she had always wanted. Every woman's dream! Money and a great lover!

JUSTIFIABLE HOMICIDE

Lacy Anderson was born in Houston, Texas, in the early 1970s. Tracy attended the public school system in Houston. While in high school, Lacy met Jerry Anderson, who was a couple of years older that she was. Lacy and Jerry started dating, attending local high school football and basketball games. After the games, they would go out and enjoy pizza. Jerry wanted to get a good-paying job with a local company. Jerry graduated with honors and started searching for the perfect job. Jerry was hired by an international shipping company who had a large shipping operation at the Houston International Airport. Jerry was selected as the assistant manager in charge of handling the loading and unloading of large cargo planes at the airport. Feeling secure in his employment, Jerry asked Lacy to marry him in 1992. Since Jerry had a great job, Lacy was allowed to stay at home and take care of the household. A couple of years later, Lacy gave birth to a lovely young girl, which the couple named Tracy. A year later, Lacy gave birth to a cute little boy whom the couple named Jimmy. From all appearances, the couple appeared to be the perfect American family. Jerry was successful in his job, and Lacy were the perfect housewife, with two little adorable little children. Appearances can be deceiving! Behind the scenes, there was problems in their marriage. Jerry was the breadwinner and controlled the family's finances. Jerry's attitude was that he would call all the shots in the marriage. Lacy was required to do everything as Jerry demanded. If Lacy failed to so, Jerry would verbally abuse her. Jerry would drink a few beers and get physically abusive and slap her around. Since Lacy had sensitive skin, the physical abuse would result in Lacy having bruises all over her tender body. Her body could not take any more physical abuse. After another beating at the hands of Jerry, Lacy felt life committing suicide. How could she get out of this abusive marriage? Kill Jerry and end it?

Lacy got more depressed with each passing year of her marriage. Jerry was very controlling and demanding. The only thing that kept Lacy going was taking care of two little adorable kids. Lacy felt that she was trapped in a hopeless situation. There was no escape from the stress of dealing with Jerry. The only time that Lacy got to herself was when Jerry was working at his shipping job. Jerry had been promoted to the night shift manager. Jerry would go to work at seven in the evening and work all night. Jerry would generally arrive back home at seven in the morning. Lacy considered a separation and a divorce. Jerry's response was, "No way." Jerry would grab her and slap her around. Her dreary life changed completely during the summer of 2002. As a part of her weekly routine, Lacy would to go to Walmart to shop for groceries and other household necessities.

One afternoon, Lacy met Peter Taylor, a very polite young man with a friendly smile. During one of these conversations, Lacy learned that Peter worked for a large stockbroker company in Houston. Later, Lacy ran into Peter at the Eisenhower school where both of their children attended. Lacy learned that Peter was divorced from his wife. After a few weeks of friendly conversations, the pair exchanged phone numbers and started talking and texting back and forth during the evening hours while Jerry was working at the airport. Lacy told Peter that she was unhappy in her marriage. Peter offered a shoulder to cry on. They agreed to meet at a convenient time and enjoy some "adult privacy!" Lacy was amazed at the great pleasure that she experienced while making love with Peter. Their relationship became more intense with each passing month. Lacy texted Peter one evening and told him that she needed him that night. Peter responded, stating that he would stop by around midnight for a quickie! Peter got to her house at twelve thirty. Lacy came out and got in his truck, wearing a nightgown with nothing underneath it! Lacy got in his truck and told him to drive down the street out of sight of the house.

Once the truck came to a rest about a block down the street, Jerry shut the truck off, and Lacy opened the nightgown, revealing that she had nothing on underneath. Lacy slid over on the seat next to Jerry and said to him in a very sexy voice, "Show me what you got!"

Peter peeled off his clothes and started kissing Lacy all over her soft sexy body.

Jerry was working his night shift at the airport when he developed an upset stomach after eating a takeout meal composed of a large greasy hamburger and a two dozen large French fries. Jerry finished his job and decided to go home early. Jerry left his airport job and proceeded home, arriving just after midnight. Jerry drove past the truck where Lacy and Peter were making love. Seeing the headlights flashing as he drove by their vehicle, Lacy immediately knew that Jerry was coming home early. Lacy closed her robe and proceeded to jump out of the truck and run back toward the house. Pulling into the driveway, Jerry saw Lacy running back toward the house. Jerry jumped out of his vehicle, grabbing his gun that he had hidden in the glove compartment. Jerry said to Lacy, "Get in the house."

She ran toward the house. Jerry turned around and directed his attention to the man that was in the truck down the street. Peter was hurriedly trying to get his clothes back on as Jerry approached the truck. Jerry yelled, "Get out of the truck, you bastard!"

Peter, seeing that he had a gun in his right hand, shoved his keys in the ignition and started the truck, hoping to race away. Seeing that the truck was leaving, Jerry raised his handgun and fired three shots into the back of the truck. The bullets pierced the back window of the truck, striking Peter in the back of the head. Since the truck was in drive, the vehicle moved forward, crashing into a nearby tree. Jerry looked inside the truck. Seeing the truck was totally engulfed in flames, Jerry turned and ran back to the house. Now it was time to take care of Lacy!

Upon hearing the crash of the truck into the tree in his front yard, a neighbor picked up his phone and summoned emergency units of the local fire and police departments to handle the emergency. Police and firemen arrived at the scene within ten minutes. The neighbor identified the Anderson as being involved in the incident. The police approached the house and rang the doorbell, inquiring as to what had happened. After questioning, Jerry was arrested and taken to the police station. Jerry was booked in jail on a charge of first-degree murder! Lacy was questioned about the incident and taken to the police station in a separate vehicle. Lacy was released and allowed to return home after being detained for a period of four hours. A couple of days later, Jerry was arraigned on the charge of murder in the district court of Harris County, Texas. Jerry entered a plea of not guilty. Bail was denied. Lacy refused to see Jerry in jail.

Lacy, with the assistance from her mother, retained an attorney and filed for divorce. Subsequent hearings in the divorce court resulted in Lacy getting custody of the kids and sole ownership of the home.

Approximately, six months later, a show cause hearing was held in Harris County District Court. Jerry was bound on a charge of first-degree murder and ordered to stand trial. The Harris County prosecutor was seeking the death penalty. Jerry was appointed a public defender to represent him at the trial. Jerry's attorney, after reviewing the transcript of the preliminary, advised Jerry to plead guilty and beg for leniency. The attorney told Jerry that Harris County juries had placed more people on death row than any other county in the United States! Jerry refused, contending that he only shot the man because he thought that the man was sexually assaulting and raping his wife. Jerry demanded to have his day in court.

The murder case against Jerry Alexander came on for jury trial in the spring of 2004. Jerry fired his public defender and employed Carl Beldon, one of the most prominent criminal defense attorneys in the state of Texas. Being experienced in defending homicide cases, Beldon demanded the that the case be remanded back to the magistrate's court for another show cause hearing. The purpose of that motion was to compel the testimony of Lacy, the former wife of Jerry. At the initial trials, Lacy, on the advice of her attorney, had refused to testify, citing the legal claim of spousal privilege, the common-law rule that dated back to colonial America. The spousal privilege rule provides that a spouse, wife, cannot be compelled to testify against their husband in any case where the husband is accused of committing a felony offense. The assigned trial judge, upon hearing oral arguments, ruled that the trial court had improperly applied the spousal privilege rule and that the case should be remanded to the trial court for a second show cause hearing. At the second hearing, Lacy was served with a subpoena to appear in court and testify for the defense. Lacy appeared at the hearing with her divorce attorney and refused to take the witness stand and testify. After being warned of the consequences for failing to testify, Lacy was cited for direct contempt of court and ordered to immediately be sent to jail and serve ninety days. The judge did indicate that Lacy could expunge herself of the contempt charge by taking the witness stand and agreeing to testify. After spending one night in the dirty jail, Lacy reluctantly agreed to take the stand and testify. At the hearing, Lacy took the stand and was questioned at length about the night of the shooting. Lacy admitted that she was friends with Jerry and that she was talking to him when her husband approached the truck and started yelling at them. Lacy testified that upon hearing her husband yelling at them, Lacy jumped out of the truck and ran into the house. Lacy testified that she heard Jerry fire several shots into the truck as she entered her house. She turned around and looked as the truck veered off the street and crashed into a tree, resulting in a large fire.

Tracy denied that she was having sex when Peter when Jerry approached the truck, yelling for the occupants to get out of the truck. Lacy emphasized that she was a loyal and faithful wife. Lacy also testified that she was the victim of spousal abuse, being subjected to physical abuse on a weekly basis. Other witnesses called by the attorney for Jerry Alexander indicated that Lacy was a regular visitor to a local Traveler's Inn, always in the company of Peter Taylor. The motel manager, reviewing his records, testified that Lacy and Peter had been visitors at the hotel some twenty-six times in the past nine months.

Jerry took the stand in his own defense, stating that he was confronted with a "sudden emergency" when he arrived home and saw his wife running down the street, yelling: "Rape! Rape! He is trying to rape me!" Jerry testified that the only reason that he used his gun was to stop the man that had "raped" his wife and that the man was trying to flee the scene before the police arrived.

After the testimony was concluded, Jerry's lawyer asserted the defense of justifiable homicide—that is, a husband is entitled to use deadly force when his wife is the victim of a sexual assault by a stranger! The magistrate judge agreed that, that was a proper defense and that the trial judge should allow the jury to consider when the case went to trial. Jerry was bound over to trial, and the case was transferred back to the trial judge. After several continuances, the jury trial for Jerry Alexander was held in the fall of 2005. More than twenty witnesses were called to testify by the state before the prosecution rested its case. For the defense, the same evidence that was presented in the preliminary hearing was presented. At the conclusion of the evidence presented by both parties, the trial judge issued the instruction that the jury could consider the issue of justifiable homicide. After closing arguments, the jury retired and deliberated for six hours. The jury returned to the courtroom and rendered the verdict that Jerry Alexander was not guilty!

Jerry was released from jail and decided to head home. Jerry arrived at the residence and tried to enter the home. The key did not fit! The lock to the door had been changed during the two years that Jerry had been locked up in the county jail. Jerry rang the doorbell. An older man finally opened the front door. The old man, visibly upset, asked, "What do you want?"

Jerry replied, "Is Lacy here?"

"No," the old man responded, "she sold me this house over a year ago!"

The old man slammed the door in his face before Jerry could ask any further questions. The next day, Jerry went down to the hall of records and checked the title on his home. Jerry was shocked to discover that Lacy had sold the house the year before to the old man. The selling price: $240,000. Jerry was in a state of shock as he left the hall of records. Jerry went to the courthouse and discovered that Lacy had been awarded title to the house and custody of both children. Jerry remembered being served with divorce papers while he was in jail, but did not appear in the court hearing on the divorce case. Jerry went to his bank and discovered that Lacy had taken all the money out of their bank account, some $3,000, and closed the account out. Jerry remembered that he had a safety deposit box that he had stashed some cash in as an emergency. Jerry retrieved the key from his wallet and asked to see his safety deposit box. Opening the box, he was surprised to see that the stash of cash had not been touched and was still in the box. Jerry pulled the stash out of the box and slowly counted it. Jerry smiled as he finished the count and came up with over $4,000. Jerry stashed the cash in his pocket and returned the box to the bank secretary. The cash would help him rent an apartment and take care of his necessities until he could get a job. After Jerry settled down, he started to complain to the district attorney's office, demanding that the prosecutor examine the case and pursue criminal charges against Lacy Anderson.

Several months later, Lacy was relaxing at home and watching television when she heard her doorbell ring. Answering the door, Lacy was shocked to see a deputy sheriff standing there.

"Madam, are you Lacy Alexander?" he asked.

"Yes," she replied.

Pulling out a piece of paper, the deputy stated, "Lady, I have a warrant here for you arrest. You are being charged with the crime of manslaughter, first degree. Turn around and place your hands behind you," the deputy stated. "I am sorry, young lady, but I have to place you under arrest and take you downtown to the sheriff's office."

Lacy slowly turned around and placed her hands behind her. Lacy was in a state of shock as the officer cuffed her. Lacy was taken out to the sheriff's car and transported down to the county jail for booking into the county jail. The formal charge was first-degree manslaughter!

The following day, Lacy was arraigned on the manslaughter charge. Lacy entered a plea of not guilty and requested a jury trial. The trial judge set bail at $100,000. Lacy was unable to post bail and remained in jail for the next eighteen months. Lacy was appointed a public defender to assist her in her defense. After a preliminary hearing, the judge concluded that the evidence did not support the charge as alleged in the complaint and information and ordered Lacy bound over on an amended charge of second-degree manslaughter. The maximum punishment for the amended charge was up to four years in jail. How could Lacy go to jail? She did not fire the gun or do anything else that resulted in the death of her friend Peter Taylor. In 2006, a jury trial was conducted in Harris County, Texas, for Lacy Alexander. The trial lasted two weeks. The jury retired and deliberated for four hours before returning to deliver their verdict. The verdict rendered by the jury was a shock to everyone!

The judge ordered Lacy to turn and face the jury as he read the verdict. The judge read the verdict, "We, the jury, duly sworn to hear the evidence and render a verdict, do hereby find that the defendant, Lacy Anderson, is *not* guilty!"

The judge thanked the jury for their service and discharged the jury. Turning to Lacy, the judge stated, "Lacy Anderson, the jury empaneled to hear the evidence and render a verdict has found that you are not guilty of the charge of manslaughter. I therefore order that your bond be exonerated and that you be released from custody immediately."

Lacy Anderson walked out of the Harris County courthouse, a free woman. Lacy granted custody of her kids to her parents and left the state of Texas two days later. Lacy moved to an undisclosed location out of the country, happy to get the nightmare over.

THE SENIOR TRIP

M ost every person has fond memories of their childhood and their friends at school, particularly if they are the only child in the house. Every person tends to bond with their fellow classmates. Girls generally make friends with other girls in their class at school, and boys tend to bond with other boys in their respective classes. Friendship formed in elementary schools continue into high school and beyond. Once high school is finished, most people part company with their fellow classmates, not staying in touch. The end of the senior year generally results in a senior trip to a resort area for the graduating class. The students select the place that they want to go, subject to the approval of the teachers and the school administration. Planning for the trip starts in the fall of the senior year, giving students sufficient time to raise the money for the trip. Fundraising is done at high school athletic events to avoid placing an undue financial burden on the family of the student. Girls would sell cookies and candy. The boys would mow yards and other cleanup work around homes in the school district. Everyone treasures the memories of the senior trip throughout the remainder of their life.

During my senior in high school, every person in our class was asked to submit suggestions on where they would like to go on their senior trip. Our class poll reflected that most students wanted to go to a large lake to fish and swim in the warm summer. The majority of my class selected Lake Gibson, a large natural water lake in the eastern part of our state. Teachers would help seniors in the fundraising by announcing the fundraising at PTA meetings and other school events. The school arranged transportation to the resort through buses provided by the school district. Two teachers and the bus driver was in charge of supervising the class as we started on our trip. The trip was planned for the third week of May, just before the graduation program on the last Friday in May. Everyone was so excited as we packed and met at the school at 8:00 a.m. The lake was about a four-hour drive from our high school building. We piled on the bus, some forty seniors. We talked all the way down the interstate highway. We arrived at around 1:30 in the afternoon. We waited in the bus while the teachers went inside to check in and get our room keys. Each student had paired off with a friend to share the room with. My friend Abby Gates and I agreed to share a room. We got our keys and headed off to our room. The room was beautiful, with a beautiful view of the lake. Abby and I thought that we had landed in paradise. Little did we know that it would end up being a trip to hell!

While waiting on the bus for our keys, we all agreed to meet in the hotel lobby in ninety minutes and proceed down to the lake together. We were hopeful that we could stake out an area on the beach all to ourselves. This strategy would allow us to bring our own coolers with ice and something to drink. While most of the girls thought we would share bottles of water and soft drinks, unknown to us, two of the boys had snuck four six-packs of beer in their luggage down to the lake to enjoy when we got on the beach. The two boys, Jack and Bret Garner, loved to drink beer. Their favorite, Coors! Two other boys had stored several marijuana gummies in the beach bags. Their plan was to eat some pot gummies. They would get high and do some swimming in their birthday suits: buck naked! Around 2:00 p.m., everyone had shown up on the beach. The class president, Debbie Myers, assigned each pair of students a particular area to set up their positions, lay out their towels, and place their drink coolers. Abby and I were fortunate to get an area down the beach about a hundred yards, away from the very loud and noisy boys. Abby and I looked around to see where the teachers were. Neither one was insight. One of the boys indicated that both the teachers were tired and that they had decided to rest and take a nap while we were tanning and swimming. What about Roy, the bus driver? We were told that he had walked down the street to a convenience store to get a twelve-pack of beer! With no one around to supervise, the boys were pulling out their cans of beer. Some of the girls wanted to drink some beers. Jack Garner took a head count and decided that some of the boys needed to go down to the convenience store and buy about ten to twelve six-packs of beer to accommodate everyone. Jack came around and took up a collection to help cover the costs of the beer. Within ten minutes, he had collected about $90 and headed down to the store. Several of the girls decided to take a dip in the water and see how warm the water was. One of the girls, Connie came back and reported that the water was great! About a dozen girls followed her back down to the water and waded in. Abby and I joined the parade. The water felt nice and warm, just like bath water! The waves of water made it feel like we were in a jacuzzi! Very relaxing after a four-hour bus ride. Abby and I swam for about twenty minutes and headed back to our towels to relax in the sun. Most of the other girls soon became tired and came back to their respective towels. One girl, Debbie, came out and looked around. "Where is Barbara?" Barbara was her roommate. Not seeing her, we glanced back into the water. Had she drowned?

Debbie became upset and started crying! Where was her lifelong friend, Barbara? She became frantic with fear, screaming and yelling. Abby and I went up and tried to console her. Other girls joined us. We decided to fan out and search the area around our side of the lake. We were desperate to find Barbara. We formed a line along the beach approximately a hundred yards long and started wading into the nice, warm lake waters. We searched for over an hour, looking for Barbara. No luck! After an hour of desperate searching, most of the girls were tired and decided to wade back to the shore, taking a break to rest and catch their breath. After resting for about thirty minutes, we gave it another shot. No luck! The search went on until dark. About 7:00 p.m., we decided to call it a day. Abby and I went back to the hotel to rest and get something to eat. That night in the hotel room, we kept hearing loud noises from down the hallway. I went out in the hallway and told the guys to "hold it down." Jack and his brother were totally bombed! The boys' room was filled with other boys who were blind drunk. I went down to one of the teachers room to ask for help to quiet the boys down. Mrs. Taylor, the senior teacher assigned the responsibility of overseeing the students, answered the door.

"What do you want?" she asked.

It was obvious from her appearance the she had been drinking. Her eyes were bloodshot, her speech was slurred, and she was unsteady on her feet, hanging on to the door to maintain her balance. I told her that the noise down the hallway by the boys were keeping us awake. She glanced down that way and turned back toward me, saying, "I don't hear anything! Get out of here and leave us alone!"

I glanced inside the room and observed that Mrs. Gilmore was holding a bottle of whiskey and pouring a drink for the bus driver, Roy. I turned away and left the area, realizing that there was nobody on the trip that would be supervising the students and their conduct on the trip. We were all on our own! No one cared or gave a damn about the students' welfare on the trip! Abby and I turned on the television in our room and switched the channel to a music channel which featured soft piano music. It took time, but we eventually fell asleep.

At about six o'clock in the morning, we were awakened by noise of someone pounding on our door. I put on my bathrobe and answered the door. I was startled to see a deputy sheriff standing there. "Young lady, we have found the body of one your classmates that washed ashore down on the beach! We need you to come down to station to help identify the body!"

I mumbled, "Okay, Officer. Let me wake up my roommate."

The deputy waited outside in the hall as I woke up Abby and we got dressed, quickly throwing on our clothes and following the deputy down the hallway to the lobby. We joined several other girls in the lobby and followed the deputy out into the parking lot. We were escorted down to the sheriff's station in several cars. The desk sergeant directed the deputies to take us back to a conference room. We were all seated and advised to wait a few minutes until the shift commander came in. About thirty minutes later, an older gentleman walked into the room and stepped up to the podium. "Ladies, I regret to inform you that a young girl's body washed ashore this morning at the back side of the lake. The medical examiner has taken custody of the girl's remains, and they are being taken to the state medical examiners for an autopsy. We need someone in your group to provide us with some personal information."

Debbie Myers, the class president, stood up and stated, "We are seniors from Classen High School. We come down to Lake Gipson for our senior trip." Debbie continued, "We were out swimming on the beach in front of our hotel about 4:30 yesterday afternoon.

Barbara Anderson was one of our seniors that was swimming in our group. We left the beach area at about 7:00 p.m. and came back to the hotel. Barbara went down to the beach with our group, but she was not with us when we came back to the hotel. Some of us thought that she had already returned to the hotel since we had been down there for several hours."

The shift commander inquired, "Does anyone know who to contact, such as her parents or next of kin?"

Debbie replied, "That would be our teacher, Mrs. Taylor."

The deputy looked around the room and asked, "Is Mrs. Taylor here?"

We looked around at each other, and Debbie stated, "She is not here. She must be back at the hotel. She was staying in room 233."

The deputy stated, "Thank you, young lady. I will have one of our deputies contact her at the hotel and bring her down to the station for an interview."

I mumbled to myself, "Good luck with that! She was drunk on her ass when I talked to her last night."

The commander looked up and asked, "What did you say, young lady?"

Oh my god. I thought that I would get in trouble for making that comment. "I tried to talk to her last night. She was tired and did not want to talk until breakfast this morning. She is probably back at the hotel wondering why all the students are not down there for breakfast."

We were escorted out of the sheriff's station and driven back to the hotel.

While we being driven back to the hotel, I wondered where the teachers were this morning and why they were not already at the sheriff's station being interviewed. Considering the fact that they were drinking and partying all with the bus driver, they were probably drunk and hungover from the all-night party. As we were getting out of the sheriff's car and walking back into the hotel, I turned to Abby and said, "I would bet they are still drunk and hungover from all-night drinking."

Abby replied, "I don't know. Let's go by their room when we get upstairs."

I agreed with her. We got on the elevator and went up to their floor. Just as we were getting off the elevator, I glanced down the hall and saw Mrs. Taylor being escorted out of the room by a deputy sheriff. Her hands appeared to be in handcuffs. Shortly thereafter, we saw Mrs. Gilmore being escorted out of the room behind her. She was also in handcuffs.

Turning to Abby, I said, "Do you see what I am seeing?" We both stood there in total disbelief as to what was unfolding. Both teachers had their heads bowed down, hoping that no one would recognize them as they were being escorted out of the hotel in hand-cuffs. After they got on the elevator and disappeared, I told Abby, "What happened to Bob, the bus driver?"

We walked on down the hallway and looked in their room. We could see in the distance that a figure that appeared to be him was lying on the floor with a sheet over his body. Abby and I gasped in disbelief as we hurried back to our hotel room. Abby closed the door, and we both sat down on the bed. We were speechless for a few minutes. Finally, I mumbled to Abby, "We better call our parents so that we can get the hell out of here!"

She agreed. Abby got on the hotel phone and placed a collect call to her mother. Abby's mother told her that she would leave immediately and head down to the lake. It was about a four-hour drive down to Lake Gipson from our neighborhood. I got on the phone and called home. My dad answered the phone quickly.

"What's wrong, baby?" he asked.

I related the fact that Barbara had apparently drowned in the lake and that both our teachers had been arrested by the sheriff's office.

My dad quickly responded, "Your mother and I will leave immediately and head down there."

"Thank you, Dad," I quickly replied.

Abby and I were totally relieved that our parents would be there in about four hours to get us out of hell.

While we were waiting for our parents to come and get us, I wondered about the boys that had been drinking all night. Were they up and aware of what was going on? I told Abby that I was going to down to the boys' room and see what was going on down there. I took the stairs down to their floor. I opened the door leading toward their rooms. The smell of alcohol and beer was all over the place. I had to cover my mouth to keep from gasping at the smell as I approached their rooms. The door was open to the Garner brothers' room. I slowly walked into their room. What a sight! There were two guys lying on the bed. There were four other boys lying on the floor and the sofa. Every guy was passed out and reeked of beer. There were beer cans scattered all over the rooms. Turning around in disgust at the awful sight, I slowly walked back into the hallway. As I passed the bathroom, I glanced inside. One boy was lying in the bathtub and another boy lying on the floor, both passed out. I could not believe what I had just seen. I almost threw up as I hurried down the hallway to the stairwell. I stumbled down the stairs, pausing at the bottom to regain my composure before going back to the room.

After regaining my composure, I decided to go down to the teachers' room to see what was going on down there. I went down to the first floor and walked across the lobby to the stairway on the other side of the hotel. After looking around to verify that no one was watching me, I opened the door and started climbing the stairs to the second floor where the teachers' room was located. I opened to door to the second floor and peered down the hallway to see if there was anyone there. Seeing no one in sight, I entered the hallway and slowly edged down to the area where the teachers' room was located. As I neared the room where the teachers stayed, I could see that the door was open and that there were people talking inside the room. Leaning against the hallway wall, I edged down to the area right outside the room. Listening carefully, I heard one man say, "Looking at the head of the corpse that was lying on floor, the cause of death appears to be blunt force trauma to the right side of his head." Looking up, the man told the officer writing down the report, "He was hit on the right side of the head by a heavy object, probably that whiskey bottle that is smashed over there on the floor. Rigor mortis has set in, so I would place time of death at somewhere around five this morning." Looking up, the man whom I assumed was the corner instructed the officer to place all that information in the report.

I walked slowly back to the stairway, making sure that I did not make any noise along the way. I climbed the stairway back to our room on the third floor. I noticed that the door to our room was closed. I knocked on the door and told Abby to let me back into the room. I heard a noise inside the room like there was some furniture being moved around. Abby unlocked the door and let me in.

"What was that noise that I heard?"

Abby replied, "I had a chair placed against the door to keep anyone from getting in our room. I was scared while you were gone. What did you find out?"

My response, "All the boys are still passed out in their room. They are totally bombed out from a night of heavy drinking. On the way back, I went by the teachers' room. The police are still in there, examining the body that is on the floor."

Abby asked, "Who does the dead body belong to?"

I replied, "It is the bus driver, Bob. The coroner was examining the body. He told the officer that victim was killed by blunt force trauma, a blow to the head caused by being hit by a bottle of whiskey."

Abby asked, "Who killed him?"

I answered "I don't know. It may be Mrs. Taylor or Mrs. George. They were both arrested. Maybe they did it, taking turns bashing him in the head."

We were both wondering what the bus driver did to prompt the two teachers to react in such a violent way.

The four-hour wait for our parents to show up at the lake and pick us up seemed like it took forever. Finally, Abby's mother showed up at 4:00 p.m. I walked Abby down to the car and assured her that my father would be there shortly to pick me. I went back up to the room and locked the door. About an hour later, my parents showed up. My mother hugged me as my dad carried my luggage down to the car! As we walked down to the car to leave, my dad stopped at the front desk to talk to the desk clerk. He asked for directions down to the sheriff's station. He wanted to find out what happened between the bus driver and the two teachers that resulted in the killing of the bus driver. We waited in the car as he went inside the sheriff's station. About thirty minutes later, he came out and drove us home. Dad said both teachers had been arrested with regard to the homicide of Ray Jackson, the bus driver. Charges would be filed in the homicide a few days later.

After a long drive back, we got home just in time to catch the six o'clock news. We all wondered if the murder case would be on the evening news. Nothing was mentioned about the murder. My dad was frustrated. He called the local newspaper and the television stations to see if they had information about the murder that had occurred down at Lake Gibson. It was great to be home. At last, I felt safe and secure. I knew that I would get a great night's sleep. I slept late the next morning, not getting up until 9:00 a.m. I was hungry. I went into the kitchen to have a bowl of cereal. Flipping on the television in the kitchen, I was pouring some milk on my bowl of cereal when I heard the news broadcast come on. With the news report headline "Murder at the Lake," the reporter said, "We have the latest news update on two local teachers being arrested in connection with the homicide of the school bus driver." He continued, "The Wagoner sheriff announced that two teachers have been arrested in connection to the homicide of a local bus driver. Janet Taylor and Connie Gilmore, both teachers at Classen High School, have been arrested in connection with the homicide of Roy Moore. Paperwork will be presented today to the district attorney's office in connection with the homicide later on. It will be up to the district attorney's office on what exact charges will be filed against each of the two teachers. We will have the latest news at 10:00 p.m."

What a shock! Both teachers had been arrested in connection with the bus driver's homicide! I had had both of these teachers during my time at Classen High School. What caused them to kill Roy, the bus driver? He'd seemed so nice and friendly toward my classmates on the way down to the lake. I was puzzled about the circumstances that led to their arrest. I talked it over with my parents, who were both dumbfounded about all the things that had occurred during our senior trip. A senior trip is supposed to be a time of celebration for having completed four years at Classen High School, not a time of tragedy and murder!

Slowly the thoughts about the nightmare began to subside. Abby headed off to college at the University of Arkansas. I enrolled at Northeastern University. I enrolled in political science, hoping to go onto law school and become a prosecutor in our criminal justice system.

During my first semester in college, I adapted to a college lifestyle, studying during the evening hours and attending all my classes. I did not go out to local taverns or smoke pot! I was very intent in trying to be an outstanding student, making good grades so that I could go on law school. I planned on attending the University of Tulsa located in Tulsa, Oklahoma. Tulsa University College of Law was rated as one of the best law schools in the United States. After nine intense weeks of hard work, I went home to see my parents during fall break. I had not seen them since August 15. On Thursday, I got to sleep late for the first time in almost three months. On Friday, my mother stayed home so we could go shopping for some winter clothes. We ate a quick bit of breakfast, and we were leaving our driveway when a sheriff's car pulled up in front of our car. We got out of the car to see what was going on. A deputy sheriff exited the vehicle and approached our car. The deputy asked, "Does Connie Stewart live here?"

I answered quickly, "Yes, sir. I am Connie Stewart. How can I help you?"

The deputy walked up to me and handed me a folded piece of paper. I opened it up and almost fainted. What was it? A subpoena to appear in court on October 30 and testify in the case of *State of Oklahoma v. Janet Taylor and Paula Gilmore*. "Oh my god! I am going to a witness in the murder case!" I exclaimed.

Getting back in his car, the deputy turned and said, "Lady, I would advise you to appear and testify." He continued, "If you fail to appear, the judge can find you in contempt of court and have you arrested and thrown in jail!" The deputy got back in his car and left the driveway.

Why was I a witness? I thought. Suddenly, I remembered that I had gone down to their room on the night of the murder and observed both of them sharing a large bottle of whiskey with the bus driver, the murder victim. I would have to testify that they were both very drunk prior to the homicide! My nightmare had suddenly returned! I returned to school on Sunday, but I had trouble sleeping, worried about my upcoming court appearance on October 30. It seemed like forever, but the day finally arrived. My mother went with me to the courthouse, trying to console me while I was waiting To testify. Finally, at three thirty in the afternoon, I was summoned to come into the courtroom and take the witness stand. I told the court about going to the teachers' room and observing both of them getting drunk with the bus driver. I was excused and allowed to go home. What would happen now? I finally found out the next day.

A lady from the district attorney's office called me and told me that both teachers had been bound over for trial. They were going to trial on charges of second-degree murder. Their jury trial date was set on the spring jury docket, which would start the first week pf April. She also advised me that I would receive a summons to appear in court on the date that the case was set for trial. The next five months were a total nightmare! I would have to go to court and testify before a jury of twelve people and be subject to cross-examination by two sharp criminal defense attorneys. I would probably be made to look like a fool! How embarrassing to testify in front of a packed courtroom. Would each one of the defendant want a separate jury trial? Would I have to testify twice? Oh my god! What a mess! It was hard to focus on my schoolwork. With all these questions hanging over my head, I finished the semester with a B in all my five classes. Not too bad, considering all the issues that were bothering me during the final weeks of the fall semester. I had two weeks off over the holidays before I returned to school in January.

The weeks flew by till spring break in March. I was home on spring break when a deputy sheriff showed up at the house and served me with a subpoena to appear back in court on April 15. The nightmares started all over again. I had several sleepless nights in the days leading up to the trial. Finally, the big day arrived, and my mom drove me to the court house. After checking in with the bailiff, I was placed in the jury room with several other witnesses. About 11:00 a.m., the bailiff came in and directed all of us to follow him into the courtroom. We were seated, and the judge entered the court-room and took his place on the bench. The judge gaveled the court to order and made the following statement: "Ladies and gentlemen, thank each of you for coming to court today. For your information, the defendant, Connie Gilmore has waived her right to a jury trial and entered a plea of guilty to the amended charge of accessory to the charge of second-degree murder. She will be sentenced at a later date after a presentence investigation report from the Department of Public Safety. As a result of that, the case with regard to the defen-dant, Janet Taylor, has been continued to the jury docket this fall. In view of these facts, each of you witnesses are released from your subpoenas today. Thank you." Turning to the bailiff, he asked him to escort us out of the court house. I was done with this mess.

I completed the spring semester with straight As. I made the president's honor roll! Over the summer, the judgment and sentenc-ing of Connie Gilmore were conducted. Mrs. Gilmore was sentenced to five years in prison, with the term to be suspended conditioned on her good behavior. I enjoyed my summer with no stress at all. In no time, the summer was gone, and I had to return to Northeastern to start the fall semester. In September, my mother called me and told me that a sheriff's deputy had stopped by to serve me with a subpoena for the upcoming trial of Janet Taylor. I was subsequently served with the paperwork when I returned home for the weekend. The paper-work indicated that the trial would start on Monday, October 28. My stress and nightmares returned.

Finally, the trial date arrived, and I made arrangements with my professors to take the week of the twenty-eighth off to appear and testify in the Janet Taylor murder case. I was required to do some directed reading and take a test in each class when I returned to campus. On the morning of the trial, my mother drove me to the court hearing, and I went into the jury room, where the court bailiff advised me to have a seat and relax. It was going to be a long day. The trial lasted for five days. I had to attend every day, waiting in the jury room to be called as a witness. Finally, on the third day of the trial, I was summoned into the courtroom at 4:00 p.m. I repeated the same testimony that I had given in the preliminary hearing. I was excused and allowed to go home. The trial finished on Friday morning, and the jury started their jury deliberations that afternoon. I was home resting watching television when a news bulletin came on interrupting the afternoon movie. The news report stated that Janet Taylor was guilty of murder in the second degree and that the jury had sentenced her to fifteen years in prison. The nightmare of my senior trip was finally over!

A MOTHER'S LOVE

One of the great moments in life is when a woman gives birth to a child. A mother's love for her children is one of the greatest feelings in the world. From the moment of birth, the mother attends to her baby's every need, nurturing the child as it grows into an adult. While there is a special bonding between the woman and a baby girl, the woman is also very attached to a baby boy. What lengths will a mother go to protect her child from the cruel outside world? Let's examine one particular case.

Connie grew up in a rural area of western Arkansas. Connie was a bright child who excelled in her education as she attended the public schools in Van Buren, Arkansas. Connie graduated with honors from Van Buren High School. During high school, Connie met and started dating BJ, the best-looking guy in school. BJ proposed, and Connie accepted. They planned to get married after graduation. Unexpectedly, Connie was awarded a scholarship to attend Arkansas State University. Connie was torn between getting married or going off to college. BJ insisted that they get married during the summer and that she could still carry through with her plans to start college in the fall. Believing BJ, Connie went ahead and got married to BJ in July. After a brief honeymoon in Eureka Springs, the newlyweds moved into a small apartment near the campus. BJ got a job at a local grocery store while Connie attended classes. Life seemed to be going great for a few months. One day, Connie came home from her afternoon classes to find that BJ was still in bed, snoring away. She went into the bedroom to awaken him. Connie discovered that BJ was drunk! When BJ finally came around, he told Connie that he had been fired from his job at the store and that he had bought a twenty-four-pack of beer and that he had gotten drunk and fallen asleep. While Connie had some sympathy for BJ, she realized that if he could not hold down a job, then there would be no money coming in to pay for food and their rent. She would be forced to drop out of school and get a good-paying job.

Connie telephoned her mother and asked for help. Her mother agreed to help Connie with her basic necessities, encouraging her to stay in school. Over the next six months, BJ continued his daily habits of drinking a dozen cans of beer, sometimes stealing money out of Connie's purse to go to the liquor store. Connie become more agitated with every passing month. BJ refused to go out and get another job. After the completion of the spring semester, Connie separated from BJ and moved back home to live with her mother. Connie, with financial aid from her mother, was able to hire an attorney and file for divorce. BJ did not appear or contest the divorce. The divorce was finalized in the fall as Connie was completing the fall semester. Finally, life seemed to be going well for Connie. Life without BJ was great! Within a few months, Connie starting dating a classmate that she met in her math class. They would study together and go out for pizza. Upon completion of the fall semester, her classmate, Roger asked her to move into his apartment. Without hesitation, Connie agreed. The next few months were a slice of heaven for Connie. They agreed to get married once they both graduated from college. During their second year together, Connie became pregnant. While Connie was totally happy with becoming a mother, Roger was upset and started becoming abusive. Roger would go out and pick up a six-pack of beer on the way from his classes. After the evening meal, Roger would down the six-pack of beer and become intoxicated and abusive. Roger would verbally abuse Connie and slap her around. At one point, the police were called. Arriving at the apartment, the officer arrested Roger and took him off to jail. Connie was forced to file for divorce again. The divorce proceedings dragged on for several months. During the interim, Connie gave birth to a cute baby boy, which she named Jaime. Roger agreed to allow her to have custody of the little boy when the divorce was finalized. Connie moved back home to live with her mother after completing the spring semester of her sophomore year of college. Connie's college education would have to be put on hold until she could afford to return to school.

During the summer, Connie applied for a student loan. Her mother agreed to cosign the loan, putting a mortgage on her house. Connie was able to return to college for her junior year with her mom taking care of Jaime while she was away at school. Being able to complete her degree without the distractions caused by domestic issues, Connie graduated with honors in less than two years. Connie was able to find employment almost immediately with a mortgage company. Connie was able to find a nice rental property in the town where she worked. Connie moved into her new home and furnished a special bedroom for Jaime. The house was only a few blocks from her mom's house. Jaime would stay with her mom during the day, and Connie would pick him up after getting off work. One day, Connie picked Jaime up and noticed that his clothes were dirty and that he had been crying. Jaime told her that he was playing with his friends in the neighborhood park when an old man approached him and offered to pay him an ice cream. Jaime accepted and followed him down the road to the Dairy Boy ice cream stand. Buying him an ice cream, the old man then offered to give him $20 if he would stop by the man's house on the way back to the park. Jaime accepted the offer and followed the man back to his house. Once inside the house, the old man slammed the door and locked it. Jaime said the old man dragged him into a back bedroom and ripped at his clothes! Jaime related that he kicked the old man in his groin area and ran of the house. Connie immediately called the police and asked for emergency assistance. A uniformed police officer came out to her house and took an offense report. The officer advised Connie that it would be a difficult case to prosecute since Jaime could not identify the man or provide an accurate description of the house where Jaime was assaulted. Connie was unsure what to do to protect her child. After spending a sleepless night worrying about what to do, Connie took the day off from work and personally take Jaime to his elementary school. After dropping Jaime off at school, Connie went shopping at a local shopping center. She was determined to buy a gun!

Connie went to several stores before she found the ideal gun, a .38-caliber handgun which the salesman identified as a police special, a gun used by undercover police detectives working on a felony crime. The handgun was light and easy to handle, the perfect gun for a young woman to use in defending herself and her children! Connie bought several dozens of rounds of ammunition to go with the handgun. After having lunch at a nearby restaurant, Connie went to a gun range outside of town and practiced using the gun, trying to get a feel of how to use the handgun in the event that she was confronted with an emergency! After two hours of practice with the gun, Connie left the gun range, feeling confident that she was ready.

Connie talked to her mother that evening, advising her mom to carefully watch Jaime anytime he was out of school or at outside the house. For the next few weeks, Connie carefully watched Jaime's activities when he went to play down in the neighborhood playground and played with his friends. Connie would sit in her car, slumped down in the car seat, and watch the kids play.

Three weekends later, Connie took Jaime to the park and sat in her car, watching the kids. About noon, Connie noticed that an older man, probably in his fifties, entered the park and sat down in a bench, watching the kids play. That old man may be the one that had conned Jaime into going to his house. An ideal opportunity for Connie! Maybe he would try to do something again. Jaime and the other boys were playing pitch and catch with a baseball when the ball rolled away and ended up near the park bench where the old man was sitting. The old man picked up the ball and hid it in his pocket. One of Jaime's friends went over to retrieve the ball. The old man denied having the ball. The kid turned around and looked around and behind the bench. Not finding the ball, the boy gave up looking for the ball and headed back to the other boys. After a few moments, the old man took the ball out of his pocket and threw it back to the boys. Connie wondered if the man was the same one that assaulted Jaime a few weeks earlier.

After a couple hours of play, the boys were tired and decided to take a break and head down to the Dairy Boy for an ice cream. Connie honked her car horn and motioned for Jaime to come over to her. "Jaime," she asked, "is that man the same one that assaulted you?"

Jaime glanced around at the old man that was still sitting in the bench. Jaime replied, "It could be, but I am not sure."

Connie looked at the old man and advised Jaime to go ahead and join the other boys for an ice cream. Connie said, "Go ahead. I will stay here and watch him."

Jaime left and ran down the street, joining the other boys at the ice cream stand. Connie turned back toward the park bench.

She watched the old man carefully as he got up from the bench and headed out of the park, walking down the sidewalk, away from the ice cream stand. Connie started her car and slowly followed the old man down the street. After a few minutes, he approached an older house and entered the house and closed the door. Taking out her notepad, Connie wrote down the address: 6911 SW Twenty-Ninth Street. It was time to play private detective!

The following day, Connie took the day off and went down to the county courthouse to check the land records and see who owned the house that the old man lived in. After two hours of diligent searching, Connie located the house and discovered that the house was owned by a local real estate company. Connie went to the city services division and discovered that the utilities were placed in the name of Carl Wesley. That evening, Connie got on her computer and did some further research. Connie discovered that Wesley was a retired railroad worker that was apparently drawing a railroad retirement in addition to social security. A police records check revealed that Carl Wesley had a criminal record, having been arrested several times on charges ranging from drunk driving to assault with a deadly weapon. Wesley had served time in jail on three occasions! Also, Wesley was on probation for two years from his last offense: assault of a minor! Obviously, Wesley was an old pervert that needed to be watched and should not be near any kids playing on a municipal playground.

Connie spent many sleepless nights! What should she do to protect the kids in the residential area from a crazy sex pervert? How could she expose him and his weird behavior to the families living in the area? A week later, Connie concluded that the best thing to do was to put up a sign in the park, warning parents of the danger of leaving young kids alone in the park to play.

The following Saturday, Connie went to the local lumber yard and bought two sheets of plywood, paint, and the posts necessary to construct the signs and get them ready to display. Working diligently that weekend, Connie painted the two signs and attached the signs to the metal posts. After her son went to bed that night, Connie slipped into her clothes and drove down to the park. The park was vacant during the midnight hours. The park did not have adequate lighting for the kids to play on the playground during the nighttime hours. Connie pulled the two signs out of the trunk of her car and placed them at the two entrances to the park. The signs read, "Parents beware! Do not leave your kids unattended in the park! There is a convicted felon living in the area!" Connie slipped back in her car and drove home, not turning on her car lights until she pulled into the driveway. Connie took a quick shower and headed off to bed, feeling confident that she had solved the problem that had plagued her neighborhood for several months. Connie got a great night's rest and went to work feeling like a million bucks!

The neighborhood was rocked with speculation about what person had placed the signs in the park. A second question was also obvious! "Who was the convicted felon that lived in the neighborhood?" Connie continued watching the park in her spare time whenever her son was down there playing. The old man never appeared during the times that Connie and her children were at the park. Curious as to what happened to the old man, Connie started driving by his house. One evening, Connie noticed that the realty company that owned the house had placed a For Rent sign out in the front yard. The old man was gone and forgotten from the neighborhood forever! Not quite!

A few weeks later, Connie was taking out her trash one evening when she saw her neighbor at the curb. The neighbor advised Connie that an old man was roaming the neighborhood, looking for a vacant house to rent. Connie inquired as to what the old man looked like. The neighbor's reply matched the description of the old man that used to sit in the park down the street. Connie became alarmed, concerned that the old man was moving back in the neighborhood. The house across the street was vacant and available to be rented. Could that old man be coming back to be near her? Connie watched diligently the vacant house to see if it was rented out by the old man. Two weeks later, a large moving truck pulled up in the driveway and started unloading furniture, taking it inside the vacant house. Curious as to who the new tenant was, Connie walked across the street and asked the movers who the new tenant was. The response shocked Connie. The new tenant was an older man who appeared to live alone. Had the old pervert returned to the area? A few days later, the new tenant arrived and went inside. Seeing the man, Connie recognized the new tenant as the old man from the park! Oh my god! What was she going to do? A sex pervert was living across the street from her young child.

Connie suffered through several sleepless nights during the next several weeks. Connie scolded her son to never leave the house without her being with him. One evening, Connie had to work late and did not get home until after 6:00 p.m. Connie drove up into the driveway and noticed that her son was playing in the front yard. Glancing across the street, Connie noticed that the old man was out on his front porch, sitting in a lawn chair and watching her boy carefully. Connie quickly grabbed her son and ran into the house. What was she going to do? Call the police? The cops had failed to do anything the last time when the old man lured the boy into his house and assaulted him. Connie had to do something else. The question was what could she do to get rid of this monster forever?

Finally, Connie came up with a plan to resolve the issue once and for all. Connie talked to Jaime and told him that she was leaving to go back to the office to retrieve some papers that she had left at the office. Connie stated that she would be gone about an hour. Checking her purse, Connie made sure that her pistol was in the purse and that it was fully loaded. Connie patted Jaime on the head and told him that he could play outside while she was gone. Getting in her car, Connie backed out of the driveway and drove off. Jaime got his basketball and went out to play in the front yard. Jaime was bouncing his ball on the sidewalk. This was the first time that he had played outside in several days. The fresh air felt good!

Connie drove around the block and parked on a vacant lot directly behind her house. Getting out of her car, Connie walked across the vacant lot that was covered with large shade trees. The trees provided perfect cover to hide her from being seen by anyone walking in the neighborhood. Connie moved carefully through the trees until she approached the back porch of her house. Connie slowly edged her way around the side of the house until she got to where she had a perfect view of the front yard. Glancing into the front yard, Connie could clearly see Jaime bouncing his basketball on the sidewalk in front of her house. Connie pulled out her pistol and checked the ammunition to make sure that it was fully loaded and ready to use.

A few moments later, Connie glanced and saw the old man come out of his house and sit down in his lawn chair on the porch. The old man's attention was focused on Jaime as he played with his basketball on the sidewalk. Nobody else in the neighborhood was outside at that time. Sensing that this his golden opportunity, the man got out of his chair and walked slowly across the street toward Jaime. The old man came up to Jaime and said, "Are you ready for an ice cream?"

Looking up, Jaime recognized the old man. Jaime answered, "No, I don't want anything from you!"

The old man moved quickly and grabbed Jaime as he turned to run away. "Come here, you little bastard!" the old man screamed. The old man, being much stronger, pulled Jaime and dragged him out into the street and toward his house.

Pulling the gun out of her purse, Connie stepped out from behind her house and yelled, "Let the kid loose!"

The old man turned around and looked at Connie. He saw the large pistol that she had in her right hand. "Don't shoot!" The old man released Jaime from his grasp and let him go.

Connie yelled, "Jaime, get on the ground!"

Jaime immediately fell and lay down flat on the ground near the sidewalk. With Jaime out of the line of fire, Connie raised her gun and yelled, "Now, you bastard, you are going to pay for your sins. You are going to hell!"

Connie unloaded her pistol! *Bam! Bam! Bam! Bam! Bam! Bam!* Connie continued pulling the trigger on the gun until she finally realized that the gun was out of bullets. The old man slumped to the ground, covered in blood as a result of the six bullets that had hit every area in his chest and neck. The old man passed out and died in less than a minute. Connie dropped her gun on the ground and rushed over to Jaime.

"Are you okay, baby?" she asked.

Jaime hugged his mother and started crying. Connie picked Jaime up and carried him into the house. After resting a few minutes to regain her composure, Connie picked up the phone and dialed the 911 emergency number. Connie advised the operator that a man had been shot in her front yard. Emergency responders and law enforcement officers arrived within fifteen minutes. The paramedics checked the old man and advised the officer that the old man had passed away. The officers directed the ambulance attendants to transport the body to the coroner's office for an autopsy. After questioning Connie and Jaime for more than one hour, the officers decided to escort Connie and Jaime to the police station for further interrogation. After four hours of further questioning, Connie was released to return home that evening. A review of the police report and the autopsy report resulted in the district attorney concluding that no charges would be filed against Connie. The prosecutor concluded that the case was one of justifiable homicide, that being that Connie had a legal right to use deadly force under the circumstances to protect her child on her own property from any intruder committing a crime.

DEADLY EVIDENCE

D etective Paul Miller had been a detective with the Riverside police department for more than twenty-eight years. While he was nearing the age of retirement, he did not want to retire. Paul's wife, Catherine, had died two years earlier, and he dreaded the thought of retirement since he lived alone. Paul's daughter, Linda, had been married for more than fifteen years and had moved out of state due to her husband's job. His friends and associates at the police department was busy in their jobs and family life. In recent months, Paul could feel the fatigue from being the senior detective with the department and in charge of most felony crimes on the weekend shift of the police department. The captain of the criminal investigation division was hinting that Paul should hang it up and turn in his retirement papers. Paul was dragging his feet on the filing of the paperwork, knowing full well that he would be gone within six months after the paperwork was turned into the municipal retirement system.

Early on a Sunday morning, Paul was awakened by his cell phone. Glancing at the phone, he realized that it was the police dispatcher at police headquarters. Paul slowly answered the phone as he climbed out of bed. The dispatcher notified him that there had been a homicide on the north side and that he was needed at the crime scene. Throwing on his clothes, Paul hurried to his car and proceeded quickly to the crime scene. He parked on the side of the street adjacent to the homicide scene. The house was located on the north side of the city, where most of the homicides occurred. The patrol officer immediately recognized Paul and ushered him in the house. The old wood-framed house was in sad shape, with fading paint on the walls and cracks in the ceiling. A typical residence in this part of town.

Walking into the kitchen, Paul glanced and noticed the victim of the homicide lying on the floor. The body was covered with a sheet, a typical crime scene, while the police officers searched the scene for possible evidence that could lead to the identity of the person who committed the crime. Paul pulled back the sheet and glanced down at the victim. Paul quickly turned away after seeing the victim, an older woman, probably eighty to eighty-five years old.

Paul quickly placed the sheet back over the body and walked over to the uniformed officer that was filling out the paperwork.

"What do you have?" Paul asked.

The officer responded, "The victim has been identified by her daughter as Linda Williams, an eighty-seven-year old widow who lives alone." The officer continued, "The daughter came by to check on her mother after she wouldn't answer her phone this morning. The daughter had a key and let herself into the house at about eight thirty."

Paul responded, "Based on the state of the body, I would estimate that she has been dead for about five to six hours. The cause of death is she was strangled to death by that electrical cord that is wrapped around her neck," Paul concluded. The officer made a note of Paul's and wrote it on the office report. Turning around, Paul stated, "Please put a copy of your report in my folder at the department when you get finished here."

The officer responded, "Yes, sir! Will do!"

Paul walked out of the house, mentally noting that this was the fifth homicide in this area involving an elderly senior citizen. Senior citizens that lived alone were clearly vulnerable to violent crimes like this one. Getting in his car, Paul slowly headed back downtown to the police station, pondering an emerging question, Was there a serial killer running loose in this city, preying on elderly senior citizens like the one he had just seen?

Paul worried that this case would be another unsolved homicide, which reflected badly on the Riverside police department. There were no witnesses to the homicide. There appeared to be no possible suspects or persons of interest that should be investigated. What was the motive for the murder? Obviously, the woman did not have a lot of money or she would have lived in a better neighborhood or in a senior retirement village type of home. What could Paul do to solve this horrible crime? Parking in his assigned parking spot, Paul exited his car and headed into his office. Paul stopped by the lounge and poured himself a hot cup of coffee. Adding some creamer and sugar to the hot coffee, Paul walked back to his office and sat down at his desk. Paul liked to read the newspaper and the *Police*

Digest monthly, keeping with the latest developments in the field of criminal justice. Suddenly, Paul snapped his fingers and remembered a recent article in the law enforcement magazine. It involved a recent decision by the United States Supreme Court. After search for a few moments, Paul located the article, the case of *California v. Greenwood*, which focused on an issue on the Fourth Amendment. The Fourth Amendment related to the law on the issue of search and seizure. The question, What are the requirements of the police getting a search warrant, and when can the police conduct a search of private property without a search warrant? The key issue: can the police search the trash put out to the curb to be picked up by the garbage truck? In the Greenwood case, the police searched the trash of a possible suspect without getting a search warrant signed by a judge after a probable cause hearing. What did the court rule? Finally, Paul found the article. No search warrant was required for trash!

Paul immediately grabbed his phone and telephoned the shift commander. Paul wanted the officers assigned to the area around the location of the homicide to see if there was any evidence that might be connected to the crime. The commander readily agreed and ordered the officers in the area to search the trash bins in the neighborhood to look for possible evidence that might be linked to the crime. What items were they looking for? Anything such as clothing that may have belonged to the murder victim. Any items that may have blood or possible DNA evidence that may help solve the crime.

About an hour later, one of the officers had located a possible item of interest, a large, man's T-shirt that had some spots of blood on it. The officer was directed to place the shirt in an evidence bag and bring it into the police station. At the end of the shift, officer walked into the police station and gave Paul the plastic evidence bag containing the evidence. Paul held the bag up to the light and observed spots of blood on the shirt. The officer, Pete McCoy, entered into the evidence log the address and location of the house and the garbage bin from which the shirt had been taken. Taking custody of the bag, Paul drove the evidence bag down to the police lab building and handed it over to a laboratory technician, directing him to have a complete analysis be done on the shirt to determine the possible identify of the possible murder suspect. Back at the office, Paul checked the land records website and determined that the property belonged to a man named Cornel Cochran. Paul logged into the state criminal records website and ran a background check on Mr. Cochran. Jackpot! A hit! The records check came back that Cochran was a convicted felon that had served time for rape, sexual assault, and attempted murder. Paul suddenly had a possible suspect in the murder of elderly woman on the north side of town.

Just as expected, it took several days to get the report back from the police crime lab. The results: the blood left on shirt matched a blood sample taken from the murder victim during the autopsy at the medical examiner's office. After reviewing the reports, Paul took the two lab reports and other crime scene evidence to the office of the district attorney. Reviewing the evidence, the assistant district attorney assigned to the case prepared the paperwork to get an arrest warrant for Cornell Cochran.

Two weeks later, Paul went to court to be present when Cochran was brought into court for his initial arraignment. Paul watched intently as Cochran entered a plea of not guilty, telling the judge that he was innocent of the charges! Paul smiled as Cochran was escorted from the courtroom in handcuffs. The killer was being held without bail since the charge was first-degree murder! Several weeks later, the case came on for the first court hearing in the case, a show cause hearing. The burden was on the state to show that a crime had been committed and that there was reasonable cause to believe that the defendant had in fact committed the crime. The hearing went on for more than three hours before the judge ruled that there was sufficient evidence to hold the case for a jury trial. Approximately a year later, the case came on for a jury trial. The defense counsel for Cochran filed a series of pretrial motions. The most important motion, a motion to suppress the introduction of the bloody shirt into evidence. The grounds: there was an illegal search of Mr. Cochran's trash! Paul was required to appear and testify. Paul related the facts that led up to the police doing a search of the defendant's trash can. The court agreed to Paul's assessment that no search warrant was required based on the ruling of the United States Supreme Court in the cases of *Greenwood v. California*. The judge complimented Paul for his hard work on the case.

Three months later, the jury, upon hearing the evidence including the lab reports on the bloody shirt, convicted Cochran of first-degree murder and assessed his punishment at life in prison without the possibility of parole. Paul was disappointed with the verdict, thinking that Cochran should have received the death penalty for brutally strangling to death a helpless elderly woman who could not defend herself. Evidence uncovered during the investigation disclosed that Cochran was involved in the murder of seven other elderly women in the area. He was eventually charged and convicted in all seven homicides. That happened far too often! People killing elderly citizens who were living alone and helpless. Since Paul's work had resulted in taking a serial killer off the streets of Riverside, Paul concluded that the Cochran case was his final case. Paul turned in his retirement papers, deciding to leave such a violent area of the country. Paul reflected on his twenty-eight years in law enforcement as he packed up his stuff and left the police department for the last time. Paul had worked on more than 200 homicide cases over his twenty-eight-year career. Paul and his fellow officers had solved more than 150 of the cases, with the suspect being arrested and convicted. All those people in the police department who thought he was too old to do his job were shocked that he was leaving. It was time for a change of scenery. Paul sold his house and moved to the Gulf Coast. Paul bought a condo on the beach and spent his final years fishing in the beautiful waters of the Gulf of Mexico.

ABOUT THE AUTHOR

Dan Brown is a well-known professional in the field of criminal justice, having served as a police officer, prosecutor, and defense counsel, handling more than five hundred felony cases in the past forty years. More recently, Dan has served as a professor of criminal justice and political science at Southwestern Oklahoma State University. Professor Brown's previous published books include *Critical Issues in Criminal Justice, Crime Victim* and, most recently, *Justifiable Homicide*.

Milton Keynes UK
Ingram Content Group UK Ltd.
UKHW040652140923
428670UK00001B/115